IN THE FIRES OF THE AFRICAN MOONLIGHT

Edythe Monserrat is the name they give the woman who appears from the forest. The natives revere her as a goddess. Desperate men are drawn to her. But within her beautiful body rages the torment of a terrible mystery. . . .

Dr. Heinrich is the strong and sophisticated physician living a life of self-imposed exile and loneliness to escape his own bitter memories. The mysterious woman whose life he saves kindles forgotten flames of passion. Then he discovers the deadly secrets of her past. . . .

Paul Marion is the young American whose love for an exotic native princess has damned him to a life of misery and despair. A false drug charge imprisons him indefinitely. Only one woman holds the key to his freedom—Edythe.

Rivers of Time

JEAN BARLOW HUDSON

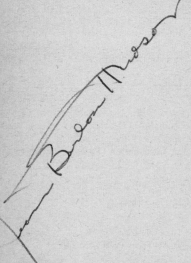

AVON
PUBLISHERS OF BARD, CAMELOT AND DISCUS BOOKS

RIVERS OF TIME is an original publication of Avon Books.
This work has never before appeared in book form.

AVON BOOKS
A division of
The Hearst Corporation
959 Eighth Avenue
New York, New York 10019

Copyright © 1978 by Jean Barlow Hudson
Published by arrangement with the author.
Library of Congress Catalog Card Number: 78-59075
ISBN: 0-380-40444-3

First Avon Printing, February, 1979

AVON TRADEMARK REG. U.S. PAT. OFF. AND IN
OTHER COUNTRIES, MARCA REGISTRADA, HECHO EN
U.S.A.

Printed in the U.S.A.

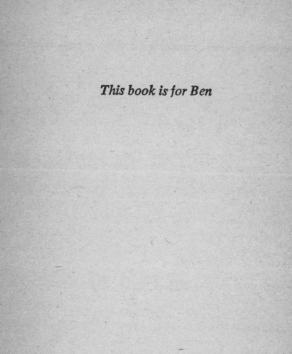

This book is for Ben

1

THE PEOPLE OF THE VILLAGE of M'Boura are a part of the Malinké-speaking people, yet so far removed in space, so isolated by the walls of the forest and the great distances of the upper plateau of Guinea, that these tall, thin black people have retained the purity and simplicity of childhood. The poetry of their lives does not change. Their village is two-thirds encircled by the forest—the forest that runs continuously from the Cassamance in Senegal to Equatorial Africa. Here and there it rises with forested peaks, the Fouta Djallon, lordly over the plateau. But the people of M'Boura cannot see the Fouta Djallon, they can only see the forests and the tall, waving grasses of the savannas.

Around their village is a small marshy area and here they grow a sparse millet for their own use, and not enough of that sometimes. They penetrate the forests to a certain depth, established in past times. Beyond that point the forest world is hostile, brutal, violent. Even the bravest become rigid with blind fear when they remain there too long, so the distance is established which they can endure. The paths end. Within this green world the sky cannot be seen, the air is without movement, overcharged with humidity, the hiss of sap springing from a tree, the rustling of the lianas as they move dry and serpentine against their host tree. Sometimes armies of red ants bar their way and the hunters must wait motionless for them to devastate the path and pass on, or else cut another way around. Above them may suddenly break the ear-

1

splitting shriek of the serval, or *chat-tigre,* as he glares down from his high perch. What warm, encompassing happiness bursts upon them emerging from the forest to the clearing!

To the west of M'Boura is a scrub land, covered with tall grasses, a wasteland dotted with the weird, grotesque shapes of the baobab, the long spindly cassavas, the peeling trunks of the mahogany trees. A few sugar palms sway in the high winds. Here live the wild boar, the lion, and herds of antelope. The jungle clearing is a more friendly place.

Yet it is across these savannas that one goes to find other tribes, and the hunters go to find food. From this direction comes the *griot,* he who sits with them and sings the legends of old, the news of today. From this direction come once or twice in a lifetime *les agentes des police,* who count people and peer into their homes and about their village, men who drive noisy machines and carry guns. From this direction came the foreigner together with one of these policemen. Because the Malinké policeman requested it from the chief, the foreigner was permitted to stay. He gave them gifts and he stayed for a long time, building his house with his own hands and the help of village men. The stranger was a white man with a black beard. He lived among them and wrote words on paper. He spent the day's length looking at plants they brought him, making pictures on the paper, and writing, writing. They tolerated him as he did no harm and took nothing from them. In fact, he had some magic that he occasionally used if they had wounds that would not heal. But sometimes he would peer at the sick or wounded person they brought to him, shake his head sadly, and go inside his hut and close the door and stay out of sight. The person nearly always died after that. They did not blame him. Either his magic had not been strong enough or it would not obey.

Now, at the time that the white woman walked out of the forest, there had been a hard rain in the night. The skies had opened with fire and great thunderclaps, and the rain had fallen in a brief, ferocious downpour. In the morning the air was sparkling, clean, and beautiful, as mornings are in Africa, the distillation of sweetness and freshness. The jungle sang in a great hum and whir and buzz of insect life, the bird songs were a cacophony of shrillness, and the monkeys leaped and chattered along the forest edge.

Midé and Kia were wading about in the mud of the marsh planting the millet. Midé's husband sat on the dry ground nearby watching them, his hands locked around his long, bony legs. The children stood at the marsh's edge holding the jar of seed. People were moving about between the huts, for the women were preparing food. Others slept in the green-gold sunlight. Children ran and shouted; a baby cried lustily, then paused and gurgled. Who noticed first the figure that emerged from the forest, the wavering figure like an apparition from the spirit world, strange and beyond comprehension, a white person in a white foreign garment, walking up the path on the slope to the village as though drawn invisibly by chains, with eyes that did not seem to see and a face that did not have a soul, hair light in color and short on the head, feet in strange sandals?

The planters in the marsh, when they saw her, first one and then the other, let out long moans of terror and dropped their sticks and seeds and ran, first this way and then that. Figures emerged from the grass huts in the village, moving together out of fear, touching each other for safety. The white woman came on as one walking in sleep, as one groping through the night. The path led only one way, to the village.

And the people moved together, making a crowd that kept away from the white figure but in some way propelled it forward and seemed to direct it to one point in the village, toward the farther edge and the hut of the white foreigner. When they were there his door opened and he emerged, like the others, shocked, disbelieving, perhaps afraid. The people stopped, the woman stopped her unsteady forward movement.

3

The white man shouted something at them in Malinké, but they did not reply. Their eyes followed the woman. She swayed. She reached out an arm and fell into the dust, crumpled like an exhausted child. Only then the villagers found their voices. They all spoke at once and the foreigner went to the woman and touched her here and there, listening, feeling; and he tried to lift her and ordered his servant, Naba, standing back with the other women, to help him, but Naba refused and moved farther away among her own people. Cursing in his own language, the foreigner finally lifted up the woman and carried her into his hut. He kicked the door shut behind him. The villagers of M'Boura squatted down and waited, conversing in low tones.

The foreigner came back out of his hut. He looked distraught and worried. He called the chief, Yago, to him. Yago came with others to stand near him, and he asked them in their language if they had heard noises during the night, of motors, of the great machines that fly in the sky carrying people from great village to great village. But they all shook their heads, for no one had heard any such noise. He talked more, saying there must have been such a passenger bird that had fallen in the forest and there may be more people lying there too hurt to walk. Would they not go and look for such people? Afraid and uncertain, Yago and the others withdrew and talked among themselves. Finally after much time and talk they collected some bows and arrows and long wooden spears and walked slowly down the path and into the forest.

In a daze, Alfoldi Santillana looked down at the woman lying on his bed, trying to remember his meager medical knowledge. Feet up in shock, he remembered. Cover with blankets. Keep warm. *Porca miséria!* Keep warm in this climate! The perspiration was running from his body with exertion and excitement. Nevertheless, he followed as best he could the precepts he knew for treating persons in shock. He ex-

4

amined the woman for wounds. No doubt about it, a nasty blow on one side of the head; blood had matted in the fair hair and there was some swelling. Strangely enough, that seemed to be all except for a long superficial gash on one arm and scratches on the legs and arms that must have been from vines and undergrowth in the forest. The whole thing was utterly beyond him. Why was she alive at all? Where had she come from? How could anyone survive a crash into the jungle? Where were the others?

He cleaned off her head and face, and tried to get water down her throat. Please, his thoughts urged her, don't die here. Come to, open your eyes, live! Finally, he ceased his efforts and told himself, she has survived this far as a miracle. Who was he to say live, live? He sat down in his one chair and watched her and tried to think what he should be doing.

His mind was in a whirl. After so much time in this place by himself he had learned to live in a certain narrow way. Rising at dawn, doing his exercises, calling the servant from her sleep nearby, going out to his self-made latrine, bathing in the bowl of tepid water brought to him with soap and towel. Breakfast outside on good mornings such as this, the delicious tea, hoarded and watched over as if it were leaves of gold in the box, the porridge made from semolina, eaten sometimes with curdled goat's milk, sometimes with canned milk. After breakfast the walk through the village to speak to people, to increase his vocabulary, to observe, then into the forest or the savanna with some of the men as companions to help him carry back plants to be catalogued and written up for his research.

By nine o'clock, usually, his walk would be finished and he would return with his treasures to draw them, and to describe them in his notebooks. In this way the forenoon passed pleasantly enough. For lunch he dipped into his larder of tinned foods for some meat or cheese, a tinned dark bread, all eaten sparingly for there was no replacing it, it had to last the time he needed to finish the work. His exchange trinkets, the

5

small goodies he gave the people of M'Boura in exchange for honey, for millet and curdled milk and wild fruits and cassava nuts, also needed to last his stay. Once a month rice came from Siguirre, along with some fresh vegetables and the mail, by Land Rover across the bush country. He often lost track of time and forgot to mark his calendar until, when he looked at it, he could not believe it had only been two weeks since the last messenger from the city had brought his mail. Afternoons were spent in sleeping and reading. He ate honey and millet for supper, a tiny glass of liquor, and then came sleep soon after night fell. This was his routine.

And now this. He noticed he was trembling. He went to his store of liquor and poured himself an unaccustomed daytime drink. It helped him to pull himself together. His mind began to work. A message must be sent for help. He would ask for a runner to go to Tarombali, nearly a day away. There were police there who would radio to Siguirre, the closest provincial town of any size, a two-day trip by Land Rover. With luck, help would come after three days. But people moved at their own speed in Guinea. With everything moving along they could get this woman to a hospital on the evening of the fifth day after today. But what if more were found in the forest? God! He shuddered at the possibility. He got up and went to the door and looked toward the wall of green. There was no movement. The village was quiet. A group still squatted near his door. He lifted his hand to them, a gesture indicating no action, nothing happening. They regarded him solemnly, and he knew behind their impassivity lay an immense apprehension. He beckoned to two of them, Nohote and Barga, to come to the door. After a delay in which they looked at each other, murmured a few words, shifted uneasily, undecided, he went to them and in their tongue said, "Come, see for yourselves."

They came cautiously to the doorway and from there poked their long heads around only enough so

6

the woman could be seen on the white man's bed, covered with a blanket, her eyes shut, her light hair neat against the wound on her head. The men looked at her, their eyes large and afraid. Santillana put his hand against the side of his head and said the word for "wound." They accepted his statement without expression and withdrew and went to their people.

It was afternoon, and he had forgotten lunch. His stomach growled, yet neither food nor rest was possible. The woman lay in her coma.

Much time passed before the men returned from the forest. They came single file with Yago leading. They came up to the Italian and reported that they had found nothing.

Santillana asked, "Nothing at all! Surely you saw the tracks of the woman?"

They nodded. Yes, they had found the tracks where the woman had stumbled onto the main path, but they had not followed the tracks back through the forest. It was so dense and the evil spirits were still waiting there for her to come back. They did not follow.

"Someone must run to Tarombali, then," said Santillana, "to get the police to come and take the woman away."

They were in quick agreement with this, to get the woman away from M'Boura. They talked among themselves rapidly. Santillana could not follow when they spoke fast and together. He waited for the decision. Yes, then Akaki would go. He was the fastest runner. He could reach Toumbi-Timbi by this nightfall, and Tarombali the next day.

"Tell him," Santillana said, "not to linger beyond the night in Toumbi-Timbi, but to go fast to Tarombali or the woman might die here."

Disturbed, they talked again and agreed that Akaki must go fast and not linger in the next village to gossip or to eat. Santillana left them to their deliberations and prepared to make himself a new bed of reeds. He disliked sleeping only on a mat on the ground. He found his hatchet and went to the marsh.

The runner was on his way, and almost immediately the drums started. As he hacked at the marsh reeds, Santillana saw the circle of men squatting behind their drums, intent looks on their faces as they beat with long, flat hands. They were driving away the evil spirits who had brought the woman. The women and children were out of sight. The birds and insects were quiet while the drums were speaking.

2

FOR FOUR DAYS the woman lay on his bed. Santillana
kept her covered, her feet up, and gave her water in
which he put some salt, berating himself for his lack
of medical knowledge. The woman tossed back and
forth. She moaned and tried to speak, but her words
were unintelligible.

She opened her eyes on the third day and looked
around like one still dreaming. He raised her to a sitting position and spoke to her in French, but there
was no comprehension in her eyes. She drank the tea
he held to her lips, but the food she would not attempt. When he asked if her head hurt, if she hurt
any place at all, she did not respond. He tried his
broken English, a few words of German, his own
Italian. Still no response. She lay back and sank into
another restless sleep. He felt she was French. The
dress had a French label in the back. He had examined the rings she wore, one a diamond which she
wore on her right hand, and the other, on her left ring
finger, a beautiful stone in an old-fashioned setting.
He thought it was a sapphire.

Naba, the girl from the tribe who had helped in his
kitchen, had left and gone back to her mother's hut.
He struggled with the fire and boiling water, making
tea by himself. He did not go to the field to look for
plants. He still wrote in his diary, only now it had become a patient's record,

Her pulse seems rapid and weak. I can't count it.

*Patient takes water. Have diapered her like a baby,
but she seldom eliminates.*

9

Removed her clothing and washed it. There was an odor of vomit on the dress. It occurs to me she may have vomited before coming to us here and perhaps this explains lack of feces evacuation. Thank God for that, anyway.

Her fingertips are bluish. Am worried.

Another entry. *Turned patient onto left side. She keeps curling feet up, cannot keep them elevated. Don't know how much it matters.*

And then, *God, I wish Laura were here. She has a way with sick people and wounded animals. I never did. Laura, Laura!*

His thoughts were all too often back in Italy with his wife, picturing her working in the garden, her floppy hat bobbing up and down among the delphiniums, shopping with a basket on her arm; moving ivory Mah-Jongg pieces across a playing table with manicured fingers, the lace falling back from her slender, blue-veined wrist. He closed his eyes and saw rose petals falling on a lacquered table on the veranda. And here he sat in this stifling hut with an unknown, unconscious woman to care for in the most intimate way.

On the afternoon of the fourth day, when the thatched hut began to steam with heat, the woman of her own accord sat up in bed and said clearly in French, "Where am I?"

Santillana, who was dozing on his small elevation of reeds and blankets, jumped to his feet and went to her.

"Bonjour!" he said, *"Grâce à Dieu!* I think you're going to live."

She stared at him with hostility, and Santillana became conscious of his own image—olive skin, balding head, black beard, rumpled khaki field clothes, black hairy arms.

"Where am I?" she asked again, a rising note of fear in her voice. He began to reduce the age he had given her of thirty-eight or -nine to about thirty. Not a bad-looking woman, even in this condition.

10

"You've had an accident," he told her in French. "You are in my hut, here in the forest in M'Boura in upper Guinea. Your plane must have crashed."

He almost said, You are the only survivor, but he checked himself.

She stared at him uncomprehending, her mouth open. Perhaps he should change the subject.

"Do you feel all right? Would you like to try standing up? I'll help you."

He seemed to remember that patients should move about as much as they were able. He helped her swing her legs onto the floor. She looked at her clothing and the cloths around her in dismay. For cleanliness he had dressed her in one of his white shirts.

"I—I've had to make some adjustments here," he said. "You've been unconscious for three days, you know. Wasn't sure you'd ever make it. There's help coming—when they'll get here I don't know, maybe by tonight. Then we'll get you to a hospital in Siguirre."

He caught her as she swayed and nearly fell onto the floor.

"J'ai des vertiges," she said, *"beaucoup vertiges."*

Santillana laid her back down on the bed. "I think this is the place for you," he said. "But I'd like you to eat something. Do you think you could? I have some tinned rice and meat. Something solid after all this time."

The strangeness of talking to another being from his world almost overcame Santillana. His voice sounded foreign to his own ears, although he was used to speaking in French.

She opened her eyes and looked at him and did not say no or yes.

"I'll fix it and you try to eat," he said. "You must get some strength for the trip to the hospital. It won't be easy in your condition. It's a hard trip on anyone. Now lie still and I'll be back."

He had to go outside to the kitchen, a lean-to against the hut, in order to build a fire in the stone

11

firebox. Naba had brought wood and left it there. Bless her for that! He took a match from his pocket and very carefully began a fire.

The Land Rover arrived that evening after dark. It brought a driver and one police officer as well as Akaki. The police agent, tall, black, uniformed, with gold braid on his cap, came to Santillana's door. He was irritated, disbelieving, in a thoroughly bad humor. He could not believe what he had been told by Akaki, that a white woman had walked out of the forest, that the plant doctor (so Santillana was called by the villagers) had said a great machine bird had fallen there. When shown the sleeping woman the officer looked frightened and unable to accept what he saw. The whites of his eyes rolled in the dim candlelight. Santillana motioned that they should go outside to talk. They conversed in French while the whole village stood around, waiting. There was apprehension and relief on their faces. Now that the police were there something would be done with the white woman. The drums had ceased.

The officer, unwilling to believe the woman was a spirit as Akaki would have him believe, still could not accept the fact that she could have survived a plane crash, or could have survived the jungle.

"I cannot either," Santillana agreed, "but there it is. She exists. She could have come in no other way. See how she was dressed—in what a woman would wear on a flight from one city to another. When we get to Siguirre, we must find out what planes are missing."

"Oh, of course, we have begun that already," replied the officer haughtily. "And when we get back they will send out troops to hunt for the plane. Everything will be taken care of."

Santillana did not reply, knowing more of African efficiency than to believe that, for things never marched along in logical sequence. And a search

12

would be made only as far and at such time as it was convenient.

They made arrangements for starting back the next morning.

"You must see that the driver goes slowly; even so, the patient may not survive the trip."

"You will come along, monsieur, won't you?" asked the officer, the thought of having the woman on his hands intolerable.

"Of course, I will come."

Actually, Santillana knew he had to see her to the hospital. She had become his responsibility, and the change of pace in his life was not unwelcome, either.

That night he wrote in his diary, *I have before me the evolvement of a M'Boura legend. I can imagine its telling and retelling, embroidered with God knows what fiction, embellished with all kinds of jujuism. I suppose this woman will draw me into this legend in the role, perhaps, of shaman. I hope it does not put the coup de grâce to my work.*

Those who had sent the Land Rover had thrown in a litter but no mattress or pillow of any kind for a patient to lie on. Furious, Santillana took his bed of reeds and did the best he could in the small space left beside the gasoline drums in the vehicle. The woman got out of bed in the gray-green dawn, unsteady and weak, and he helped her to get ready for the journey. She drank a little tea and, half choking, ate more of the cold rice. All the while her face wore a kind of rigid, frightened look. She didn't talk. When Santillana led her slowly out of the hut, the officer and driver were waiting. The group of watching villagers moved back. The officer bowed to her slightly, whipped out his notebook, and with ballpoint pen poised over it, asked her to please give him her name.

She stared at him in bewilderment, and Santillana exclaimed, "For God's sake, can't this wait until the hospital? She's ill and for all I know still in some kind of shock."

13

The officer grimaced, flipped his notebook shut, and marched ahead to the Land Rover. The driver took his place. The woman did not want to lie on the reeds in the back, so Santillana helped her into the seat and climbed in beside her.

"Please overlook my arm," he told her. "I must be sure you do not fall and bump yourself, so I shall keep you steady."

A slight lurch, a curse and a command from the officer, and the driver turned the Land Rover around and headed it across the trail of the savannas. The villagers stood impassive, watching them leave.

"I will be back," Santillana called, waving to them.

3

THE FIRST HALF of the long, hard journey to Siguirre was not unpleasant. The woman sat on the seat supported by the Italian. It was February, still the dry season, although at M'Boura, on the forest's edge, there was little distinction between the seasons. Yet, a short distance away on the savannas, the difference was distinct indeed. The grasses were yellow and brittle dry. The gnarled, twisted trees and brush looked plucked of their foliage, whether by the wild life grazing or their own dryness. The ground was rock-hard. Anthills, tower-shaped, often higher than a man, stood here and there on the plain. There were great, dry, clay-covered depressions within the sea of long-stemmed grasses and one had to peer carefully ahead to see them. The driver was alert enough to watch for the worst dips and cracks in the earth, and the officer, acting as a navigator, would call out, *"Dambos!"*

And the driver would slow down, change gear, change course, if possible, to avoid the jarring descent into the depression.

As they drove, Santillana's mind wrote terse notes in his mental journal.

Grasses, Andropogon, *showing extreme dryness.*

Flock of tisserin flying south, searching for water.

Saw le martin-pêcheur à tete blanche *sitting on the baobob. Don't the* indigènes *say it is a sign the dry season will soon end?*

The driver called out, *"Le bubale,"* pointing to a beautiful huge antelope who stood observing them. The Land Rover hit a rock and swerved. Santillana

15

tightened his arm on the woman's shoulders as they pitched sideways.

"Watch your driving, you idiot, and leave off the sightseeing," shouted the officer angrily.

"*N'est pas bubale*," Santillana shouted above the din of the motor. "*C'est l'eland géant.*" And to himself said, *Taurotragus derbianus*, making the mental note in his journal and the distinction between the giant antelope and the bubale in his mind.

By noon they had reached Toumbi-Timbi. It was a village larger than M'Boura, but still only a cluster of round, thatched huts with pointed straw roofs. There were a few sparse cattle grazing nearby and a well, its machinery broken. The women stood at the well lifting up a bucket on a rope. The water was cloudy. Santillana used his own canteen of boiled water and gave some to the woman. She appeared exhausted; he could see it plainly enough. She was struggling to maintain her upright position. There was a flush on her clear skin and her eyes wavered between open and shut.

Patient showing signs of fever now, his scientist's mind continued its recording. *Worried she will never make it to Siguirre.* Then he corrected that entry. *Patient will be flat on her back by the time we arrive.*

When they reached Tarombali that evening, they slept in the police quarters, Santillana tending to the housekeeping chores for himself and the woman. He knew that by the evening of the next day, barring any breakdown, they would reach Siguirre.

On the second day, as they drew near the provincial capital, Santillana had tired of his observations and the mental-recording game. The woman lay on the little bed of reeds, her face flushed, her breathing short and quick. She seemed unconscious of the sway and jerk and bounce of the journey. None of the occupants of the Land Rover spoke in the last hours of the trip; each of them was folded into his own endurance of the heat, the thirst, the wearing bounce of the trail through the savannas.

Alfoldi's thoughts had turned to the hospital ahead and to his friend, Dr. Heinrich Fink. He and the doctor had met soon after his own arrival in the plateau country, when he was staying in Siguirre until official paperwork for his work in M'Boura could be completed. He had been referred to the hospital by the commissioner's office, for gamma globulin and cholera shots, and after that he and the doctor met whenever he was in the town. In fact, Santillana had found that here in this remote place he had developed, in a very few meetings, a closer relationship with another man than any he had had since his youth. Although he often observed the long, tattooed number and the red triangle on the doctor's left forearm, they never discussed the past, the war, or their own parts in it. Nor did Santillana ever question why the doctor was living in this remote part of Africa. He did not appear to be a man with a mission. Santillana felt the doctor must want obscurity and peace, that the limited environs of the hospital and Siguirre were all he wanted. Now, glancing back at his patient, he thought to himself, I am bringing him another survivor—another miracle swept up with the flotsam of this century.

As they came into the provincial town, the Italian felt the lift and excitement he always experienced after weeks in the bush. The dusty streets were a marketplace, crowded with movement and life. A great team of four oxen pulling heavy logs moved toward them. The Land Rover swerved aside. An ancient Peugeot taxi, honking steadily, sped around them, pedestrians jumping aside. Bicyclists passed them, peddling with reckless speed from both directions. A herd of sheep being driven into town for the next morning's market, moved this way and that trying to avoid the vehicles, their small hoofs sending up spurts of dust.

People thronged the streets, for it was the hour to shop for the evening meal. At the same time, workmen in their dirty, knee-length *kenbe,* white tunics

17

and turbans, threaded their way home through the street traffic. Young girls wearing only short wrap-around skirts darted in between the throng, carrying parcels wrapped in newspaper held tightly against their thin chests. The Malinké women, beautiful with their shining skin and fine features, their *m'boubous* flowing around them, their turbans fluttering, walked on the edge of the streets, their gaze straight ahead. A chauffeured limousine cut across the path of the Land Rover, an elegant black official sitting in the back, as isolated in his grandeur as the French had been before. The driver of the Land Rover, happy to be back in town, chattered to the officer, and, now and then, waved and shouted to acquaintances in the crowded streets. He honked continuously, as much to assert his high social position as a driver as to avoid the traffic, animals, and bicyclists. Occasionally the officer leaned out and shouted Malinké curses to help clear the way.

They passed the railway station. The evening train from Kankan was in, still puffing smoke, the depot overflowing a human river. Mammylorries were pulling out, bursting with passengers, bodies clinging to the steps, the sides, the back. A woman wearing only a skirt tied at the waist crossed the street with the crowd. She balanced a tray of sweets on her head and called her wares in a high, singsong voice. Her full breasts glistened with perspiration.

The Land Rover turned onto the main avenue of the town, a wide, brick-paved street, Avenue de Sékou Touré, and here traffic was orderly. Only vehicles were allowed in this street, people must stay on side-walks. Smartly uniformed police with whistles directed the flow of evening traffic.

As they approached Rue de Jean Jauré the Land Rover drew to a halt against the upraised, white-gloved hand of a policeman. Leaning out, the officer called and signaled to the policeman, and immediately, in deference to his rank, the policeman turned and held his hand in the opposite direction stopping the onslaught of traffic, sweeping the group from M'Boura onto Rue de Jean Jauré. Santillana then could see the broken-down front fence of the hospital grounds and he sighed with relief. The Land Rover swept into the curving drive of the entrance. Glancing back at his patient, he murmured, *"Grâce à Dieu,* she made it. She's still alive."

4

THE TWO-STORIED brick hospital building, seared and warped by the constant sun, despoiled and deteriorated by heavy usage and insufficient maintenance, presented no image of its accomplishments. The dried-up grounds and discolored building fit in with all other Siguirre buildings, sun-faded into one washed-out pastel. It had been surrounded once by a high wrought-iron fence. Sections of the fence were broken now, lying flat on the baked ground. Bougainvillea flourished on the remaining upright parts, transforming them with its hardy, variegated blossoms, tender against the artistry of iron. Jasmine and oleander bushes sprawled against the hospital walls and a pepper tree drooped its graceful branches with their delicate pointed leaves over the dry, scuffed earth of the compound. Partly obscured by these willowy branches was a weathered upright sign, *"l'Hôpital Niger Plateau Supérieur."* A circular tarmac drive wound under a portico of this structure. Here patients entered and families stood and waited to be allowed inside. Brick steps led up to the wide doors.

Built in the sudden flurry of activity in the fifties when France's African colonies began slipping from her fingers, the hospital was so inadequate for the task that confronted it that when the present doctor came to take charge, he immediately began solicitation of every charity agency in the region for money to make additions and improvements. The United States, in its season of indulgence, responded, and the new wing of the hospital was constructed. It was in this new concrete and glass addition, planned as the doctor wanted it, that the important work of the hospital went on—the rooms for surgery, the laboratories, the kitchen, the emergency and delivery rooms. The old part contained the wards, the storage rooms, the apothecary and business offices, the wide spacious foyer. The doctor guarded the new wing as an autocrat his kingdom. He knew that otherwise it, too, would bow to the twin ravagers, time and man.

The three nuns assigned to the hospital by their order in France, Sisters of Mercy, understood the fervor of the doctor's guardianship, having watched with dismay the deterioration of the original building in a mere six-year period. Besides, they adored him and would never have questioned his dictates.

A frame house only fifty meters or so from the hospital had been built for the nuns at the same time as the new wing. Like most of the wooden houses in Siguirre, it was built off the ground, supported by strong wooden timbers treated with wood tar. Three steps led to the narrow screened porch that ran around three sides of the cottage. Within were cloister-sized bedrooms for each sister, a common room, a washroom and toilet, and a room for a chapel with an altar and votive candles and a small statue of Our Lady of Mercy. Here, services were held when Father Donnegan came from Conakry to take their confessions and administer communion. Here, each sister came to pray and meditate upon the strange, unCatholic, inexplicable world they lived in. Here, they sought to find again the source of strength they had thought they would possess forever, but now knew they must forever seek and find again—the strength and fortitude to withstand relentless toil, tedium, and isolation.

Murmuring a few final words to the Virgin, Sister Hildegaard rose from her knees, genuflected once more, and with her accustomed short, careful steps crossed the cottage and the porch and stepped down, holding carefully to the handrail. As the screen door banged behind her, two weaverbirds feasting on a ripe squash darted up and took refuge in a banana tree. A tiny brown lizard slid out of the sun to the safety of an overhanging leaf.

Sister Hildegaard's white habit made a sudden cool contrast to the hot, vivid colors of the tropical growth. The small plot which the sisters tended was enclosed by a crude fence of palm fronds and flat reeds, the kind used in weaving produce baskets, a fence that could not withstand a determined goat or a stray ox. Many times they had had it replaced, for it was a delineation of their privacy and it discouraged the passing locals, who liked to stand and peer into their cottage.

Sister Hildegaard always felt blessed by the garden. Sister Caroline teased her occasionally, saying the garden took the place of a pet, something to stroke. Sister Hildegaard often did not understand Sister Caroline's sense of humor, and now as she looked at their garden sprawling in the afternoon heat, in need of water and attention, she wished she had time to put it to rights. Squash vines straggled underneath hardy marigolds, those precious seeds sent to them in the mail from the sisters in Conakry. Yellowed onion stalks grew alongside hardy zinnias, too leggy and sparse to form the bank of color that had been intended. Yams grew beyond them, with a local type of chard. Sister Hildegaard bent and yanked out a few weeds and then crossed to the gate, making a mental note to herself to pick the squash no later than tomorrow morning or the insects and birds would have it all.

She carefully hooked the gate with its string hook and crossed the side yard of the new wing and into the hospital. She would do her afternoon work in the sterilizing room and then go upstairs to relieve Sister Caroline in the wards so she could go for tea and a rest. After that, hopefully by seven o'clock, she would be free of duties for the day. That is, unless some emergency came to disrupt their schedules, which was more likely to happen than not.

Working deftly with the tongs, Sister Hildegaard put

together little bundles of sterilized cloths picked from the autoclave, rolled them up, fastened them together tightly, and stacked them on a tray. It was a pleasant task. The heat in this room was always intense, but she was used to it. A high screened window opened onto the front of the hospital. Her mind had learned to shut out all but the most unusual sounds. She would automatically sort out cries of anguish, which meant a hurt or frightened patient being brought in by his family or friends. She could hear the approach of vehicles and sort them out as being usual, or unusual. This left part of her mind free to murmur prayers when her thoughts were not free of spitefulness or self-pity, free to plan menus for the staff dining room, free to make lists of things to order. At the moment, she was planning a list for Emma to take to the market the next morning. Emma was the only person she could send who might get what she wanted.

Her thoughts were interrupted by the approach of a Land Rover. She wouldn't have described it that way, but she detected that it was not a Siguirre taxi, was not an official limousine, was not a lorry. Yes, she could hear voices in French asking if *Monsieur le Médecin* was in. Dear, dear, a new case, and time for the doctor's final round of the wards before he went home. Poor man, was there never an end to his work!

Steps came running down from the front desk of the hospital. It was Fatou, the receptionist, calling for Sister Gertrude, for the doctor, an excitement in her chatter. There was a quick command from Sister Gertrude and the steps receded. Sister Hildegaard carefully closed the door of the small autoclave and with her apron wiped away a few specks of dust and lint. It was their most precious hospital possession. She picked up her tray and carried it into the examining room.

Sister Gertrude, her long white skirts snapping about her ankles, took the steps to the main hall, avoiding the incline used by carts and stretchers. Another case this time of day, Dearest Lady, give me

23

patience and humility to accept the labor and give the doctor the physical strength to keep going. Where is that Monsieur Diallo and that lazy young man, Sy? Closed and gone for the day, nine until five. We must struggle with the paperwork as well as the rest. Ah, that Italian scientist from the jungle! He's bringing in someone, bless the man. How he must need some good Catholic person to turn to now and then. Oh, if only we had a parish in Siguirre!

"Follow me, please, messieurs." Sister Gertrude bowed to the group with the litter, glancing at the patient. A young woman, a white, of all things. Our Lady of Mercy, where did she come from? Light short hair, high clear brow, high flush on her cheeks, blue-veined eyelids. Poor dear, how exhausted and sick she looks.

Fatou stood by, flustered and curious. The procession followed the straight back of Sister Gertrude down the hall to the new wing and into the examining room. Sister Hildegaard helped Sister Gertrude lift the woman onto the examining table, looking at her with amazement. The driver and the hospital guard were waved out of the room with the empty litter. Santillana stood at one side, waiting. Doctor Heinrich was at the sink, scrubbing his hands.

"So, Alfoldi," said Doctor Heinrich, "you made the trek again. Where did you find this patient?"

"You won't believe it, Heinrich," said Santillana.

"Probably not," said the doctor, and he walked over to the patient, still drying his hands and arms. "She's out, isn't she? Don't tell me you found this woman in your part of the forest."

"I said you wouldn't believe it," said the Italian. "She walked out of the jungle into M'Boura, Heinrich. Literally. That's six days ago. I presume she miraculously survived a plane crash, unless we have here an example of transmigration."

"Incredible," was Heinrich's comment. "Has she been conscious at all?"

"Yes, a little. She was improving until this journey.

24

It was too much for her. But she told me nothing at all, not even her name."

The doctor was ready now. He said to the Italian, "Alfoldi, go find Sister Caroline. She is on duty upstairs. Ask her to show you who else is a patient here. Then wait for me."

The doctor began his examination.

As Santillana started down the hall, Sister Hildegaard caught his sleeve.

"Professor," she whispered, "first you should come to the dining room and have something. After that trip you must be thirsty and hungry."

He looked at her gratefully. "Indeed, Sister, I am both. Just a bite to see me through until dinner."

Sister Hildegaard took the Italian to the staff dining room and after a few moments in the kitchen she came out with a pot of tea, cold water, a bowl of soup, and some biscuits. Gratefully, he ate and drank, and the strength seeped back into his weary body. The sister sat watching him eat. She urged more on him, refilling his water glass.

When she dared interrupt, she asked, "Now tell me, Professor, where did that woman come from—in those clothes? She certainly isn't from around here!"

"No, Sister," Santillana said, wiping his mouth on a small napkin. "We have here a miracle beyond a doubt. She walked out of the forest alone, as I told Heinrich. And then, of course, she collapsed, practically by my door. I know it is unbelievable. It has to be the crash of a plane in the jungle. I sent the village men back to look for more survivors, but they wouldn't go off the beaten paths, scared to death of evil spirits, you know."

He rumpled his hair with his hand and looked at Sister Hildegaard. "I've been terribly upset about it, you know," he concluded.

"What else could you do!" she said. "What a thing. I've never heard the like of it in all my years here.

25

Never. Didn't she have bones broken, internal injuries?" she asked then.

"Not as far as I could tell," Santillana said. "A bad head bruise was all I could find. I bathed her, washed her clothes—they were a mess. She was conscious after a couple of days, ate and drank a little, but the trip in was too much for her. She went out again."

"Concussion," said Sister Hildegaard, and her round, fleshy face quivered in sympathy. "What a task for a man alone. You deserve a lot of credit."

"Oh, they came promptly enough after we got a message through. But it was a rough trip. The savannas are so baked it's like driving on rough asphalt. Who does Heinrich want me to go upstairs and see?"

Sister Hildegaard shook her head again, as if there was more to accept than she could tolerate. "Yes," she said, "you go upstairs. Sister Caroline is there. She will show you. I must see about the supper trays right now. I expect one of us will be needed with this new patient tonight."

She heaved herself wearily up from the bench and disappeared into the kitchen.

Santillana wandered through the hospital and upstairs in the old part. There was no elevator. He wondered why the building had not been stretched out on one floor like the new wing. Like so many other things in Africa, it made little sense. Whom was Heinrich referring to that was a patient? He knew few people in Siguirre. He had come to know the hospital staff. As for other acquaintances, well, there were not many. He saw Sister Caroline enter the upstairs ward as he came to the upper hall. He called to her and she signaled that he should wait. An *indigène* nursing aide in a blue cotton uniform went by him, giving him the Malinké word of greeting. She carried a bundle of towels and disappeared into the ward. There was a clatter of trays as two young orderlies appeared at the head of the stairs carrying a cart loaded with food for the evening meal. Sister Caroline hurried out of the ward at the clatter and bang of the trays to give them a few orders.

Finally, she came to the Italian and they shook hands.

"Monsieur Santillana, what brings you to town again? Are you bored with all your work, or have you finally come to the end of your cataloguing?"

"I am very seldom bored, Sister, and I'm not finished either. No, I brought in a patient from M'Boura." He did not elaborate, feeling it was not his prerogative at that point.

"Oh," she said. Her gray eyes searched his. He always had the feeling with Sister Caroline that she read much more from a few words than one intended her to do.

"The doctor said I should have you show me some patient. I cannot think who it would be that I know."

"I see," she said, and then she laughed a little at her monosyllabic answers. "Yes," she said, "I think you will be concerned. Come."

He followed her back toward the stairs and beyond to a corner of the hall where two private rooms were situated, and then the Italian noticed with a start that a military guard stood at one of the doors, his rifle slung on the back of a straight chair. He had evidently been sitting until they came his way. Now he saluted and stepped aside as they approached the room.

"You don't mean Paul Marion!" exclaimed Santillana.

"Indeed," said Sister Caroline gravely.

They stood at the doorway. The patient, a slight form beneath the sheet, was asleep; the white face was thin, the skin pulled taut against the bones, the chin faintly shadowed with beard. Alfoldi gazed a moment at the pale face and then backed away to the hall and they walked slowly together.

"The dysentery," said the nun. "He was in terrible condition when they finally brought him, but he's improving now."

27

"He looks awful!" said Santillana indignantly. "How disgraceful! Do the Americans know?"

The sister shrugged slightly. "It is not their problem, you know. He is a prisoner of the State and treated like any other. The Americans stay out of the picture. Still, the food they serve at the prison, it is difficult for a foreigner to survive on it. And Paul isn't a robust type."

The Italian sighed deeply. He had believed when he saw the young man imprisoned a year ago that he couldn't survive the prison life. "Does Heinrich think he'll pull through?" he asked.

"Bien sûr!" said Sister Caroline. "He's responded very well to the treatment. He takes liquids now and keeps them down. Tomorrow we will begin a soft diet."

"I'll come to see him in the morning. It will be early, as I have to go back again tomorrow."

"Sister Hildegaard may be on duty," the nun said. "Come when you like."

They parted at the head of the stairs. He descended to the foyer to wait for the doctor.

The plight of the young American lay heavy in Santillana's thoughts. Paul had come to West Africa originally with the American Peace Corps, but when his tour of duty was finished and he was debriefed in his own country, he had shipped back to the West African coast by freighter and found work at the Catholic Mission in Conakry teaching English. He had been drawn to the life he had experienced in the French-speaking countries. When he met Barbette, a lovely black student in the boarding school of the mission, he fell in love with her. Barbette was the daughter of the governor of Malinké Province, the province encompassing Siguirre and all the upper Niger plateau country. The friendship between these two had become a kind of "Paul and Virginia" idyll, idealistic, innocent, and joyous.

When Barbette returned to Siguirre on vacation, Paul Marion went along. Perhaps he had invited himself in his brash, Western way; perhaps she had encouraged him to come. Her family, to say the least, was surprised at the white guest she brought, obviously adoring, obviously wooing in an open, hearty way. It was nearly unbelievable to Barbette's Muslim parents and a society where suitors were usually chosen, or at least approved, by the head of the household and followed very rigid procedures in their courtship.

People later asked why, if the girl knew this, she had allowed him to come? Why had she not warned him, or had he disregarded her warnings? Or had she had some other motive in bringing the American boy home with her? These questions were never answered.

But the governor had been courteous to his guest, the mother saw that he was hospitably housed and feasted, and the numerous relatives, brothers, and sisters all stood around staring at the stranger and forgetting how to converse. Barbette and her young American chattered together interminably or they walked, touching hands sometimes when it seemed that no one was watching.

And then, in a way that Paul could not explain or understand, the atmosphere had changed. Barbette had been sent to her room to stay, and he had found himself on the station platform in Siguirre with his return ticket in his hand, waiting to board the morning train. As he had made his way through the train, unhappy and confused, a policeman had tapped him on the shoulder and asked to inspect his suitcase. Surprised but compliant he obeyed, and when it was opened the police, before the eyes of curious onlookers, found a brown-paper parcel containing five pounds of hashish. Paul was arrested, tried, found guilty of drug trafficking, and sentenced to five years in prison.

Doctor Heinrich, hearing of the case at the Railway Club, found it easy to doubt the young man's guilt, as did Alfoldi Santillana. Santillana attended the trial during one of his sojourns in the city. They believed the boy had been victimized by a jealous suitor of Barbette, perhaps in collusion with the girl's father

himself. The American consulate, called in on the
case, had no way of proving Paul Marion's innocence,
and the lawyer they provided him was ineffectual.
Since the boy was proven to have possessed drugs and
to have broken the law, he was incarcerated in the
Siguirre prison to serve his sentence. The girl, Barbette, had been taken by her family to school in a
neighboring country.

The three nuns sat by themselves at their supper in
the staff dining room. They had not expected to see
the doctor eating at the hospital this evening since the
Italian scientist was in town. The two men would be
eating at a local restaurant.

"It is good for Heinrich that the Italian came in,"
said Sister Hildegaard, breaking off a piece of hard
bread and wiping up her plate with it. She made that
same remark each time Monsieur Santillana came to
town, and no one replied to it.

Sister Gertrude said, "A very strange thing, a handsome woman like that, dressed in those clothes, walking out of the jungle."

"It's like a miracle of some kind," put in Sister
Hildegaard. "Perhaps it really is a miracle. Imagine
that, up there in M'Boura."

The nuns were always curious about their white patients. There were so few of them, and they could
speculate upon their lives more than with the *indigène*
patients, whose ways were largely incomprehensible to
them in spite of their years there and constant contact
with them.

"We have two unusual cases now," murmured Sister
Caroline.

"The doctor is interested in this case," said Sister
Gertrude. "He examined her very thoroughly, as
though she were a creature from another planet."

"He'll have her fit again in no time," said Sister Hildegaard with confidence.

For a few moments they ate in silence and then
Sister Hildegaard spoke again in a pensive voice.

"I've always wondered why the doctor doesn't marry. Of course, I know there's no one around here for him, but he could go out and find someone, go back to Europe. But he never does."

"I never knew for sure," said Sister Gertrude looking at Sister Caroline, "if he was married before, before the war." Sister Caroline was always looked to for facts and theories; somehow she gathered both in her quiet, steady way.

"I understand that he was engaged to a young woman," said Sister Caroline, "when he was in medical school. They were waiting for him to finish and get into practice."

"I suppose she was shipped off to the death camps," said Sister Gertrude. "What a terrible tragedy, to have to remember all one's life."

"But he was there himself," said Sister Hildegaard. "How did he ever get away with his life? I suppose they even used Jewish doctors, sometimes."

"Heinrich was a political prisoner," Sister Caroline said. "Didn't you know that? That's really the reason he survived. Political prisoners helped each other."

"He never talks about it," said Sister Gertrude.

"I know," said Sister Caroline. "I was told all this in Paris before I came out. That's how I know."

"Well, the dear man gives too much of himself," said Sister Hildegaard, stacking her dishes neatly. "I wish he would rest more."

"You will be sitting with the new patient tonight, sister?" This from Sister Gertrude.

"Yes," answered Sister Hildegaard over her shoulder. "As soon as I say my devotions I'll be in, and you can tell me what I should do."

5

Darkness lay over Siguirre by the time the two men emerged from the dining room of l'Hôtel l'Ivoire. Santillana always stayed at this small hotel on the quai. It was a second-class hotel on the shabby mercantile street, but after coming in from M'Boura he never felt up to the pomposity of the Victoria over on Avenue de Sékou Touré. And he liked being close to the river. He liked the sounds he could hear from his room, the soft lap of the water against the anchored boats, the guttural calls of the fishermen as their boats docked in the dawn, the sibilant chatter of those who came to market on this street, the cries of the water birds.

Feeling an aura of pleasure in each other's company, the two men stood for some moments under the portico of the hotel. Streetlights were dim and far apart. Now that the heat of the sun was gone, the night, though still hot, was soft and seductive, the air a mixture of scents—the sweet perfume of jasmine and frangipani blossoms, the smell of fish, a sweet-sour smell of decay, a tangy odor of spices drifting from the river cargo that lay baled and waiting for shipment.

Above the town was the junction of the Tinkisso and Niger rivers. Here it was one, the great Niger, running past the city on its long, curving trek through the wastelands to the Mali border, on to the capital of Bamako, and then into Niger, down into Nigeria, and finally to the sea.

A beggar approached the men, whining his song,

waving his stumps of hands. To avoid him they turned and began walking slowly. Darkness had emptied the streets. A mammylorry with only a handful of sleepy passengers rumbled by and turned up toward Rue de Jean Jauré. A group of night people, painted, polished, in *les grands boubous* and caftans, strolled past, turning faces that shone and glittered toward the lights.

The men had been talking of the white woman all during dinner and of the plane crash they felt must have occurred.

"If the woman were not now my patient," said the doctor, "I'd be inclined to think this incident a result of some hallucinogen that you've been taking there in the wilds."

"Exactly!" said Alfoldi. "As a matter of fact, I still doubt my senses. They should send out troops to search the forest for the plane. It can't be far off the beaten path."

The doctor said, "The commissioner will say, 'But we have no orders from Conakry,' or some such nonsense. The trouble is, no one in Conakry is going to believe this woman exists. And locally they will stall and stall. They hate forays into jungles such as M'Boura has."

"Surely they will go when word comes that a plane is missing. Conakry will insist."

"Yes," Heinrich answered, "and our patient will be able to tell us the story."

"What is your prognosis, Heinrich?"

"I don't see anything beyond the concussion. Still, one can't always tell with head wounds. She appears to be a person of good general health. Damned attractive, isn't she?"

Heinrich spoke lightly, yet he felt strangely stirred and excited by this woman who had been brought to him and placed in his care. There was something about her that spoke to the sensual part of him that he did not ordinarily face. An essence had come from her that he was not used to encountering. As he had examined her, his hands and his eyes giving him their usual medical messages, some new sensation also stirred in him, and because of it he felt exhilarated and alive.

"Yes, I think so, too," Santillana replied. And they both laughed a little, foolishly, shaking their heads at the whole thing.

They were out of the business section now. The road curved by the river. Small houses, built off the ground, stood in the shadow of the trees. A bicyclist passed them, his white garments flapping ghostily. They had reached the end of the good road, only a path continued. On the river's edge stood an immense dead tree, erect still, one of its leafless limbs pointed across the river in enduring dignity. The two friends turned to retrace their steps.

"Did you get your mail?" asked the doctor.

"Yes, a packet of letters from Laura. A real treat."

Santillana didn't say more about them, although the thought of the letters that he would read again and again was a warm thing. He had heard that the doctor never received letters except for occasional communications from the Paris Missionary Board.

"Do they always make you homesick?" asked Heinrich, as if the letters must be spoken of.

"*Certainement, certainement!*" exclaimed Alfoldi. "But I've promised myself to finish the work by the time the rainy season begins. In six weeks or so, I'll pack up and go home. I can't spend another rainy season here."

"The rains may be late this year," said the doctor, the dismal fact that Santillana would depart settling heavily in his thoughts. "Anyhow, that's what Bakary, the cook at the hospital, says."

They were back near the docks now, and the hotel. A small crowd had gathered near the river, standing close together watching the water. They joined the group. Out from the darkness on the river could be heard the sound of a motorboat, and they could see an arc of light moving back and forth across the water.

"What is it?" the doctor asked a man in a long, gray caftan standing next to him.

"A prisoner escaped," was the reply. "The police are searching for him. They think he has a small boat."

The district prison for Malinké Province stood at the other end of the quai, some blocks away. Its tower light was circling the area. Santillana and Heinrich waited with the others, peering into the dark waters, wondering what drama was being played out there. Suddenly there was a shot, followed by another, then silence again except for the boat's motor. The crowd seemed to sigh.

The man next to the doctor said, "They must have gotten him, poor bugger."

The crowd murmured, grumbled, and then drifted apart. The two white men crossed the quai to stand in the shadows away from the hotel portico.

"Tell me about Paul," said Santillana. "Sister Caroline took me to his room, but he was asleep. He looked bad to me."

"So you saw him. I was going to talk about him, but then this woman has been on my mind. Yes, we've had him a week. They were afraid he would die in their prison, the dysentery was so bad. Damned food they shovel out there."

"Is it under control yet?"

"Yes, finally, and actually Paul is improving rapidly although he looks ghastly. But give him another week and we'll see a change. The sisters will fatten him up soon as he can eat."

"And then back to that jail and the bad food again," Alfoldi murmured.

"I have a plan," Heinrich said. "I'm going to talk to Commissioner Equilbecq and ask him if we can send food to Paul twice a day from the hospital. It's the only way to get him really healthy again. I'll scare the commissioner. They don't want the publicity of an American dying in their prison. I'll manage Equilbecq."

"Good for you. The boy's plight troubles me. I've

35

been tormented by it since I wandered into his trial a year ago."

"God, has it been that long!" Heinrich said. "Is my life pouring away from me at such a rate! Alfoldi, come home with me for a drink of good whisky. We need it."

"I know, and thanks, Heinrich, but I'm dead tired. And tomorrow it's back to the bush for me, if I'm to be finished by the time the rains begin."

"Confound it, Alfoldi, I thought you'd stay longer."

"Ce n'est pas possible, mon ami, but I will be up at the hospital early to talk to Paul and take another look at your latest patient. You've two from outside now."

"Well, then," Heinrich said sadly, feeling already bereft. "Look for me in the morning before you leave. And take care. This is the hardest time of year to stay well."

"I know. *Au revoir,* Heinrich."

"À demain, friend."

6

LIGHT. Gray shadowy light. Where, oh where . . .
white high walls up, up, a window over there, a door
standing open, this narrow bed, rough strange sheet,
this coarse garment on me, my arms held by tape to
boards, bottles up there dripping fluid into my veins,
where, oh God, oh God, I'm trapped, bound, who,
where, who, where. . . .

Her thoughts burst into a scream and then another
and another. To Sister Hildegaard in the next room
the screams held deep terror. She came running, her
loosened sandals dragging on the floor, the large white
wings of her headdress flapping back and forth, her
face contorted with anxiety. She had fallen asleep in
her chair in the early morning stillness. Quickly she
placed restraining hands on the woman's arms and
spoke soothingly to her, murmuring comforting words
as one would to a child.

"There, there, do not worry, do not be afraid. You
must lie still. You are here in our hospital, now. You
are safe. Everything is all right. There, there now."

The screams ended. The woman gasped a few times
and looked at the white, concerned face above her.

"You will be all right, now," said the sister again,
drawing up a chair with one hand, keeping the other
touching the woman. "Do you have pain?"

The woman rolled her head back and forth. Not
pain, no, not pain as people think of pain, but this
pressure—I must escape from this pressure. I cannot
stay in here, I am so alone, I cannot think, it is like a
locked room here, I cannot think, why am I here,
where did I come from. . . .

The woman's mouth opened and closed and no
words came out.

Sister Hildegaard said, "They told me I could take this one bottle away as soon as you awoke. Now, just hold very still and I will be as quick as possible."

And as she spoke the sister released the patient's right arm from the board, took off the adhesives, and gently withdrew the needle from the vein. Reaching into her apron pocket she brought out a bandage, which she deftly opened and stretched across the hollow of the forearm. Sister Hildegaard was not a graduate nurse, but in her years of work in Africa she had learned much, and she did nearly everything that Sisters Caroline and Gertrude did.

"There," she said, pushing the one apparatus away from the bed. "At least you can move that arm. Now, would you like to have some tea or coffee? It's too early for the kitchen help, but I can make it myself."

The woman reached her free arm and caught the sister's apron.

"Non, attendez."

Her first words. Sister Hildegaard sat down, pleased the woman had spoken, and in French, too.

"It doesn't matter. I shall stay. They will come to the kitchen before long. Perhaps you can sleep more now."

Kind face, warm firm hands, stay close to me, I cannot tell you how terrible it is, there is an abyss inside, a chasm, and when I look over the edge I nearly fall into it, dark, bottomless darkness, and nothing nothing else. I cannot recall one thing of how I came here, nor do I know even who I am, whose body this is. . . .

She opened her eyes and tried to will away the blackness, the panic blackness, from her thoughts. She moved her hand to touch the hand of the sister. The sister's hand responded, moved upon hers. She looked up at the broad, anxious face above her. Slowly she relaxed. There was enough residue of the medicine the doctor had given her the night before to cause sleep to come again, and without knowing it she surrendered herself to oblivion.

7

SISTER GERTRUDE OPENED THE DOOR to the new wing and smelled the fresh coffee in the kitchen. Bakary was at work, a clean apron over a dirty uniform. He gave her an open smile full of the goodwill and sweetness of the new day.

"Porridge ready, Sister," he said, speaking French with her as he was proud to do. And he dished her a bowl of hot farina. "And here the milk."

Reconstituted milk, porridge, hot coffee. Sister Gertrude eased her ample frame onto the bench at the common table, the only person in the staff dining room. She could hear sounds of conversation in the examining room, where Mamady was cleaning floors and Kouindo, an orderly, was distracting her with his gossip.

She ate with small, neat spoonfuls, erect on the bench. After cleaning the last bite from the bowl she returned with her dishes to the kitchen. There she gave a critical look around, even though it was not her special domain, and then she went to relieve Sister Hildegaard from her vigil.

The new patient was sleeping like a child. Sister Gertrude listened to Sister Hildegaard's report and sent her off duty. Then she went on a routine check of the downstairs women's and children's ward, and on her way scattered the gossipers in the examining room with a sharp look and reprimand. Kouindo sped away to his duties and Mamady moved to a dirty part of the floor and slopped more water onto the tiles from her bucket.

It was a forty-eight-bed hospital. Heinrich Fink was chief surgeon and resident physician, assisted occasionally by Dr. D'jala Diop, a young Guinean doctor who had his own clinic in Siguirre. The hospital was funded by President Touré's government, which provided the administrator, Monsieur Diallo. The salary of the doctor was paid by the Paris Missionary Board, an arrangement that would have been completely unacceptable to the proud and violently pan-African government had they not needed the hospital and the doctor so desperately. But the President's feeling for his countrymen outweighed his embarrassment at accepting French money, even from nonofficial sources. The help was accepted and the government sent the operating funds from the capital, inadequately but regularly.

Returning to the new wing, Sister Gertrude found the doctor drinking his morning tea alone.

"How is the new patient, Sister?" he asked in German.

Alone, the doctor and the sisters often spoke in German, which, except for Sister Caroline, was their first language.

"She still sleeps, Doctor."

"Then sit down a moment with me. The road has already arrived, Sister."

She sat down across from him. The doctor was referring to the Peul proverb, "No matter how early you rise the road always gets there first." He was right—she pushed too much, too hard. If she could only learn not to try to get everything done. She looked humbly, seriously at the doctor.

"What do you make of her, Sister?" he asked.

In the early morning his eyes were pouchy and heavy. His shoulders, too big for the rest of his body, hunched forward in the white coat. His thick, brown hair resisted any neatness. His hands, strangely small to contain so much skill, were locked together around his teacup. He looked tired and older than his forty years as he regarded Sister Gertrude seriously.

"We don't know one thing about her yet except that she walked out of the forest into M'Boura with a concussion, some scratches, and that is all. I'm tempted to accept the native version of witchcraft."

"Doctor Heinrich," Sister Gertrude replied, almost primly, "it is not witchcraft, but God's will that this woman lives. You might call it a miracle if she has survived a crash of a plane. God must have wanted her to live."

"Ah," said the doctor, a hint of teasing in his eyes, "so God wanted her to live and the others to die. Very friendly, nice fellow, your God."

A flush suffused the sister's face. The doctor was teasing, and he had every right to the cynicism she knew he felt, and yet it always hurt when others made fun of, or disbelieved, her faith.

"Perhaps God has need of this woman, Doctor," came the gentle reply. "Or perhaps God feels she must learn more before she dies."

"We all must do that," he sighed, "or die in abysmal ignorance, which sometimes I am certain I shall do."

She looked at his face, disturbed by the sadness in his voice.

They were interrupted by Mamady standing with her pail. Speaking in Malinké, she said, "Come, Doctor, Sister, come see."

They went quickly. Mamady was pointing to the room where the white woman lay, and then they heard the sounds, deep waves of sobbing.

Hurriedly, Sister Gertrude went and touched the woman and said in French, "Dear child of God, do not weep. We are here to take care of you. You will soon be well and happy again."

The woman turned her face to them, contorted with her crying. "It is so terrible, so terrible," she said.

"Is it pain?" asked Sister Gertrude.

"Non, non," came the reply, "not pain."

The doctor touched the woman's skin. He looked

into her eyes, pulling down the lids and peering closely. He felt her pulse.

"How do you feel this morning?" he asked gently.

She looked at him and did not speak, her hand pressed over her mouth.

"I think you are much better," he said. "So much better that you are beginning to realize you are a part of the world again. It is almost a shock, isn't it, to find that you have another chance at life."

He drew up the chair to the bed. "I am Doctor Heinrich. Now, why don't you let Sister Gertrude and me help you? Begin by telling us who you are. We shall put it here on your chart. What are you called now? What is your name?"

The woman looked up at the two attentive faces. She made a strong effort to stifle the scream that wanted to burst out. She could not put into words any of the horror of her thoughts, a kind of looming, overpowering emptiness, a nothingness. But patiently they waited and finally she managed to speak.

"I don't know. That's just it, I can't remember who I am. I cannot find myself at all. I can't find anyone. It is so awful!"

"You do not know your name?" asked the doctor. This had never happened to him before. He had had black patients too frightened of a white doctor to speak their name, or patients too wrapped in pain or delirium to say their name, but this, "I don't know" . . . ! He picked up her left hand, looking at the sapphire on her ring finger, and the right hand with the diamond.

"Are you married?" he asked.

She stared at him and at her rings as if it were the first time she had seen them. The doctor turned the ring on her left hand.

"This looks like an unusually nice sapphire. Where did you get it?"

She whispered, staring at her fingers, "I don't know."

"Where were you born?" he asked.

42

She shook her head. He tried again, "What city do you live in?"

Again, nothing but fear on her face. "Is it Conakry?" he probed, "Freetown? Monrovia? Dakar, Paris, Nice?" Nothing.

The eyes, he noticed, were beautiful, green like the sea on a windy day, and large and dark-lashed, but now full of anguish and trouble.

"No, no, no," she moaned, her head moving back and forth.

"We shall not torture you any longer," he said. "You will remember all when your mind is ready to remember. You have had a concussion, but this memory loss will wear away. Do you understand? Do not distress yourself. Be glad you are alive and in as good shape as you are. You have good, French-speaking friends here in the sisters, who will help you. The important thing now is to be quiet, to rest. Rest for many days."

He turned to the sister and said, "Sister Gertrude, we'll do the routine tests—blood, urine, so on. Take the vital signs twice daily. Let her eat whatever she wants, as much as she wants."

Turning to his patient he placed a hand on her shoulder for a moment, and then turned and left the room, followed by the sister.

Lying alone, the woman thought of the doctor and the nurse, Sister Gertrude. They have names to be called, she said to herself. I have none. I do not know the name that belongs to me. There must be one that people—people someplace—call me, but no one here knows. Even I do not know. That is really being lost. I am lost from myself.

For a moment the panic threatened to engulf her again, but she caught herself and murmured out loud all the Christian names she could remember, saying them aloud as one might count, but none of them sounded like her own.

"Oh, who am I?" she gasped in despair. "God, God, I do not know who I am. I am empty!"

She wept into her pillow, but this time not as long nor as hard, nor as frightened. There were gentle people nearby. Perhaps life would go on. Yet, what if there was someone waiting for her someplace, frantic to know of her safety? She fingered the rings she wore, staring at them. I have no memory. How far back can I go? I remember vaguely walking in the forest, vines pulling at me, stumbling, the sound of my own cries. I remember the taste of fear in my mouth, I remember a path, thinking it would lead out. It was dusk there. The path widened and something soft hit me in the face. I screamed and hit at it with my hands. It was just a bunch of feathers hanging from a tree. Then I saw the clearing and I was out and there were black people running away from me. How did I find the white man, the Italian? I can't remember. But he took care of me in his hut. That horrible long trip to this hospital. Oh, I can't remember anything more. That's all there is.

Lifting the rough hospital gown, she looked at her own body. It was neither young nor old. Her breasts were firm fruits, peach and pink, her belly flat, a light brown bush at her crotch, her legs smooth, and she noticed the contrasting whiteness of her breasts and loins to the rest of her skin—a bikini, she thought, marveling at her own recognition. There was no mirror in the room; she could not know what her face looked like. She had no image of her own face. She felt her hair. It was cut short and close to her head. She felt her nose, her lips, trying to judge. Chin rather pointed. Teeth? They felt strong. On her right arm a scab was beginning to form on a long gash. It was painted with medicine, but unbandaged. She touched her head and it hurt on the one side, tender and slightly swollen. I must lie still, as the doctor said.

She lay back, tired from her self-examination. Who am I? What kind of person? Who misses me, wonders where I am? If only I knew. Surely someone is looking for me and will find me.

44

When the doctor left his new patient, he went about his rounds preoccupied with the thought that he very likely had his first case of amnesia. He had never been confronted with such a situation before. In any place in Europe he could go and call another doctor, a specialist, to come in and consult with him or take over the case, someone who knew about post-traumatic amnesia. Poor woman, how frightened she looked and how lost.

Now he had two lost children, in a manner of speaking, although the woman was certainly a mature person and not a child at all. But she and Paul Marion were both lost as far as their own worlds and cultures were concerned. Surely any day now there would be some word from the authorities about who this woman was, and she would be claimed. She probably would not be with them for long.

8

IN THE FOLLOWING DAYS the woman slept much of the time. Through her open door she could watch the comings and goings of the hospital personnel. She learned the names of two of the sisters, of the doctor, of some of the aides. She was fed, bathed, rubbed, and fussed over, and the doctor came often to see her.

After several days they came one morning with a stretcher on wheels and Sister Gertrude said cheerfully, "Here we go now, *ma chère,* for a long ride."

"Where?" asked the woman, apprehensive of the high stretcher, of the orderlies who stood by the door, waiting. "Where are you taking me?"

"Upstairs, to a room of your own. A nice room." Sister Hildegaard helped Sister Gertrude with the sheets.

"Oh, dear." She didn't want to move. She was comfortable there, and used to it by now. But she was lifted up and strapped onto the stretcher, the sheets tucked neatly around her. The orderlies grasped the stretcher front and back and rolled it down the tiled hall of the new wing. The woman panicked at the swiftness of the movement and reached out her arm. Sister Hildegaard spoke sharply in Malinké and the orderlies went more slowly. There was a slight bump and the sound the wheels made changed; it was a rumble now, over wood floors. Then she was aware of a great openness around her and the feeling of the out-of-doors being close. There were many voices and new sounds, faces flashed past, black faces, looking at her. The sound of the wheels changed again, now a dull solid sound, the bricks of the lobby. Then the stretcher was lifted up by the orderlies and they began to ascend. It was a frightening feeling, being lifted up. The sisters, one ahead and one behind, talked constantly to the bearers, admonishing them now in French, now in Malinké, to carry it level, not to move so fast, not to bump against the railing or the wall. Finally, after what seemed an interminable length of time, they set the stretcher down on solid floor once more, and she was wheeled into a room. It was a small room, but it gave her a feeling of freshness, of cleanliness, of light. The walls were light green, the window long, open, and screened. The top of a tree could be seen. The sisters lifted her onto the bed. Sister Hildegaard sent one of the orderlies for a fan, the other disappeared with the stretcher. The fan, when it arrived, was small and ancient, but it was placed on the floor, its breeze directed at the bed. There was a small bathroom off the room with a toilet and lavatory, a table by the bed with a lamp, a carafe of water, and a glass sitting on a round tray.

"This is one of our best rooms," laughed Sister Hildegaard. "It is reserved for dignitaries. You have two sheets. That is special. Most of our patients prefer lying on a mat on the bed with nothing over them but their hospital garment. That we do insist upon."

Before she left Sister Hildegaard explained, "Across the hall you may sometimes glimpse a police guard standing with his gun. This has nothing to do with you. The patient in the room across the hall is a prisoner, so they keep him guarded."

"A prisoner!" the woman exclaimed, afraid again. "Why does he have to be here?"

"Because he is sick," explained Sister Hildegaard patiently. "But you needn't worry. He's not dangerous." She laughed a little, thinking of the boy's helplessness. "He's just a young man, twenty-two or -three, and harmless. He's an American," she added. "Poor soul."

"But why is he here?" persisted the woman on the bed, "I mean, why is he a prisoner?"

"He was so ill in the prison they had to bring him here," the sister said. "The prison part is another story. The doctor may tell you if you ask him. And now," she paused, standing in the doorway, looking around to see if all was as it should be in the room, "when the doctor comes tomorrow morning, ask him if you can begin to get up a little, to walk around your room and to bathe yourself."

She came back to the bed and smoothed the sheets and adjusted the pillow again. Then, with a motherly pat on her patient's shoulder, she went out, her sandals flapping softly down the long flight of stairs.

During that day, Sister Caroline paid the new patient a visit. The nun entered the room with a cool swish of her long, white skirts. She was younger, smaller, and thinner than the other sisters. She had a grave, attractive face. Her wide mouth was held in a firm line as though it must always be controlled and disciplined, but it was her eyes that revealed her personality. No matter what she did with the rest of her face, her luminous gray eyes were unwavering and and loving. Sister Caroline drew the one chair in the room close to the bed and sat down, her back straight, her hands clasped in her lap.

"I am Sister Caroline," she said to the patient, who regarded her cautiously. "I am in charge of the spiritual and temporal care of our patients. I have been trying to find some time to talk with you, but they keep us so busy." She paused, embarrassed to hear herself complaining. Then she continued softly, "Believe me, my dear girl, you have been in my prayers. Tell me, are you beginning to find yourself at all? Are you remembering anything about yourself?"

The face on the pillow returned her direct gaze, disturbed yet guarded. She shook her head. "No," she said. "I remember nothing. Nothing at all." She played with the edge of her sheet while looking at the nun.

Touching the woman's arm, the sister said, "God, our Father, has not deserted you. He knows where each of us is and He is waiting to be in touch with us. He is more than memory. He is everywhere. He is here. He is with you. Do you pray, my dear?"

The head on the pillow shook again. "I said that I do not remember."

Reaching in her pocket, Sister Caroline brought out a rosary. She held it up. "Do you know this?"

"It's a rosary."

"Can you say a rosary?"

A thoughtful look, a frown, and then a shake of the head again.

"No, then perhaps you are not of our Church. I doubt if you would forget these prayers. Would you like me to teach you to tell the beads?"

The woman said nothing. The sister urged her to repeat the words of the litany, but she lay unresponsive and uninterested.

"Your time will be well spent if you say these prayers as you lie awake," the sister continued evenly, and she pressed the rosary into the woman's hand.

"Now, Dr. Heinrich has told me you very much need a name. He says he cannot continue just calling you 'that woman.' Have you thought about what we should call you?"

A slight interest showed in the green eyes. She had heard someone in the hall earlier in the day referring to "the white woman" and she didn't like being referred to like that.

She said, "I find it impossible to say, Sister. I cannot make up a name for myself. I don't like anything that I think of. It seems too unreal."

"May I try to help?" asked the nun.

The woman shrugged. "If you wish," she said, passively.

Sister Caroline looked at her patient steadily for a few moments. She felt as though she were forcing her way to communicate with her, yet this was a chore

49

she had become accustomed to in nursing the sick and the disturbed. Resolutely she went ahead.

"Would you accept the name Edythe? Edythe Clare Monsarrat. It is only until we find your real name, of course. That shouldn't be long."

The woman on the bed seemed to be thinking of the name and she repeated it softly to herself.

"It isn't a bad name, Sister," she said. "Where did it come from?"

"Out of my head. It belongs to no one," answered Sister Caroline, smiling. "Do you like it?"

The woman looked a little amused and sat up in bed. "Edythe Clare Monsarrat," she repeated. "Well, it certainly makes me a fictitious character, doesn't it? I feel as though I am a character in a play."

Sister Caroline looked startled. Yes, she could see how a person might feel that way, a name meant a role. Yet the character was not yet delineated.

"And what will Edythe Clare Monsarrat be like in this play?" she asked.

The woman looked at her, smiling a little. "I suppose I shall create the character," she said, "or perhaps just discover it. And the sort of play it is going to be. Is there a mirror, Sister? I would like to see this character named Edythe."

"Oh, what a pity, and that reminds me of another thing," said Sister Caroline, flushed and excited with the success of the naming. "In the morning I shall send Emma to you. Have you met Emma? No? Well, she is of the Fulani people. Most of the hospital employees are Mande or Malinké—that is the same. Emma lived with the nuns in Conakry for some time, and then she worked for a French family there. She can read and write a little, and understands something of our way of life. She does for the doctor in his cottage, does his laundry, makes him comfortable." Sister Caroline heard as from a distance her own words rattling on. She quickly continued.

"Emma does very useful things for us here, too. She knows where to find things we need in town, and she does many errands for all of us. Often she is able to translate a patient's words when no one else can understand. She knows Pular and Susu, as well as French and Malinké. Now, Edythe, tonight you think of what things you need, personal things, such as a mirror, comb, brush, toothpaste and brush, talcum, underthings. Look, I have a little pencil and notebook here in my pockets where I carry everything but the dispensary." After a little rummaging around, Sister Caroline found the pencil and pad which she laid on the bedside table.

"Order stationery or notebooks, if you like. I think it would be helpful for you to write your thoughts and your dreams. Perhaps it would help you to remember something. We have some money for such purchases. You must begin to try to live a normal life, as you feel stronger day by day."

Sister Caroline rose and quickly kissed the woman on her forehead. "I shall leave you now, Edythe Clare. Sister Hildegaard will be here soon with your supper. God be with you."

The patient did not respond. The sister turned and went down the hall and down the stairs, with a vague, dissatisfied feeling. She went to the hospital chapel, seldom used since the sisters conducted their devotions in their own small chapel in their cottage. It had rows of benches and an altar with a white plaster statue of Christ wearing a wreath of thorns. The sisters kept prayer candles burning at one side of the altar. Sister Caroline lit one now for the woman upstairs and then she chose a place to sit in the dimmest part of the room. She needed to examine her thoughts. She was disappointed by the unresponsiveness of the woman upstairs, by her seeming lack of gratitude. A woman more or less her own age, who spoke her language (although truly Sister Caroline could tell that French was not the woman's first language), a woman from the world beyond the upper Niger plateau. Sister Caroline felt that she was committing a sin in thinking these thoughts and letting the woman bother her. She

51

herself had never been in such a predicament, with no memory of who she was or where she came from. She should not sit in judgment of her attitude. Yet she could not help but remember the woman's hands lying on the sheet, hands that showed no signs of toil—manicured, soft, uncallused. The lovely rings she wore, not ordinary at all. She thought of the perfect body tan and knew it must have come from hours spent in indolence on a beach or terrace. She had seen those women, wearing the briefest of bathing costumes, reclining on bright towels, voluptuously soaking in the sun's rays; she had seen them strolling the streets dressed for shopping or for parties, the rich tan on their arms and legs, the lovely clothes. This was the kind of person who now lay in their hospital, a person from the upper classes, such as she herself had left years ago. This person who was taking the name Edythe Clare Monsarrat.

She was glad the woman had liked the name. Edythe Clare had been the name of a doll she had owned as a child, an exquisitely dressed china doll. She had been the most beautiful thing in the world to her then. Yet Edythe Clare was not the doll she took to bed with her or held closely when she cried or was lonely. That had been another, homelier, softer doll. Monsarrat was a surname she had just pulled out of the air because it went well with the rest.

How different their two lives were. Perhaps God was testing her in exposing her to this new relationship, testing her commitment to her vows. The nun slipped to her knees and prayed.

The woman now named Edythe Clare Monsarrat lay staring into the dusk, her fingers toying with the rosary. From her window she could hear the sounds of the muezzin calling the Mohammedan faithful to evening prayer. A shiver of ecstasy passed over her. She listened, her fingers touching the Catholic beads, but her emotions carried her beyond the hospital, the pepper tree, the town itself, on the wailing cry from the mosque. She was no longer earthbound; she was borne up and away on the air of the evening. Then silence fell again and she saw that the shadows had absorbed the light in her room, turning it from gold to amber and then to darker and darker shades of blue and gray.

A nursing aide came in on the evening rounds. She set a glass of juice on the bedside table, straightened the bed linens, and checked the bathroom. Edythe heard guttural male voices across the hall and decided that the night guard must be coming on duty. There were heavy sighs and the shifting about of a chair. She told the aide to close the door.

It had been an eventful day. She was in a different room, well enough to be by herself. She now had a name, even though it was fictitious and temporary. Strange how important it was to have a name! Though all the layers of memory that make up the adult mind still remained mute and inactive, she felt she had secured one small portion of firm ground. Images raced through her thoughts as she hung on the edge of sleep. Sometimes she was a caldron of soup that sat on a fire too feeble and sputtering to bring it to a boil, and the soup refused to bubble; sometimes she was the soup, sometimes the one who stirred and waited. Again she was a great lump of clay lying on the earth waiting for a skilled potter who dawdled and waited nearby to come and make her into something —she was in the clay, crying mutely, trying to move while the potter sat stupidly gazing into space. And then she was a tiny animal who was caught in a great lake and could not swim, and she caught desperately at bits of drifting debris. She saw the name Edythe Clare Monsarrat come drifting by and it was easy to catch. Now her hands had something solid enough to hold her. She would not go under. But there was still fear of the depths beneath and she clung desperately to the name. Would she ever reach the shore?

Just before sleep came, the face of the doctor floated across her thoughts. She could see the calmness about

53

his eyes and brow and remembered how she had felt an immediate trust and a response to that face. There was also a sensuousness around his mouth that stirred her. She tossed and turned, smiling a little. The sister had mentioned the girl, Emma. She was nearly asleep, but she remembered that Emma would come in the morning and she must make a list.

9

HEINRICH SET DOWN his empty teacup and switched
off the BBC on his shortwave. It had degenerated into
a sporadic crackle that spoke of lonesome distances
and nothing more. He stood up and stretched. He
glanced toward Emma, who was asleep on her mat in
a corner of the room, curled up, one arm over her
face to shut out the light. She liked to sleep around
people. She had thrown a yardage of bright cotton
across herself, but her strong, smooth legs were already tangled in it, pulling it half off. The tiny, wiry
braids of her hair, unturbaned, fell in all directions.
Beside her on the floor was a basket of her sewing
things. She was often sewing on some garment or other
as a pastime, having been taught to do careful work
by the nuns in Conakry.

The overhead light flickered and Heinrich pulled
the cord to turn it off. The electric power of Siguirre
was erratic, it flickered often and the least storm or
hard wind sent it off altogether.

Standing in the darkness at the window he smelled
the night air. It was heavy and sweet. He decided
suddenly to go to the hospital. He fastened his loosened trousers, slipped on a white jacket without bothering with a shirt, and pulled on his canvas shoes.

Outside, the street was empty. The only light showing was on the corner of his street and Rue de Jean
Jauré, where a dim streetlamp flickered and the bugs
danced around it. At the hospital two lights on either
side of the portico were lit. The doctor came up to
the front entrance, which he never used in the day-

time when people were around. Tonight he enjoyed the feeling of going up the uncluttered steps. He felt as though he were entering his own mansion. In the main entrance hall he saw no one. To the left, in the chapel, a place he never entered, the candles burned eternally. He went on to the new wing.

Kouindo, the orderly, was on duty on the first floor. Heinrich found him in the examining room. He was sitting on the doctor's stool talking to a man in a loose white caftan who sat on the floor in a relaxed manner, his hands clasped around his upraised knees. Heinrich recognized him as a patient recovering from a hernia operation. He was nearly well and ready to be dismissed. The two got to their feet when the doctor appeared in the doorway and looked at him anxiously.

"Is everything all right?" Heinrich asked.

Kouindo replied, "This man, he can't sleep, Doctor. We just talking."

"Yes," said Heinrich. "Well, I will check the wards. I didn't feel like sleeping either."

"I come with you, Doctor?"

"Yes, you should be closer to the ward, you know. And you," Heinrich nodded to the patient, not remembering his name. "You should go to your bed."

"Yes, Doctor," the man said, and padded down the hall to his ward.

Heinrich visited the downstairs ward for women and children. He went from bed to bed, listening to the breathing of the patients, sometimes touching them. A child, ill with abdominal pain, tossed and turned and complained in his sleep but did not wake. An old woman lay awake and as he bent over her she said in Malinké, "Home, I want to go home."

"Tomorrow, perhaps, Mother," the doctor answered. He patted her thin, withered hand, as cool and light as water.

Seeing that Kouindo was at his proper station, Heinrich went upstairs. Two nursing assistants were on the upper floor; the nuns slept. The assistants followed the doctor around, wondering why he had come. The wards were quiet. Still, Heinrich checked the records and observed the patients. Some of them, lying awake, were comforted at the sight of the doctor moving through the room. They closed their eyes and found sleep ready for them. Heinrich felt a great affection for the Malinkés. They complained so little, and the depths of their spirits both mystified and soothed him. He went down the hall to the two private rooms. The guard at the prisoner's door had been dozing and now he stood up at attention, wiping his face and trying his best to appear alert.

"Why is this door closed?" asked the doctor sharply, seeing the woman's door pulled shut.

"She asked me to close it," the young Malinké aide replied. "I think because of the guard."

The doctor opened it and they went in. The woman slept, one arm hanging down from the bed. The doctor carefully raised it and placed it by her side.

The rosary had fallen to the floor. He picked it up and placed it on the table. Sister Caroline was here, he thought. The hall light shone partially into the room, illuminating the sleeping woman. He lingered, looking down at her. He felt a great curiosity about this person who had survived a plane crash and had walked out of the forest into M'Boura and now was here with no memory of her past at all. He remembered a primitive legend of Asherah, the Moon Goddess, who rose up out of the forests, taking the form of a woman. He felt a sense of awe and mystery, but then told himself that this woman was very much the same as the rest of them. She had a pulse and a blood pressure and a nervous system. Yet she could not remember anything! As if to confirm the miracle!

The aide stirred a little, but still Heinrich stood thinking about the patient. Should he send her to the hospital in Conakry? But the trip would be risky, and they had no specialized help there either. Perhaps in a few days she would regain her memory. He knew amnesia could be a temporary thing.

There had been occasional white women in the hospital in his years in Siguirre, wives of French provincial businessmen or farmers, but they were provincial, noisy, small-minded, and very much aware of their social status in this backward country. He had found them abrasive. This woman, even in her amnesic state, possessed a subtle natural elegance he had not known in a woman before.

Heinrich turned and went out. They closed the door but he told the nursing aide, "Check on this patient every hour."

In the room across the hall Paul Marion lay awake. A candle burned on the bedside table.

"I couldn't sleep," he told Heinrich, welcome on his face, "and the candle is company. Sister Hildegaard let me have it."

Heinrich sent the aide away and sat on the side of the bed. He and Paul talked together in French. Heinrich detected the stain of tears drying on the young man's cheeks and sensed his loneliness and despair.

After a few questions as to his physical condition, he asked, "Has anyone told you about our new case, the white woman who walked out of the jungle at M'Boura?"

"Come on!" said the youth. "The sisters have mentioned the woman across the hall in rather a mysterious tone. What's it all about?"

And the doctor told him about the woman and her amnesia, feeling his breach of professional ethics could be justified as Paul needed something to occupy his mind.

"Wow!" Paul exclaimed when Heinrich finished. "I never knew anyone before with amnesia. Were there other survivors? What kind of a plane? Where did they come from?"

Heinrich had to say reluctantly, "They haven't found the wreckage. They haven't found anyone else. It is a miracle she walked away from it. And I haven't heard from the commissioner if they know what plane is missing in the area."

Paul was silent a few minutes. "Then you're only

assuming there was a plane crash," he said. "Christ! It's some story, isn't it! And she's across the hall there. What does she speak?"

"She speaks French."

Then Paul jumped to another subject, afraid the doctor would get up and leave before he had said everything on his mind. "The guard told me there was an escape from the prison the other night. He said a guy took a boat across the river."

"I know," said Heinrich, "but he didn't make it, Paul."

"Oh," said the young man. "Then it was true. I thought the guard was lying about that."

"It was true."

"Well, he probably only had a native pirogue. Now a motorboat would be a different thing."

"Don't get any ideas, Paul. You couldn't make it. They shot him down on the river."

"Oh, don't worry. I'm too weak to escape from a chicken coop, now. But . . ." His voice trailed off.

"How about trying to get some sleep, Paul?"

"Yes, maybe I can. I'm glad you came in. Oh!" And Paul sat up again. "Do you think there's any chance I might get me a pardon—now that they've had their pound of flesh for a year and I've been sick and all? I heard the Pardon and Parole Board meets the first of April. I mean, do you think there'd be any chance?"

Heinrich caught his thread of hope, his plea. "It's possible, isn't it!" He caught some of the hope himself. This hadn't occurred to him; he knew nothing of the Pardon and Parole Board. "How would you go about applying?"

"I hear all kinds of forms and signatures are necessary," said Paul. "I know you're too busy, but I wondered if there is anyone who could—anyone who would do it?"

"The American consul, possibly?" asked the doctor.

"No," was the reply. "They won't touch it."

"I know Alfoldi would," said Heinrich, "if only he

were in here. But I don't know if he'll return soon enough."

"Yes," said Paul, "I thought of him, too. He's my only other friend, really."

Disturbed by the thought that there might be a chance for a pardon wasted, the doctor felt the burden of Paul's needs. He turned and blew out the candle.

"Leave it with me now, Paul. Sleep. I'll look in on you tomorrow."

"Goodnight, doctor," Paul turned and curled his body. Heinrich went out, leaving the door ajar.

The burden and despair of too many lives were laying their claims upon him. Resentment surged. His own life's burden was enough, really. As he walked back to his cottage through the dark street he had a feeling of wanting to push away these intrusions from the outside world, these people like Paul and the white woman who came from out there and demanded that he become involved with their lives. His work was here in this hospital; this was his job. He had made it his one area of concern for ten years now. He had carefully built a life for himself in Siguirre, with rare trips down to Conakry, and then he always hurried back. How long since he had been in Europe—my God! And why should he go? Out there, the malignancy of a decaying West. Here, primitivism and simplicity, yes, and a kind of purity. He had chosen it; he was glad he was here, hidden in the interior of Africa. Since his escape from the despair of Europe he wanted only peace. He was driven by no mission except an instinctive drive to find peace; he wanted no demands upon him except professional ones, no moral burdens anymore, no challenge to his manhood because he was a Jew or believed a certain way. Indeed, what did he believe anymore—in what? He had ceased to think along such lines. He thought with his hands as he worked. His mind beyond that drifted and was content. He didn't want to become involved in Paul's attempt to secure a pardon. Somehow he felt it would not work, anyhow. Let Alfoldi do that. Alfoldi knew about such things, didn't mind becoming involved; he had tried at the time of Paul's trial to secure a change of venue, hire a better lawyer, but he was too late on the scene to accomplish anything. He would send a note to Alfoldi about this thing; beyond that, he would not be involved. Reaching his cottage, he went to his bed and instantly fell asleep.

10

WHEN THE WHITE WOMAN opened her eyes the next morning to a room full of sunlight she felt she was not alone. Standing near the door was a tall figure, resplendent in a *m'boubou,* the garment of West Africa. The person took a few steps closer to her bed. The cotton print she wore had a dizzying effect on Edythe. Huge, stylized figures in red leaped and cavorted on a white background over which zigzag lines, like black lightning, fought for dominance. A turban of the same material was bound about her head and tied by a knot in front, the two ends sticking out like gay antennae. This exotic creature must be Emma, whom Sister Caroline had told her about. The girl's skin was brown and clear, so shining and pellucid that the image of pearls came into Edythe's mind. Her nose was fine, her cheekbones high. Only her full lips defined her African heritage. She smiled uncertainly and shyly at the patient in the bed and touched her fingertips together.

"I Emma," she announced, speaking French. "Sister Caroline send me."

The woman raised herself in the bed. *"Bonjour,"* she said. And she tried to draw her eyes away from the amazing print of the girl's costume.

"I go to market now," said Emma, smiling shyly as she regarded the white woman. "I have money from Sister Caroline." She reached in the bosom of her dress and brought out a handful of francs and showed them. "See," she said, pleased to show so much money. "Many francs to buy things for madame."

"I haven't made my list yet," Edythe said, reaching for the pencil and pad that Sister Caroline had left. "Please wait a few minutes."

"I wait."

The woman indicated the chair with her pencil. "Sit down, Emma."

The brilliant figure obeyed, sitting erect on the edge of the chair, and the woman who now thought of herself as Edythe began to list the things essential for her personal needs, although she could not resist stealing glances from time to time at the figure on the chair.

"There," she said finally, and handed the list to Emma. "Can you read my writing?"

Emma bent over the list and slowly pronounced the items aloud. At the underwear items she paused and looked at Edythe.

"What size I buy, madame?" she asked.

Edythe was taken aback. Her size? Of course, she didn't know. She looked down at herself, up at the other woman, embarrassed.

"I think the same as you, Emma," she said. She could not explain to this girl that she remembered nothing.

Emma regarded Edythe's figure briefly and said nothing more. Actually, Edythe thought, I guess I am smaller than she, but she let it go. She felt so irritated, so helpless. Emma had finished the reading; she folded the piece of paper and tucked it away

"I go now, madame." She stood up. "*À bientôt.*"

"*Merci*, Emma. "*À bientôt,* I'll see you soon."

The girl went out, leaving the door open behind her. Edythe noticed that she went across to the room opposite and, ignoring the guard, rapped lightly on the door and went inside. I suppose, thought Edythe, she is shopping for that prisoner, too.

Sister Gertrude, passing through the hall, caught sight of Emma as she moved unhurriedly toward the stairs.

"Ah, Emma. You are very splendid today. Which patient did you visit?"

"I saw the white woman, Sister, and the prisoner, too. I go to shop for the white woman. Sister Caroline has given me francs."

Sister Gertrude paused beside Emma. She was carrying a blood pressure bag over her arm and a tray of thermometers.

"And nothing for the young man?"

"He asked me for a comb and a nail file, Sister."

"Very good, Emma. Shop carefully. And did you get Sister Hildegaard's list?"

"I go now to Sister Hildegaard, Sister. She work on her list."

"You will need help, won't you? With so many things to buy."

"I take Moussa, nephew of Bakary, Sister. He will carry."

"Good. And don't be all day, Emma. They will be needing the kitchen things."

"No, Sister."

Emma went down the stairs, her red, white, and black *m'boubou* trailing behind her. She went through the hospital to the kitchen area. Sister Hildegaard was looking for her.

"Here you are, Emma," she said, relieved. "The list is ready and here is the money. You'll have a lot today. How shall you manage? Moussa is too small to carry everything."

"We find other boy, Sister," Emma replied serenely. *"De rien."*

"Well, I hope you manage. And don't be all day. Have you seen Sister Caroline?"

"Yes, Sister."

"Bientôt, Emma." Sister Hildegaard hurried away to the laundry.

In the kitchen the workers at the sinks and tables looked up at Emma, admiring her attire. They spoke a few joking remarks to her, comparing her job with theirs, offering to exchange. They laughed as they talked, their white teeth flashing in broad smiles. They called warnings after her for the marketplace, as they did each time she went. Emma closed the screened door. Outside, Moussa squatted, tossing pebbles at the snails that still had not found refuge against the day's heat. Seeing Emma with the baskets he jumped to his feet and took two of them from her.

Passing the nun's garden, Emma paused to observe a small drama taking place there. The bird the sisters called the weaverbird and the natives call the whidah bird, whose tail was nearly a foot in length, had been eating away at a squash, when a stray cat, watching for hours for such an opportunity, had pounced upon it, catching, instead of the bird itself, the long, droopy tail feathers. These he now held with his teeth and claws while the bird struggled to pull free. Emma and Moussa stood by the garden fence, watching.

Moussa's eyes gleamed with interest. "That old whidah bird, he not get away from that cat!" he predicted.

Emma said nothing. She could see that the cat was sharply considering its chances of letting go of the tail and seizing the body of the bird before it could fly away. She watched the bird's fluttering struggles against the vine leaves. The cat had a very good chance of success; the long tail feathers, the sign of the mating season, would deter the bird from lifting off suddenly and quickly. The cat had the odds. Above, in the tree, the weaverbird's mate called, "Cui, cui, cui."

"Shame on you, cat," Emma said. Then she ordered, "Moussa, throw something at that cat."

Moussa dropped the baskets with glee and hunted for a clod of earth which he threw vigorously at the cat. Startled, the cat let go and the weaverbird lifted himself and his ridiculous plumage up into the casuarina tree overhead. Its mate continued to scold and cry.

"That old cat find his breakfast someplace else,"

Emma said. She continued her way down the street, Moussa bumping along behind.

She loved going to market. She talked to many people. She loved buying and bargaining, taking pride in her ability to select things well and to buy cheaply. She loved the jangle of sounds around her—the calls of the sellers attracting their customers and their back-and-forth chatter, the yells of the workers unloading the carts and trucks, the pounding of the butchers at the meat stalls, and the delicious smells from the cooked-food vendors, but even more than these, she liked looking at the textiles, the jewelry and baubles. Usually she stole time from shopping to look at these things, but this morning her list for the white woman would take her to these sections of the marketplace.

The white woman! At first when she heard about her from Fatou and the others she was nervous and afraid of her—they said she had walked out of the forest and was perhaps an embodied spirit. But when she saw her sleeping there in the bed, her mouth partly open, Emma knew she was a woman like any other woman. Emma had lived in Conakry, known white people, seen and heard the airplanes at the airport. It was not unbelievable to her that the woman had been in a crash of one of those airplanes. She was not covered with bandages, however. They said she was hardly hurt at all. But something was wrong with her. No matter, the doctor would make her well, whatever it was. The doctor was a clever man. And kind, too. She would look to see if the papayas were good today. He liked them very much. Of course, next to mangoes, but the mangoes were not in season yet. She looked behind. Moussa was still trudging along with the two empty baskets. He flashed her a comradely grin.

It was mid-morning. Edythe had breakfasted and showered and, wearing the rough hospital gown, she lay propped against the hard pillows. She was restless, fidgety, wishing there was something to do, even though a tiredness hung over her body. Her mind was restless, dissatisfied, yearning. She examined her hands, even her toes, wondering about this person whose body she inhabited, but there was so little she could learn. She looked forward to Emma, who would be back at any time with the things from the market. And then she came at last, carrying a basket with the purchases.

Smiling uncertainly, Emma spread them on the bed. They looked at everything together. Edythe took the mirror first and regarded herself for some time. She was glad to discover that the face she saw was an attractive face, with good skin, a straight nose, and a full mouth, but the eyes that stared back at her were serious and questioning, not telling her anything. A stranger's eyes. It was a person she did not know. Panic and a feeling of hysteria swept over her. But she was not alone. The African girl waited. Edythe laid the mirror face down on the sheet.

She glanced up at Emma, who stood beside the bed regarding her in return, her eyes shifting, not knowing what was expected of her. Did Emma know that she was a stranger to herself? What would she think? Would she be frightened of her if she knew?

"My name is Edythe Clare Monsarrat, Emma," she said quite firmly.

"Yes, madame," replied Emma. "The sister told me."

"Oh," said Edythe. She wanted to say more, to confide in this girl, but she did not dare.

"You bought nice things," she said. "You even found a lipstick." It was not a bad color and, in fact, Edythe could not remember having put it on the list. "Thank you for your trouble," she added, aware the girl had tried to please her.

"De rien," murmured Emma. "It is nothing."

She remained in the room and Edythe liked having her there. There was a quality about her that gave her spirits a lift. Perhaps it was her youth and beauty. No, it was more, it was a repose she had—she seemed ordered and serene.

"I think the doctor may let me get up today," Edythe remarked.

Her dress of crisp, white linen-like material, with neckline, pockets, and armholes ribbed in brown, hung on a wall hook. She had already examined it curiously, reading the label that told her only that it was French-made. Emma followed her glance.

"Shall I help you dress, madame?"

Why not, thought Edythe. I'll be dressed when the doctor comes around. Then he'll see that I'm ready to get up and move about.

"Yes, please, Emma."

Putting aside the bedsheet, she swung her feet onto the floor. She reached her hands out to Emma, who pulled her up. Emma's hand was warm and rough. She steadied her. Edythe moved about, feeling no dizziness at all. She had been up before to go to her toilet and shower and then sink onto the bed again, exhausted. This time she intended to walk.

With Emma's help she put on the new underwear, which fit perfectly, and the laundered, mended dress. The dress hung loosely as though she had lost weight. She slipped her feet into the sandals waiting there. They were stylish compared with those of the sisters and Emma. And then she moved about her room, aware that Emma was watching her movements. Somehow Edythe felt her dress scanty, her arms so naked and her legs so bare. Emma's *m'boubou* hung gracefully from her neck, falling over her arms clear to the ankles. Underneath was the matching blouse and wrap-around skirt. Edythe's own dress was more like an undergarment.

"I would like to have a dress like yours," said Edythe. "Not the same print, of course," she added, "but a dress like you wear."

She thought of the sisters in their white garments that covered them somewhat like the African dress. She would be the only woman in such brief, unsuitable apparel. It was her own dress. At some time, in some place, it must have been just right.

"Le grand boubou?" echoed Emma, disbelief on her face.

"Do you suppose there is enough money, Emma, to buy me one? It would be better than this dress—this dress belongs someplace else."

"I ask Sister Caroline," said Emma doubtfully. White women she had known never wore *m'boubous*.

"Oh, well, I shall ask her myself when she comes by. Emma, thank you for all you've done for me. It was kind of you."

It was a dismissal. Emma moved toward the door. "Shall I go now, madame?"

"It is all right. I don't need anything just now. I must wait for the doctor to come. *Salut.*"

"Salut," replied Emma, the tips of her *m'boubou* drifting behind her as she went soundlessly down the hall.

Left alone, Edythe gathered together the purchases and put them into the drawer of the bedside table. My worldly possessions, she mused.

"I am well," she said aloud to herself. The words echoed hollowly back to her, followed by the frightening thought that she was still incomplete, crippled by that closed door in her mind, that abyss. Here in the hospital she was only a cipher, a woman with a made-up name. She felt the belittling weight of it upon her. What was it the doctor had said she had—retrograde amnesia induced by trauma? She got on her bed again and sat cross-legged, hunched over her knees, depressed and frustrated. There must be a way to open that sealed door of her memory!

She heard the doctor and Sister Gertrude approaching; they were talking together. Then they stood by her bed looking down upon her.

"Ma chère Edythe! You have been up already," said Sister Gertrude, using the new name carefully and placing a friendly hand on her shoulder.

Doctor Heinrich regarded her gravely. "It seems we are losing our patient, Sister," he said.

"I am afraid you cannot lose me, Doctor," said Edythe morosely. "Where would I go?"

"But, of course, you will go nowhere yet. I did not mean that. But we want you well and strong, not sick and helpless. I am glad to see you dressed. You are looking fresh and natural in your own clothes."

Everything he said was meant to be kind and encouraging, but she could find no comfort in his praise. She sat unresponsive, depressed.

"Are you ready to try walking in the halls?" asked Doctor Heinrich. "It will be good for you to move around—strengthen your legs, improve your circulation."

"Yes, I would like to walk, Doctor, but . . ."

"Yes?"

"Doctor, I still can't remember anything." She heard her voice plaintive and childish, but she continued, "I don't know who I am. I can't remember anything at all. What am I to do? What will happen to me?"

The doctor had no answers for her, but he replied, "My dear, be patient. Your illness, for that is what we must call it, may leave you as suddenly as it came. It will pass. In the meantime, get yourself strong physically and relaxed mentally. I can give you some tranquilizers to help ease the strain."

She shook her head stubbornly, and the doctor did not push his suggestion, for he was cautious in prescribing drugs.

After a few more routine questions he and Sister Gertrude turned to leave, but Edythe caught his arm and said urgently,

"Doctor, how old do you think I am?" She was embarrassed to ask the question, but it seemed important.

He turned back to look at her. "Can't you tell that as well as I?" He noticed the mirror still lying on her sheet.

"It is hard to be honest with this face I have seen for the first time," she answered.

Then he spoke more gently. "Edythe, I have seen thirty-year-old women who I thought surely were forty-five or more. I have seen the reverse, although not as often, I must say. I would imagine you to be around thirty, thirty-two, perhaps."

"Yes," she said. "Good. But, Doctor, can you tell me, have I had children? I need to know."

"Judging from my initial examination, I would think not. Yet it is hard to tell with some women. It's possible, yet I'd say probably not."

"Oh," she said, feeling both relief and disappointment.

Doctor Heinrich put his hands on Edythe's shoulders. He could feel the tenseness of her muscles. His hands moved to touch her throat and then her skull, feeling the fine bones beneath the short, soft hair. "Is it tender here, Edythe?"

"Only a little, Doctor."

"You must learn to wait for your memory. It will come."

"But what if it doesn't? Or if it takes years? You don't really know." Her green eyes looked at him, asking for his certainty.

"It will come. Have faith." He removed his hands from her head, and he and Sister Gertrude went across the hall to the other private room. Edythe sat thinking how good it was to be touched. She felt more like a whole person. But then she thought again, No, there is this abyss waiting inside for me. I must know who I am, who I am!

EDYTHE STAYED IN HER ROOM. She had looked out in the hall only once, to find herself staring directly into the face of the guard who stood by the closed door of the room across from hers. Frightened a little by this symbol of imprisonment and authority, she had withdrawn and closed her door. It would have been much pleasanter to have it open. She wondered about the prisoner in that other room. They had said he was an American, a young man. She must ask Dr. Heinrich about him. A prisoner, always with a guard. How awful. She wondered what his crime had been. Was it something horrible? But Sister Hildegaard had not seemed to regard him as dangerous. Perhaps it was something to do with politics.

Edythe sat in her chair by the window and tried to begin a journal. The month was now March, the date she did not know. She wrote her new name, the names of the sisters, of Emma, of Doctor Heinrich. What was the rest of the doctor's name? And then she regarded her handwriting with interest. It was a confident, educated kind of writing. Still, it did not tell her who she was. She stared at the ring on her left ring finger, turning it back and forth. Was it a ring that meant marriage, or engagement? Had someone put it there, or had she? She tried to summon up a face, a face of a lover or husband, yet none came. Perhaps whoever it was is dead, she thought. He did not walk out of the jungle with me. Perhaps he was not in the plane. I may have been on a commercial flight and he waits, wondering when I am coming. I should think if I had a husband he would be searching for me. If not, then he must be dead and I left him alone to die. I wonder if he was a good man, if he was handsome, if I loved him. It seemed more convincing, putting the tense in the past. Still no memories stirred. Her mind was a peat bog, inert and unresponsive. For what were her memories waiting? When would they stir and open the past to her?

Sister Caroline came into her room and found her sitting there twisting her rings.

"Our patient is feeling well enough to be bored, I believe."

"I am a little, Sister," Edythe replied. She wondered why this sister, obviously a remarkable person, nettled her ever so slightly.

"We should have some books or magazines for you," said Sister Caroline. "I will look for some. The sisters and I seldom have time to read, except in our breviaries."

"I would like to read," said Edythe.

"How about handwork?" asked Sister Caroline. "We always have mending in the hospital that needs to be done. Or crocheting?"

"I don't think I know how," Edythe replied. "Sister, what is the rest of the doctor's name, after Heinrich?"

"It is Fink," said the sister.

The woman looked surprised. "How strange," she said slowly. "It doesn't seem to fit him. I guess I am getting a little daft about names."

"I understand that in German *fink* is the name of a small, rather common bird," said the sister, smiling a little at the thought. "I agree with you, it doesn't fit the doctor. Yet, we don't put much importance on names here. Most of the names we hear seem impossible."

Edythe looked at her, aware of the sister's intelligence, her perceptiveness.

"So now you have permission to walk about," continued the nun. "Would you like me to walk with you the first time?"

"Yes." And then Edythe continued. "Sister, I want to have a *m'boubou*. Perhaps a white one, or one with a small print."

Sister Caroline felt annoyed. It was not so much a request as a demand, and didn't they have enough to do without worrying about such things?

"Le grand boubou?" she said. "You are a free woman, Edythe. With us it is only a matter of finding the extra money to advance you. Still, I wonder why you would want to wear a *m'boubou* like the *indigènes*. I doubt if you are accustomed to wearing such a garment."

Even as she said this, Sister Caroline felt she had spoken intolerantly.

Edythe was engrossed in the thought she was pursuing. "Here in this hospital, in this short sleeveless dress, I feel so naked. You sisters are covered, Emma's *m'boubou* covers her. I don't feel right, walking about in this—this little dress."

She was aware of another feeling she had not expressed, a feeling of not wanting to be conspicuous. It is because I feel so much like a non-person, she thought. That must be why the dress has become such an issue.

Sister Caroline said, "If you want a *m'boubou* you shall have one. It may be we could borrow one from Emma to see how you like it. That is, if Emma owns one that isn't as wild as the one she wore today. Come, take my arm now and we shall walk down the hall and you will see what the hospital is like from the vertical position."

The two slowly walked the upstairs hall, ignoring the guard whose dark eyes flickered ever so slightly at the sight of Edythe. At her request, they descended the stairway to the main floor. They stood a few moments in the foyer, but the faces of Monsieur Diallo and Sy Kanadu and other office help were peering at them so openly curious that they turned and walked again. Fatou at the reception desk smiled shyly at Edythe, but Sister Caroline introduced her to no one.

They walked as far as the hall of the new wing and then slowly retraced their steps to Edythe's room. She was exhausted and sank onto her bed.

Sister Caroline stood in the doorway, ready to go. "Now perhaps you will enjoy a rest," she said.

"The reading material," said Edythe. "Don't forget it, Sister."

"I shall try to find something. *À bientôt.*"

Downstairs, Sister Caroline met the doctor in the hall. As they passed, he asked, "And the new patient, did she walk with you?"

"Yes, we walked quite a bit. She's tired now, but she did very well."

"*Très bien.* Anything more?"

"Well, this concern of hers over what she will wear —now she wants a *m'boubou,* of all things!"

"Surely you understand," replied the doctor, looking into the troubled face of Sister Caroline. "It shouldn't take a psychologist to see that the nakedness she feels is not really a physical nakedness."

The sister was contrite. "Now I see, Doctor. I should have thought of that myself."

He touched her arm. "It's the heat and the work. They are too much for us. Try to take more time to rest, Sister."

"I'll try, Doctor. Oh, I've been intending to mention something about this patient."

"Yes?" he asked.

"Well, she isn't French. Not of French origin, that is. French is a second language to her. I've been intending to mention it."

"So!" said the doctor. Sister Caroline would know about this. She was from Paris, and French to the core. The other two nuns were from Alsace-Lorraine, where German was the preferred language. "Then what do you think this woman is?" he asked.

"I would say either English or American," said the sister. "Does it help us any?"

"Not yet," he replied. "But we shall keep it in mind,

75

and I can pass the information along to the commissioner. Finding out where she is from is his job, not ours. *À demain.*" And he hurried on his way.

Sister Caroline and Emma brought the *m'boubou* for Edythe the next day.

"This is one of Emma's; she let me choose it from her wardrobe," Sister Caroline explained.

"It is not a good *m'boubou*," said Emma apologetically, "but sister want this one."

"It is a good choice," observed Edythe. "Thank you, Emma."

The *m'boubou* lay across her bed. It was a rough blue cotton with a tiny white figure. She could see it would not be Emma's favorite, but the sister had chosen well. The two women helped her don the pieces of the African garment, first the collarless blouse with short sleeves, the wrap-around skirt, and then over the head with the great flowing outer piece that fell gracefully to the floor over the other garments. A little smile played about Emma's mouth as they worked and arranged. Edythe wondered if she were amused or displeased or proud that a white woman was wearing her clothes. When they were finished, Edythe moved about the room, and they nodded their approval, the sister in spite of her mixed feelings about the garments.

"Now," said Sister Caroline, "I must fly. Doctor waits for me. We operate at eleven. Emma may stay if she likes."

"Sister," said Edythe, "the books, remember?"

Sister Caroline gasped. "I forgot, didn't I? I'll try, Edythe." She waved goodbye and hurried away.

Edythe turned to Emma. "Would you walk outside with me?"

"Outside?" echoed Emma, looking reluctant.

"Just in the halls, Emma." Edythe knew she could not walk alone in this dress. She felt too strange.

So Emma walked with her, a little ill at ease, and Edythe felt the whole thing had been a mistake. The other ambulating patients stared at them curiously and

Sister Gertrude, hurrying past with a tray of medicines, looked around with a start. Edythe sensed that an orderly and one of the nursing aides in her crisp, blue hospital uniform, were whispering about her and looking amused. The walk ended and Emma did not linger.

Alone, Edythe spoke to her walls. "All right, now I know. The *m'boubou* was a distraction. It didn't matter that much. The real trouble is still here. I am a stranger to myself. I am hollow. Oh, who am I?"

With a groan of despair, she threw herself onto the bed. She thought of the person across the hall who was guarded night and day. A prisoner, she thought, like me. We are both prisoners.

A girl from the kitchen, Seitou, brought Edythe's luncheon tray and with it was a hastily written note from Sister Hildegaard.

"My dear Edythe, We are extremely busy today. Sister Caroline says you need reading material. I send you all I can find at the moment. Yours in God, Sister Hildegaard."

There were two Catholic tracts, called "Walks with our Lady of Mercy in Foreign Fields," a French schoolbook—*Matin d'Afrique*—and a very ragged, thick paperback copy of *Le Comte de Monte-Cristo*. Edythe sighed at the collection but settled herself to read during the long afternoon. Without surprise she found the Dumas romance familiar. Somewhere, she thought, I read this. I suppose as a schoolgirl. As she read, a part of her mind yearned for that adolescent she had once been when she had read *The Count of Monte Cristo* before.

Late in the day, Edythe sat on the floor by her window. Below in the hospital yard the families of the patients were gathered, waiting for their evening visit, laden with food from home—foo-foo, the lumps of pounded yam and cassava wrapped in cool leaves, small packages of guinea corn, papayas, bananas. Babies lay sucking in their mothers' arms, children stood clinging to their skirts. The men squatted together in groups talking softly. They waited for the signal that they could enter for the allotted time.

From her window Edythe looked down upon them. How peaceful and whole they seemed, the families, those mothers, how needed and loved by the little ones. Even the vendor of kola nuts who strolled among the crowd, her basket tray on her head, crying her wares in her singsong voice, was at home in this place; she belonged there. She had an identity, and the beggars looking for handouts of food for their suppers knew there was a place for them, too, an existence that could be maintained on the edges of their society. As Edythe watched the signal was given from the hospital door and the crowd poured into the foyer below. She continued to sit by the window, knowing no one would be coming to visit her. Outside, the vendors of fruits and sweets drifted away, sales finished for this time. The beggar drifted down the street. One figure remained, seated on the ground next to the iron fence. It was a blind woman who sold charms, talismans, and jujus against the evil eye. She leaned her ancient head back against the fence and began to sing. It was a meandering, unmelodic song, a song of the great river that flowed past the city, and of the length of the river's journey, of the burdens carried by people who came to the river's edge, of the blessings they carried away with them. It was a strangely strong voice from such an emaciated-looking body.

Edythe rested her head against the wall and closed her eyes. She let the street song pour over her. Each exquisite pinprick of sound cascaded over her, becoming steel points of pain stabbing the tendrils of her nerves. She went to her bed, lay down, and pounded her fists against her pillow. Stop, she cried, please stop. When Sister Gertrude came around much later for bed check, she was sound asleep in her clothes.

12

EDYTHE LAY ON HER BED dressed in the blue-and-white
m'boubou; the ragged copy of *Le Comte de Monte-
Cristo* had fallen from her hands. Her fan had been
taken away for someone who needed it more and the
heat of the afternoon, like a great cat, curled around
her and drowsiness made her sleep. And then as if
from far away she heard a voice speaking, and she
jerked up and saw a short, white man with a shock of
dark hair and a dark beard, wearing dusty clothes,
standing in her doorway looking at her apologetically.
He took a step into the room.

"Don't be frightened," he said. "I am Alfoldi
Santillana."

Was this someone from her past? She felt she should
know him, he looked so familiar. She sat up and regarded the stranger.

"That African thing is nice," he said, indicating her
dress. "It's the most practical garment for this country."

"You look familiar," Edythe said.

"I should think so," her visitor remarked. "But you
don't remember. You were in rather a bad way then.
It was I who brought you here, who found you—or I
guess more accurately, you found me."

Yes, now she knew. She had been wanting to see
this man again who had nursed her in those first,
blurred days. She offered him her hand and they
shook formally.

"Don't you live very far from here—it was in the
jungle, wasn't it?"

79

"I do," he said, "but I had to come to Siguirre on business and Doctor Heinrich said I should stop in to see you."

"So you are Monsieur Santillana," said Edythe. "Please sit down. Would you tell me about how I came to you—how I found you?"

Santillana sat down by the bed. He told her how she had walked out of the forest and fallen in front of his hut, about the villagers and their fear. Heinrich had told him about her amnesia. It was hard for him to grasp the idea of a person without a memory. Now, as he spoke, her face was a mixture of confusion and tension. When he finished she sat for a moment, looking into space.

"How did I get there?" she asked, intensely.

"My dear girl," said Santillana, feeling helpless. "It just has to be that you survived a plane crash. How else!"

"And the others?" she asked sadly.

"I sent the villagers to look. They found nothing, but then they wouldn't go far off the path. It is terrible, but we could get help no sooner."

"Yes," she said. "It is terrible. I can't bear to think about it very long."

"The doctor tells me you are doing well now, getting stronger, and your head has healed. It gave me a lot of worry, I can tell you. No experience with that sort of thing." He twisted his hands together, brown and rough from the sun and the handling of plants and contrasting sharply with the white skin that showed at his wrists and throat. When Edythe asked why he lived in the remote village he told her briefly about his work, hoping it would divert her from more depressing thoughts.

"How often do you come to this place—what is it called, Siguirre?"

"Usually every six weeks or so. It's too hard a trip to come more often, but I got a ride in with some of the military fellows who came out to look for your plane. They didn't find anything, of course. I don't think they looked any more thoroughly than the *indigènes*. I had something to do here for the young prisoner across the hall before the end of the month."

He jerked his head in the direction of the hall.

"Oh, are you connected to that young man in some way?" she asked, curious.

Santillana gave a little laugh. "We are all very dependent upon each other out here," he said. "I had no idea this was the way it would be when I first came. It is only in that way that I am connected to him."

Back at work again in M'Boura he had suddenly remembered the date April first, and the fact that a couple of months before he had heard, perhaps it was from Paul himself, that that date was when the Parole and Pardon Board met in Kankan—an annual meeting—and that any request on Paul's behalf would have to be submitted by then. He knew he had to do it for the boy; it was a chance. He felt irritated with himself for feeling that he must do this. He should be getting things wrapped up before the rainy season set in. Here he was getting involved with people's lives that had nothing to do with a comprehensive encyclopedia of tropical plants of West Africa.

"I understand they call you Edythe now," Santillana said.

Her face brightened. "Yes," she said. "I am no longer anonymous. I am Edythe Monsarrat."

"They told me you cannot remember. I am sorry. It occasionally happens to people after an accident or a shock—or both, like you had."

"Doctor Fink says I will get over it," said Edythe.

"Who did you say?" asked Santillana, looking surprised. "Doctor Fink?"

"Yes, Sister Caroline said that was the doctor's name. Isn't it?"

"Oh, yes, I guess I've heard that. We just never hear it used."

"It doesn't fit him at all," Edythe said. "I don't wonder." She sighed, and looked away from her visitor. "The days drag on so slowly. There's nothing to do, and reading makes me sleepy."

"My feeling is," said Santillana, "although I'm no doctor, that it is important for you to be busy, for you to keep your thoughts occupied."

She didn't answer, but picked at the hem of the *m'boubou*. "It's the emptiness, the sort of falling off into nothingness in my mind that is so ghastly," she said finally.

"Each of us has an abyss within," he said, "a place we try to ignore, something deep, dark, and so dangerous we can't bear to face it. We sense it is there— or else we know damn well it's there—and we're afraid. We stay away, trying to forget that it lies waiting."

She was interested and her eyes stayed on his face as he talked. "Waiting?" she asked, "Waiting for what?"

"Why, for us to get too close and look into it, get dizzy and fall and be lost."

"Ah, yes, that's right. That's why I'm staying away as much as I can. It's fairly easy sometimes, but other times I'm just drawn to it, I can't help myself." She felt that she and the Italian understood each other.

"You must keep busy," he said, "happy, if possible, or interested, like Heinrich with his work here."

"Does he have an abyss?"

Monsieur Santillana shrugged, whether in assent or uncertainty, she was not sure. "My dear, with some it lies in the past; with others, I suppose, sort of everywhere; with others, the future—old age—sickness— death—God knows!"

"And you, Monsieur Santillana, have you an abyss?"

When he looked at her, she thought she saw a curtain being drawn in his eyes. "Each of us has trouble enough without wondering about someone else's, my dear girl." He stood up. "Perhaps next time I come you can walk out with me. There's a little restaurant

82

down on the quai that fixes fish with a superb peanut sauce. We could go there—take the doctor, too."

"You're very kind," Edythe said. "I don't know." Somehow she could not plan for the future for she had not yet found a past.

"Well," he said, "I will go now. I must find Sister Hildegaard. I brought her a pail of honey. Then I've errands to do in the city. But ask the doctor to take you to talk to Paul across the hall."

He made a formal, rather old-fashioned bow as he left, promising to come back. She felt when he was gone as if he was some relative who had been to visit. Should she ask the doctor to let her meet the American? Monsieur Santillana seemed to think it a good idea, and now she found herself thinking of it eagerly.

13

THE MEETING WAS ARRANGED. Doctor Heinrich took Edythe across the hall one day after giving her the details that had led to the young man's imprisonment. He spoke a few words to the prison guard at the door, who nodded and stepped aside.

Edythe saw a thin, pale young man propped against some pillows. His white skin had a yellowish tinge, his eyes were blue, dark-lashed, his brown hair hung long and unevenly on his shoulders. Certainly he did not look the least like a criminal. There was no boldness or slyness or even defiance in his face; somehow she had expected something like that. If he had strengths, they were not obvious physical ones. There was something about him, though, that seemed vaguely familiar. But she did not know him. Even if she could remember again, she would not know this boy, would she? Later, when she thought back on her meeting with Paul, she thought of him as the sisters often referred to him, as *"le jeune,"* the young man. He had such a young look, young and hurt and vulnerable to more hurt.

When the doctor introduced them, Edythe wondered if she should explain that the name she was using was not really her name, but she said nothing, just stood fingering the edge of the blue-and-white wrap-around skirt. The young man spoke in fluent French.

"The doctor told me about you," he said. "That's a nice name they've given you."

Relieved that he knew about her amnesia, Edythe smiled at him and followed the doctor closer to the bed.

"It sounds strange being introduced with my new name," she said, "yet it could be my real name, for all I know."

"I never knew anyone before with amnesia."

She looked at him, impressed with his directness. "It's awful not to know who you are. It's like standing with your back against a high wall. You can see forward but nothing behind. Sometimes it's worse than that. In the first days I thought I was falling into an abyss."

"Try saying something to her in English," Heinrich said to Paul.

Paul spoke to Edythe in English then, saying, "The doctor wonders if perhaps you know English. I'm American. You look American to me, in a way. But you look French, too."

Amazed, Edythe understood him. She tried to answer in English, searching for words hidden in her mind, buried beneath the French. Gradually she was able to speak.

"How strange to be speaking English. I *do* know it, yet it's as if I seldom spoke it." She looked at Paul and the doctor, feeling dizzy. She put a hand to her head. Did this mean she was from an English-speaking country? Yet she had felt sure she was French—at least, she hadn't questioned it. How confusing everything was.

"Edythe, come, sit down." The doctor took hold of her arm, led her to the chair. "I am sorry we have added to your confusion. I only thought we should try to find out what we could about you, that it might help us."

"I'm all right," she said, sitting in the chair. "At first I was confused." The doctor's voice was friendly and warm, as if she were more than a patient, as if she were a friend.

Paul stared at her, his face anxious and intent. "Well," he commented, "you don't sound English-English. I think you're American."

They discussed the possibility, yet she was obviously at home in a French-speaking society. Edythe turned the talk to Paul.

"It is awful for you being under guard all the time. I wish I could help you."

He shrugged his shoulders. "It's better here in the hospital than in the prison," he said simply.

"Are you getting better?" she asked.

"Oh, yes, I'm glad of that, of course. The dysentery was terrible. I guess I have jaundice, too. I thought I was a goner, you know, back there in the prison. Even after they brought me here. But now I'm much better. Dr. Heinrich's medicine." They both looked at him.

"Did you understand?" Edythe asked the doctor in French.

"Not a word. Paul talks as fast as a monkey in English. Why don't you speak slowly, Paul?"

"Like the French?" asked the boy, looking amused at the doctor.

"Yes," said Heinrich, "like the French. No—like the Germans, who speak distinctly and separate their words properly."

Edythe answered in French. "He was grateful that your medicine is making him well."

"The wonder drugs earned their name this time," he said, "and now he's begun to eat again. We must get some fat on those bones before he has to go back."

"Can you get up yet?" Edythe asked Paul.

"I've started getting up. But, of course, they won't let me leave my room."

"Oh," said Edythe, wondering if he had seen her walking so freely in the halls. "Will they allow me to come in and talk to you?"

"I'll ask the guard," Heinrich said. "I think he could be persuaded to let us do that."

"I hope so," the boy said. "It gets awfully lonely."

So it was settled, as the guard could see no harm in the arrangement.

14

DOCTOR HEINRICH AND ALFOLDI SANTILLANA sat in the doctor's cottage, drinking. The doctor was in his white hospital trousers and naked from the waist up. Alfoldi had unbuttoned his shirt and let it hang loose. The ceiling fan swept each of them in turn with its breeze that relieved ever so slightly the steaming heat. They had finished discussing the weather and when the rains might come. It was the constant topic this time of year. And they had discussed Edythe, the futile search in the forest made by the local troops, and the fact that there was still no word about a missing plane.

"Unbelievable how people can disappear and no one seems to care or to be looking for them!" Heinrich said. "I don't understand the world anymore."

Alfoldi shrugged. "I think I do," he said. "It's the red tape, a cable mislaid, sent to the wrong place, waiting on someone's desk or still on the dispatcher's table under the newspaper. If not the red tape, the boredom of life in this climate. I can believe it. I've told Laura never to worry when she does not hear from me, to believe neither good nor ill until she sees me or my body, and then she can believe her own eyes."

"And so you've come into town to help Paul apply to the Pardon Board," said Heinrich, regarding the other. "I must have telegraphed my thoughts to you. After he mentioned it the other night it's been on my mind, but I've had no time to do anything about it. And here you are!"

"I'm really a fool, that's what. I should be getting

on with my work. But I had heard about this Pardon and Parole Board that meets the first of April and had entertained the thought that someone should apply for Paul's sake. And then—I suppose with the excitement of finding your newest displaced person, Edythe—I forgot about it until a few nights ago when, lying awake staring into the darkness, it hit me. God, I hated to make this trip again. But it might mean a year of that boy's life, so I couldn't forget it."

"It might mean his life, Alfoldi," Heinrich said. "I'm not at all sure he'll survive the prison. I'm an expert at diagnosing prisoners."

"Puttana miséria!" groaned the Italian, using one of his favorite laments. "The papers involved in the business, the signatures one must get. Equilbecq tells me a parole is out of the question since Paul is not a citizen, so the pardon is the only thing possible. A pardon must be submitted in sextuplicate, requested ostensibly by the American consul in Conakry. I'm getting the forms filled out, but the consul or his representative will have to sign them. I've called them twice by telephone and they've agreed to it. And then I have to run around for local signatures, the local *commissariat de police,* the chief prison warden, and two character witnesses—that's you and I, by the way. Then I have to see that it gets to the board in time."

"You're so involved you'll never get out of Africa, my friend."

Alfoldi shrugged again and drained his glass. "May I have another, Heinrich? Imagine it, ice with your whisky. What happiness!"

They went to the kitchen and made more drinks. Happy in his friend's company, Heinrich pushed away the thought of the day ahead when he would leave. Alfoldi was a part of his life in Siguirre and he looked forward to his occasional visits, to their walks through the city, their convivial visits to small bars and restaurants, their conversations in his living room. He knew but hated to recognize the difference between them. Alfoldi was not only free to go, but he *must* go.

Guinea was only a laboratory project for him. His work lay in Rome. It was different for himself. He had nothing to go to out there, nothing and no one. Here he had the hospital and all its needs, the constant stream of sick and no one else to fill his place. His family were the missionary sisters, the local staff, and the girl, Emma, all in greater and lesser degrees. No, he was not free of this country in the way Alfoldi was. He was envious of the Italian, envious but attached to him in a bond of brotherhood. They had shared many good hours together, had shared Paul's sad affair and now the problem of Edythe.

As they carried their drinks back to the other room, Santillana said, "She referred to you as Doctor Fink."

The doctor looked a little amused. "Oh, she did!"

"Yes, she said the name didn't fit you." Santillana knew he was probing, but it was his way. He was curious about his friend.

The doctor parried, "How can she tell it doesn't fit? She doesn't know me." And then he turned suddenly candid. "She's right, actually. My name is Lange. Fink was my mother's name. I took it after the war."

He didn't want to try to explain his reasons; in fact, so many years after the war, they no longer made much sense except that they were bound up with the wounds of his life, the tenderness he felt for his mother, the horror of her death.

Santillana sensed the dark web of the past wound around his friend's thoughts. He was ashamed of his curiosity and turned the conversation back to the white woman.

"So my forest spirit remembers nothing at all—she's an anonym. And very anxious and tense about it, of course. Is this a genuine case of amnesia, Heinrich?"

"It would seem so, Alfoldi. Frankly, I've never had one before. Let's hope it's a temporary state, brought about by the accident. It's rare, but it does happen. I would give anything for someone to consult with."

"But there would be little anyone could do, *n'est-ce pas?*" said the Italian. "The situation is sad."

"Indeed it is," the doctor echoed, looking down into his glass as though answers might be found there. "The hands we are dealt by fate," he murmured, "are strange. More often than not remembering is a penance. How many of us find it a pleasure to peruse the pages of our past lives? Damn few. For most of us, when faced with such thoughts, it is *la peine forte et dure*, either hell or the act of contrition."

"Yet the young woman over there begs and struggles just to remember one thing from her past," answered Alfoldi.

"Yes," said Heinrich, smiling wryly. "She doesn't understand the freedom she has been given, nor the opportunity."

Alfoldi's thoughts turned to his wife, Laura, and he said, "There is one thing that can alleviate this burden of remembering—if I may, for a moment, risk sounding sentimental—and that is love, the love relationship."

Heinrich regarded his friend curiously and said nothing, waiting for him to go on.

And Alfoldi said, "Love camouflages, hides in its mysteries, all we would remember and thus regret. Perhaps for some, like our sisters here, it is the love of God; for others, that of a mortal."

"Is love really that powerful?" Heinrich asked. "Well, there's another antidote, too, which is also the sovereign of love, and that is death. It will alleviate very well the pain of remembering."

"Come, we are too gloomy, Heinrich," said Alfoldi, getting up. "Now I have got you into a black mood and I am sorry. And I have to go about my business in the city so I can't even cheer you up again."

"Don't worry, friend," Heinrich replied, "I'm too busy to stay moody. The work drives it out of me."

Alfoldi left, and Heinrich returned to his chair. Alfoldi was probably right about the effect of their conversation. He felt he was drifting into a mood. His thoughts turned back over the day and he thought of the woman they had been discussing, remembering when he had touched her the last time, feeling her throat, her face and head, remembering the smooth, soft skin, the fine bones, the soft hair, and he thought how it would be if his hands were to move lower across her shoulders, down around the ripeness of her breasts, lower across the smooth, tanned stomach, down to the light hair covering the vulva and the introitus. He passed his hand across his face to try to wipe away the feeling of sexual hunger that swept over him. She was, of course, someone else's woman. Or had been. Was the man rotting now in the jungle, or did he still live in a safe world someplace else? The doctor got up impatiently and went to the kitchen to refill his glass.

Well, the woman belonged to the world out there and he, Heinrich Fink, belonged now to this peaceful, isolated world of Siguirre, the plateau country. It was enough to have. He was useful and busy at the hospital, his hospital. He had a modicum of companionship. He was safe from many of life's complications. Living out there a man would be constantly challenged. Professionally, he was probably behind the times. He seldom read the medical journal that was sent to him by the Missionary Board in Paris; it had so little application to the practice of medicine in this backwater town on the banks of the Niger. Perhaps he would have to be requalified to practice in France or Germany today. He dreaded facing the problems out there. Their residue drifted up to him in this place—Paul with the drug charge, rumors of the new morality or irresponsibility, of young people who no longer cared for standards. He would have to cope with all that if he went back again. He had had enough of such things.

Interned in Auschwitz and then Buchenwald, he had learned one thing—survival. True, he had seen heroism, perhaps been something of a hero himself, but he had also seen depravity of the basest form. Before the war he had been an overworked medical student, but his past had held warm ties, family, friends, a fiancée. These were gone now and those scars were healed, or nearly. But the black despair that some-times swept over him came pounding in on the heels of such recollecting. He was a machine who patched bodies. He had lost his youth and now what did he have to look forward to? He turned away such thoughts with a determined effort. I don't want to change anything, he told himself. I have a good life here.

15

EDYTHE SENSED AN INCREASED TEMPO in hospital activity. The halls were busy with movement of patients and nursing aides. The sisters had no time to linger in her room to talk and the doctor seldom came at all. She heard from Sister Hildegaard that Professor Santillana had returned to his work at M'Boura.

She went often across the hall to talk to the young man, Paul, who waited for her visits. They usually spoke in English and she found herself remembering idioms and slang phrases that seemed to spring up naturally from somewhere. I am remembering, she would think; this is remembering.

"I am getting more fluent," she said to Paul, sitting near his bed, half facing him. "I don't believe I'd been using English for some time."

"You must have lived here a long time—I mean in West Africa, or maybe France."

"Yes, that must be it," said Edythe. "I wish I could remember more, though. I feel so caged. Caged in a small room inside my head." She put her hands to the side of her head, pressing against her skull, which was hardly tender anymore.

"I'm glad my mind is free," said Paul, "even though I am actually caged. I'll never keep another pet that has to be tied or caged, never in my life." He spoke earnestly, his eyes looking into some other time.

"We're a pair, aren't we!" said Edythe.

"You will be out before I," Paul said.

"Have you thought what could be done if the pardon isn't granted?" Edythe asked, hating to mention the possibility but wanting him to face it.

There was a silence, and then Paul said dully, "I don't know. I just don't know."

"Does your family have any money? Perhaps there are ways, you know." Edythe made a movement with her wrist.

"No way," he said. "They're poor to begin with, and then, it's all beyond them. They can't visualize this place."

He told her how his father was in charge of the field equipment for a large truck farm in Tennessee and had never been farther away from home than Knoxville. "They can hardly conceive of West Africa as a place where civilized people live," he said, "much less how to do anything toward getting me out of here. But I'll give the pardon thing a try since Monsieur Santillana is going to all this trouble."

"Yes, it's a chance, of course," she said.

"A slim chance," Paul said gloomily. He felt so hopeless sometimes that even applying for the pardon seemed an exercise in futility. He looked away from the woman, alienated from her by his hopelessness.

"Come on," she said. "Let me rub your back for you. Turn over."

Paul rolled over onto his stomach and buried his face in his arms. Edythe took the lotion on the bedside table and with long, pressing strokes she worked his back, up and down, and around and around. Somehow, she thought to herself, she felt an ease within herself as she worked at her task. Her eyes often strayed to the long, brown hair lying on the boy's neck. It was as if she should remember something. Something unfinished.

"I will come and visit you when they take you back," she said out loud, wondering at the same time if she would actually dare to visit a prison.

"Oh, you'll find your family soon. You'll be gone, too."

Her family? Who was that? There was no world outside of this one. Walls closed in tighter around her.

94

"I must be going back to my room now," she said, getting up. *"À bientôt,* Paul."

"So long," he said dully, his face muffled by his arms.

16

IT HAPPENED as they all knew it would. Captain Naby, the warden of Malinké Province Prison, came to the hospital to see for himself how the prisoner, Paul Marion, was doing. Sister Gertrude took the warden to Paul's room. She stood silent, her mouth drawn tight, while Paul was questioned. Paul said very little to the warden. He knew the difference between his present condition and that when he had been brought into the hospital, more dead than alive, was clearly obvious. The jaundice was fading away, his eyes were bright again, and the warden was a keen observer. He knew the prisoner was better.

Exchanging a few questions with the guard, the warden then asked Sister Gertrude to find the doctor for him. Straight-backed and silent, the sister took him to the doctor's office. There she told him to wait. Finding Heinrich in the examining room she murmured, "It's too soon. They shouldn't take the boy yet."

Heinrich went to his office and the men exchanged greetings.

"The prisoner is improved, warden," he said. "You can see that, of course. Still his condition is not stable. He needs more days of convalescence on hospital food and care. We have just recently gotten back onto a soft diet."

"He is well enough," replied Warden Naby, a short man with short, gray hair tightly kinked. He had powerful shoulders that bulged beneath his white Western-style shirt. "There are much sicker men than he in their cells now. We can have no exceptions. Tomorrow I shall send a truck and take Marion back."

"No," said Heinrich firmly. "He is still too weak and very susceptible to a relapse of the dysentery if he goes back now. I cannot dismiss him yet."

"We have a new cook now," the warden said. "We fired the other one. The food is better. The prisoner must be returned now. Tomorrow."

But Heinrich held out for another four days, and finally the warden gave in surlily. Doctors had power and he wanted no trouble. He said the truck would be there the following Monday. He left without a good-bye, and drove off in an official chauffeured car.

Heinrich sat awhile in his office. He seldom even came to this room unless there was a conference where privacy was needed. His work was in the operating room, the examining room, the wards. But he had the feeling he should spend more time here, thinking about things, planning. He was used to letting his hands do the work, and now he had the problems of the woman they called Edythe and the prisoner, Paul Marion, and both were pressing demands upon him, upon his conscience. He felt resentment in spite of himself.

As a doctor he wore social blinders blocking out everything extraneous to the illnesses and surgical needs of his patients. He examined wounds and treated them, listened to explanations of illness and pain and prescribed; he studied X-rays, acted on his knowledge. As he operated, his mind worked fluidly, instantaneously within the channels of his training and experience. But beyond this he did not go. He performed his duties so as to return his patients as quickly as possible to their normal lives. And now he sat and thought whether or not he was moving in the right direction.

He decided he had to pay a visit to Commissioner Equilbecq, and he carefully thought over how he would phrase the requests he had to make. He and the commissioner had met at the Railway Club, a relic of the French days. Heinrich patronized the club mainly for tennis. The commissioner did not play tennis; with his weight he could not move about on the courts fast enough to return a ball, but he was a billiards player, and occasionally Heinrich had played with him at the club tables and had a drink with him on the veranda. Yet it could not in any sense be called a friendship. More an acquaintance, for Heinrich kept his reserve where anyone even faintly connected with the police was concerned, and the commissioner was number-one man in the Malinké Province police.

Heinrich hung up his white coat and put on the clean sport shirt he kept in his office. He left word with Fatou that he would be away for a while, and he asked Sy Kanadu to hail a taxi for him. He would have liked to walk, but the late afternoon heat made it unwise.

A rickety Peugeot was hailed and it lurched to a halt under the portico while the doctor climbed in, and in fifteen minutes it deposited him at the door of the main police headquarters. Squaring his shoulders for the interview ahead, Heinrich entered the building and threaded his way through the ragtag traffic in the hallways, stairways, and doorways—a potpourri of informers, supplicants, touts, hustlers, and delinquents. Upstairs, down a hallway, was the sanctuary of the commissioner, whose outer office was as full of supplicants as the hallways. Heinrich was not kept waiting and was taken out of turn.

A massive black man, Equilbecq, in red-and-gold braided official jacket, sat behind a huge desk, awesome in its size and shining mahogany grandeur. Upon it were only a pad, an inkstand, and a telephone. It was said that Equilbecq had an indefatigable memory for names and faces. His underlings jumped like marionettes when he roared for something. He had no need for a cluttered desk. When the doctor was shown in, he greeted him jocosely.

"So, *Monsieur le Médecin,* I do not come to your

place of work so you must come to mine! Well, one day, one day. *Voilà,* sit down, Heinrich!"

Heinrich sat down in the straight-backed chair in front of the desk, an intuition surfacing in his mind that this goliath in uniform worried about his physical well-being, and well he might, with all that weight.

"So how is that champion tennis game, eh?"

"In this weather!" replied the doctor. "No, Commissioner, I haven't been up to it. Much too busy, anyhow. Be glad you are not a doctor, especially this time of year."

"*Bien,* be glad you're not a policeman, even top-dog policeman." The two men smiled at each other, Heinrich playing for the commissioner's good humor.

"How can I be of service to you, Heinrich?" the commissioner asked.

"I have two things on my mind, commissioner," said Heinrich, and he chose the least controversial of the two to begin. "First there is the matter of the white woman brought in from M'Boura."

"Ah, yes," said Equilbecq, stroking his chin. "The woman who walked out of the forest. And how is she, Heinrich?"

"Much improved, but I don't know if you have heard, the situation is complicated by the fact that she has amnesia as a result of the accident. She does not know her name, nor where she is from. Not one jot does she remember from her past."

The commissioner leaned forward. "*Jésus!* Is this so! A real amnesia case, Doctor," he explained. "She doesn't know who she is?"

"That's the way it is," the doctor replied, seeing that the commissioner was jolted. "It is what we call retrograde amnesia, induced by trauma. So we have to find out for her who she is. And that's what I want from you. She's well physically, although still not strong, perhaps. But she needs her family, if she has any left after that plane crash."

"This makes quite a problem, doesn't it," the commissioner said. He felt the doctor was directing it right into his lap. "And *if* there was a plane crash, Doctor. My men went into the forest and they found nothing."

"Where else could she have come from?" Heinrich asked sharply, feeling that surely this man could not believe in witchcraft. "It is a dense, large area, the forest beyond M'Boura. How well did those men search?"

Equilbecq shrugged again. "I must assume, Doctor, that my men did their job. They reported that they found nothing, nothing at all. I cannot go myself and search in the jungle. I have passed that."

Heinrich fidgeted in his chair. It was so ridiculous, so unbelievable.

"Surely there must be word of a missing plane in the area. People don't just disappear without someone missing them, looking for them. What does Conakry say?"

"Let me see if anything has come in today," Equilbecq said. And he roared out an order to an assistant waiting outside the open door, and the man sped away. "To my knowledge there is nothing yet, Doctor. Somewhere there has been a slip-up. Perhaps the plane did not file flight plans."

"But there should be relatives, business associates, somebody!" said Heinrich.

The assistant returned and stood in the doorway.

"Yes?" roared the commissioner. "What is it, Xanatu?"

"There is no news, sir. Nothing on the matter of the white woman."

"I can't understand it," said the doctor. "What do you think this means? It is three weeks now."

The commissioner admitted, "I don't know, Doctor. I am only a policeman. Like you, I would think there would have been contact made when the plane —presuming there was a plane, of course, we do not know this for a fact—departed. And presumably, they were due to arrive someplace else. Somewhere

100

the control has been lost. This is probably the case. We must wait and see."

His own explanation seemed to satisfy him.

The doctor moved in his chair. It was hard to control his irritation. But he had no one to be irritated with, only the vague, the elusive ogre, called Control —or Red Tape—or some other depersonalized name. Nothing to help this woman they called Edythe.

"Commissioner, this patient needs help," he said. "She is without friends or family. She has no funds. It is an unhappy situation and deteriorates daily."

"I agree," said the commissioner, "for this woman it is no doubt a desperate plight. Could you not try the International Red Cross, Doctor?"

To himself Heinrich thought, Commissioner, it is your job, tracing this woman's family. Aloud he said, "Well, we shall do what we can with the woman's problems at the hospital, and assume that you will have some information for us soon. They are bound to be tracing this plane."

"We are chasing a myth, perhaps," observed the commissioner. "We have no evidence except for one woman who has no memory."

"But she exists!" said the doctor, "and one person is enough. One person demands attention. It does not take a whole village or—a nation."

"*Naturellement,* Heinrich." The commissioner spread his plump hands in a gesture of agreement. "Believe me, we shall do everything in our power."

Well, I have to believe him, thought the doctor, and then he said, "The other thing is about the prisoner, Paul Marion. You know a pardon has been requested. Monsieur Santillana has spoken to you. I'm sure you have influence with that board. I was hoping, Commissioner . . . " he let his voice dwindle away, hoping the commissioner would get his message without his having to spell it out.

"Doctor," said the commissioner in a tired, bored voice, "this case has been properly handled by the Guinean authorities from the beginning and it will con-

101

tinue to be. Pardons are given on merit. The request will be considered along with the others we receive. In the proper time."

The enthusiasm Equilbecq had shown at the beginning of their interview had crumbled into a querulous tone.

"*Ça va*," said Heinrich. "The thing now is that Warden Naby is demanding his return to the prison. Marion will go Monday, barring any relapse. However, he is still weak, the jaundice has not entirely disappeared. I want your permission to let the hospital send him two meals a day."

Seeing the frown rising on the commissioner's face, Heinrich hurriedly continued, "It will not be out of hospital funds. I shall finance it out of my pocket. It will be arranged with Diallo's office in proper form. But the two meals, morning and evening, will come from the hospital kitchen, and I shall have my girl, Emma, carry them in a basket to the prison. Otherwise, the prisoner will be ill again in a few weeks or sooner."

The commissioner drummed upon his desk with a pencil, thinking, while Heinrich paused, inwardly praying for his consent. Then Equilbecq shrugged, and Heinrich knew he had won.

"I can see no harm, Doctor, in your doing that for a temporary period. I am sure the warden, however, will have to take precautionary measures as a matter of form, of course."

"*Bien sûr*," said Heinrich, elated. "This is really kind of you, Commissioner. I shall not forget the favor. Will you send a chit on to Naby so he knows you have given permission?"

"Yes, it shall be done, Doctor." The commissioner moved impatiently. Since he had been magnamimous he must now show his authority. The doctor got to his feet.

"There is only one stipulation I'd like to request in connection with the food, Commissioner, and that is that the prison officials let Emma go directly to the

102

cell and hand the basket to the prisoner himself. Under the guard's scrutiny, of course."

"That is not necessary, Doctor," Equilbecq growled, looking up at Heinrich.

"Yes, it is, Commissioner. You know as well as I do the way of prisons. The prisoner would see a small part of that food if we didn't take some such precaution. A little here, a little there."

"Very well. Now then, as you know, my waiting room is full."

The interview was concluded, and Heinrich made his way out. Outside in the thick heat, his taxi driver sat sleeping over his wheel.

"Back to the hospital," Heinrich said, nudging the driver awake.

17

ON MONDAY the prison truck came for Paul Marion. A guard carrying handcuffs joined the one at his door, and they bantered back and forth, happy the hospital duty was finished. Paul stood tentatively by his bed dressed in the clothes he had arrived in—ragged jeans, now carefully laundered and patched by Sister Hildegaard, and a too large denim workshirt. He was shaky but determined to walk by himself to the vehicle waiting for him. He had told Edythe goodbye earlier, and when the handcuffs were snapped on his wrists, he was glad her door was closed.

He stood at the top of the long flight of stairs for a moment, realizing he could not hold onto the bannister. The thought of throwing himself down the stairs crossed his mind. But he was not ready for that. He couldn't do it, or even let himself fall. Sister Gertrude appeared, moving aside the guard with her heavy figure and a commanding word. She took Paul's arm firmly and they walked down the stairs together, the guards following.

Heinrich stood in the front hall with Sister Caroline, Sister Hildegaard, Emma, and several of the office staff. Heinrich went up to Paul and kissed him on both cheeks, saying he would be in to see him in a few days; then he stepped back, waving the group on. The others stood silent. As Paul's glance swept over them, they smiled their encouragement. The group went out to the prison truck waiting under the portico. It was a high-bed truck with staked sides. One of the guards got on and the other hoisted Paul up to him. The motor roared and with a jerk the truck took off for the prison.

From her window, Edythe saw the truck leave, and she glimpsed the slight figure with the long hair leaning against the back of the cab. Her head ached with tension, and depression settled upon her like the noonday heat. She felt isolated, bereft, now that the young American had left. The staff of the hospital seemed so much busier these days. No one had time to linger in her room and talk or to do things for her. They rushed in and out again. She did not like walking in the halls anymore, for everyone seemed too busy and by contrast her idleness more oppressive. Even Emma, who used to come now and then, did not appear. Edythe asked about her but was told that she was busy elsewhere.

When Sister Hildegaard brought in her luncheon tray, Edythe asked her plaintively, "Why is it you all seem in such a hurry these days? You never have time to stop and talk."

The rotund face of the sister was contrite. "You are right, we don't, my dear. This is the way it goes at this hospital. Some days, many days, it will be calm, then—poof! Like an epidemic they pour in with all manner of illnesses and accidents, too. The time of year affects everyone. This season we are always overloaded. We work in a frenzy."

"But why, sister? I don't understand."

"There are more sick, Edythe. It is the *hivernage,* the hot humid season before the rains come; the water is bad, the food is bad, the people are weakened. This is the worst time of year."

"You need more help, Sister."

"Indeed we do, *ma chère.* Yet God gives us the strength."

"And the doctor—can he keep up?"

"He is tired, Edythe. In the operating room this morning from seven until eleven. Patients this afternoon. Sister Caroline and Sister Gertrude assist him and Dr. Diop comes in to do the anesthetics."

Edythe listened, envious of the busy people.

"I must go, child. Be patient." And the sister, with

short hurried steps, disappeared down the hall and down the stairs to her chores.

Edythe looked disgustedly at her lunch of yams and pork, chard and pudding. A weight seemed to settle upon her—a weight of loneliness, of dissatisfaction, of frustration. I want to leave this place, she thought. I am no longer sick. No one has time to pay attention to me anymore. Yet where can I go? I am a person without a place to go. I am no one. I am a burden to myself and to the others. Who am I? Who am I? I am alive and have a right to a place like everyone else. She choked on the food and put the tray aside. She walked around and around the room, not wanting to go out to the halls where the nurses and orderlies hurried back and forth on their business, and yet feeling the walls of the little room pushing in upon her.

She tried to concentrate on *Le Comte de Monte-Cristo* until the heaviness of the afternoon heat caused her to sleep. In her sleep she dreamed. In her dream a figure hooded in white handed her a tray on which were many pieces of folded paper. This figure, in spite of its hood, seemed to smile sardonically as it said to her, "Pick one."

She chose a piece of paper, opened it, and read "Edythe." She thought to herself, fine, but still that is not enough. The figure presented the tray a second time, saying, "Take another, then."

Edythe reached out her hand and hovered over the folded papers. Which one to choose? Finally she chose one. The tray was withdrawn and she opened her paper. It was blank. She awoke with a cry of despair.

In the late afternoon she sat by her window watching the people below. The supper trays had been brought and taken away. The patients were ready for family visits. The crowd down in the yard pulsed against the hospital entrance. On the side street coming from the rear of the hospital Edythe glimpsed a familiar figure—the doctor, in a white, short-sleeved shirt, looking different without his hospital coat. Be-

106

side him, but a little apart, walked Emma. She carried a cloth bundle. So they walked down the cross street past the hospital and disappeared. Where do they go, Edythe wondered? What is it like where he lives? The families poured into the hospital and the yard was deserted.

Edythe cried into her lap. I must go, she told herself. Anywhere, anywhere. And then she thought, I have no money. It takes money to move in this world. Her predicament was intolerable. Were there no authorities who could help someone like herself? Yet in reality she knew of no place to go. She remembered no home. She wiped the tears from her cheeks with her hands. Perhaps I shall go mad, she thought. I feel as though I am beginning to shatter into little pieces.

When Sister Gertrude came around later in the evening she looked with concern upon Edythe's tear-streaked face and hollow eyes and the hands that moved restlessly.

She said, "Would you like to have a sleeping pill tonight, Edythe? The doctor has told me you may have it when you need it."

A sudden fierce resentment burned in Edythe. "No, Sister," she said crossly. "I don't want a pill."

The night was long and tortured with sleeplessness. When, finally, over the gray stillness of the dawn there floated from the mosque the Islamic call for the faithful to awake and pray, Edythe slept.

Again another morning, another day, and again the hospital routine began. Doctor Heinrich looked in briefly on his rounds, this time with Sister Caroline, but he looked so tired, so harried, that Edythe offered none of her complaints. With an encouraging comment to keep on walking about, the two continued on their rounds. Edythe turned her sober face, tears surging to her eyes, to the blankness of her walls. The tension mounted inside her. She felt nauseous and she pulled at her short, cropped hair, never noticing the pain.

18

SISTER HILDEGAARD WALKED into the kitchen and inspected the luncheon custard that Bakary had finished. She looked at the vegetables, tasted the soup and suggested more salt, poked at the lamb, stewing in its juice. All was in order. She talked with Seitou about cutting up the fruit for the evening meal, explaining how many papayas, oranges, pineapples, and bananas to use.

"And wash your hands first, Seitou," she reminded the girl.

"Bien sûr, Sister," the girl answered. The *indigène* help called Sister Hildegaard "the wash-hands sister" behind her back, for she always, always added that to any order.

Sister Hildegaard passed on into the staff dining room and checked on how the morning's chores had been done there. She could hear the murmur of Sister Gertrude's and the doctor's voices in the examining room. She was about ready to call Mamady to come and help with the luncheon trays when Fatou came running down from the foyer.

"Sister, Sister, come!" Fatou said breathlessly, "The white woman upstairs. Come."

Sister Hildegaard sensed the urgency and started to run. As she passed the door of the examining room she called to Sister Gertrude and kept on running. It was a long way to the upstairs. She slowed considerably on the stairs and was pulling herself up the last few steps by the bannister. She hoped Sister Gertrude had responded to her call. Yes, she could hear the steps behind her. At the door of the little private room she paused in dismay and caught her breath. The room was a scene of destruction. The bedcovers had been torn off the bed and thrown about. The small toilet articles purchased for Edythe were thrown everywhere. The lamp had fallen, water spilled, the glass broken, the chair fallen over, and Edythe was standing by the window systematically tearing up the books, pages lying around her. Her face looked wild and her eyes large and tormented. As Sister Hildegaard grasped her hands, she broke loose and struck at the nun. Both Sister Gertrude and the doctor came into the room, taking all in at a glance. Edythe cried out, *"Allez vous-en, allez vous-en."* Go away.

But Doctor Heinrich took her arms and backed her against the wall. Though she struggled like a held rabbit, he pressed his own weight against her, and then very suddenly she crumpled against him. He held her with his arms and she began to sob. As if she were a child, he stroked her, his hands moving on her hair, her face, her arms. Behind them the sisters began to put the room in order again. A small group of hospital people stood at the doorway, watching. The sisters waved them away.

The doctor said over his shoulder, "Sister Gertrude, bring me Largactile, a two-millimeter vial." She sped down the stairs.

Sister Hildegaard straightened the bedsheets and led Edythe to the bed. The doctor laid her down and sat by her side, a hand holding her arm. She still cried, the sobs spurting out as if she were in deep pain, lunge after lunge, her whole torso heaving with its tension. Sister Gertrude returned, breathless, with the syringe on a small tray. The doctor turned Edythe on her side and uncovering a buttock quickly injected the tranquilizer. Then he withdrew the needle and turned Edythe to the other side. He released the rest of the vial's contents. She did not quiver from the shots, only the weeping shook her frame.

At a nod from the doctor the two nuns left the

room, and he sat there until Edythe gradually relaxed. The sobs ceased, her eyes, violet-lidded, remained closed, and she slept. He drew the sheet over her lightly and went below.

The sisters were together in the dining room. They had been discussing Edythe. They looked at him a little guiltily when he walked in.

"Sisters," he said, "let us eat. And then afterward please meet in my office. We have things we must discuss."

19

Such conferences were held erratically, as need demanded. This time each sister sat with troubled face and waited for the doctor to speak.

"As you know, Sisters," he began, his tired face looking heavier and sadder than ever, "we have a problem in this woman we call Edythe. A psychologist might be able to help her. At least he might have been able to avert such a breakdown as she underwent today. We have no such professional help to offer her and we work short-handed as it is. You must not bear too personally this incident, yet perhaps we should examine the whole situation again."

He paused a moment and, swinging his chair part way around, gazed thoughtfully out his window. The sisters waited. A tear fell onto Sister Hildegaard's hands, folded in her lap. She sniffed audibly. Then he faced them again and continued.

"Do you realize what burden this woman carries?" he asked. "She not only has no identity, no place where she belongs, no past memories to fortify her in her loneliness, no person who cares for her in a personal way, no one for her to care for, yet she is well, healthy, with energy now, and intelligence, and she sits up there with nothing to do in an alien country."

He looked at the sisters and they returned his look comprehending the truth he spoke. Sister Caroline bit her lip and her eyes narrowed.

"This woman is a prisoner of ours. She cannot leave, for she has nowhere to go. She hasn't a franc to spend of her own. Why, she doesn't even own a handbag with identification, much less francs. Can you imagine a Western woman without a handbag!"

He broke the seriousness of his talk with a mirthless chuckle. Yes, he could imagine even Western women without handbags, his thoughts flicking back to the women arriving at the camps during the war, and as quickly he switched off the picture and came back to the present.

"Something must be done, or else this will happen again. I am open to suggestions." He looked at them and to himself he thought, I am hard on these dear, overworked sisters. I am asking too much of them.

They sat with their thoughts for a few minutes, and then Sister Caroline spoke.

"Doctor, I am the one who is remiss. It is I who should have taken more time with this woman. May God forgive me." Her face quivered slightly, but she went on strongly, "I do not see how we can put Edythe out. As you say, she has nowhere to go until we find her people. Is nothing being done by the authorities?"

"I talked with the commissioner only a few days ago," replied Heinrich, "and advised him of the seriousness of her need. I feel sure they've had no success. I am wondering if we should not have Monsieur Diallo go to Conakry to make an investigation for us?"

At this, Sister Gertrude's face brightened, and she said, "Yes, Doctor, a good suggestion. Édouard could do that, and he loves any excuse to go to Conakry."

But Sister Caroline said, "I think you should go, Heinrich. Then we would be sure. I doubt if Édouard can manage this problem."

"No," answered Heinrich, hastily, pushing away the idea, "I am needed here. Édouard can manage."

Sister Caroline said then, "You must instruct him well."

"I shall do my best," Heinrich answered, "But meanwhile, we cannot be idle in Edythe's regard here at the hospital."

"May I continue, please?" said Sister Caroline. "I believe it is important that Edythe feel useful and busy. Could we not give her a job? A *real* job. She needs to earn money so that she can consider herself performing a useful function and can be independent."

They all agreed with this and discussed the various things that were needed to be done at the hospital, discarding some ideas, trying others.

Finally Sister Gertrude said, "For a long time I've felt the need of help with our testing laboratory. I am the only person, aside from the doctor, who does tests, makes the slides, runs the samples. And you know how busy I get when there are many operations. The laboratory is the place I neglect. It needs a thorough reorganization, the shelves and equipment need to be cleaned and rearranged. New labels should be put on containers and bottles. I can see two weeks devoted entirely to the lab, and it isn't a job that any of our *indigène* help can do."

"Could you teach Edythe what she would need to do?" asked the doctor.

"Yes," answered Sister Gertrude, "I believe Edythe could do it. The thing we have not considered is whether or not she would be willing to work. I have the feeling she is not used to working, and we cannot insist."

"I think she will be glad to be busy," Heinrich said. "We must offer her the opportunity. I like your idea. Now—about a small salary. This is tougher."

They fell silent again. Money was scarce, for the hospital budget was rigid. Then the doctor spoke again.

"Sisters, if you would promise me to keep this just between us four, as I don't want to set a precedent, I would be glad to use an amount of my own salary to pay this girl. After all, what are a few hundred francs? I would not be taking it from anyone for I have no family. And in a few days or weeks she may well have her memory back and be gone from here. What do you say? *D'accord?*"

"Absolutely not, Doctor," put in Sister Gertrude. "This is *verboten*. Your money is your own, it is for your old age. You must be more practical. I won't let you do this. Perhaps the Diocese will help us."

But there was so little chance of this that the other sisters just looked at her sadly.

"Let us not waste our time worrying about my old age," said Heinrich, "and get on with our plans. This afternoon I shall go ahead and send Édouard to Conakry."

It was decided that the next morning, if Edythe was well enough, the doctor and Sister Caroline would talk to her about working in the hospital as one of the staff.

As they prepared to leave, Sister Hildegaard, with a perturbed look, said, "It seems to me that we're overlooking something. Is this poor woman to continue living in a hospital room? If she is no longer ill, then she shouldn't be confined here."

They were annoyed with themselves for not having seen this. The doctor exclaimed, "You are right. She can't continue to live as a patient."

It was another question to be resolved. Yet other duties pressed upon them. It was time for outpatients to be seen; they were lined up in the hall outside the examining room. Sister Gertrude said, "Let's talk about it tonight when we meet for supper. We shall find some solution."

In relief, they agreed and filed out of the doctor's office, each going directly to duties for the afternoon.

20

SISTER CAROLINE WENT UPSTAIRS and looked into Edythe's room. She was in a deep sleep. There were faint blue lines beneath her eyes and her mouth was slightly open. Looking down on her, Sister Caroline felt that Edythe was so much more vulnerable to life's wounding tentacles than most of them were. Her defenses had been taken away from her. It was a child-like state. Sister Caroline looked around the room. It had been made neat again. She picked up the pile of torn pages from *Le Comte de Monte-Cristo* and, bending over Edythe, kissed her on the forehead, knowing she would not be doing that if Edythe were awake, and knowing too that this room would always in her mind be Edythe's room, no matter who else stayed there.

She went about her nursing chores in her usual efficient way, but she was thinking as she worked that she was more to blame for Edythe's breakdown than any of the others. She was supposed to anticipate such crises, to avoid them by helping a patient talk out and express his needs and problems so that the emotional struggles did not interfere with the physical mending of his body. She knew now she had been aware of Edythe's desperation but, being busy, had chosen to avoid it. She had done little things for her, but she had failed in the big turmoil going on in this woman's psyche.

As she worked she tried to put herself in the other woman's place. She had not really done that before, had not really imagined how it would be with no memory. She had, when she took her vows, cut herself off from her own past. She had told her family good-bye, dismissed them from her life. That had been a hard thing to do, but she had been willing as part of her calling. Yet even though she had cut herself off from those years of her girlhood, she was aware that they had always remained in her consciousness, forming a pillar upon which she, the adult Sister Caroline, still rested. And wasn't she always aware of the child Caroline, the young girl Caroline, the university student Caroline? Didn't sunshine in a garden remind her fleetingly of walking hand in hand with her father in the family gardens in Neuilly? Didn't a certain bar of music take her back to the cathedral in Strasbourg and to the great resounding voices of the cathedral choir? And certain tastes would send her suddenly skimming back over the years to a time in childhood, a chocolate shop, a summer picnic? How memories of past experience and past people moved about in her thoughts as she lay awake at night! She tried to think of how it would feel if there were no past at all, no layers of memories, no knowledge of childhood dreams and events, of family, of friends, of decisions made and external events occurring that influenced growth and shaped maturation. Nothing, nothing, nothing right up to the brim of, say, last week! Sister Caroline touched the rosary she carried in her pocket and murmured the words that brought a measure of peace to her heart. "Oh Mary, Mother of God, Pray for us sinners, now and at the hour of our death."

Heinrich, as he worked that afternoon in the examining room, thought about this patient who was challenging him for help in ways he was not used to. They had given her a name—Edythe. Yes, but still it did not give her an identity. It did not cure the amnesia nor fill the void that burdened her. We must draw this young woman out of herself, he thought, at the same time as his skillful fingers were examining the

116

swollen ankle of a local country worker and assessing the extent of damage to the tendons. She must be brought into our society here at the hospital as a well person, not as a patient.

He went through the afternoon from patient to patient, acknowledging with an inward grimace a strange contrast between himself and Edythe. She was so desperate to know herself, to find her past, and he, in all the years since his liberation from Buchenwald, had been making a determined effort to forget his past and take a new identity. The DP camps had helped Heinrich Fink survive. Now here he was faced with a survivor of a different deal by fate, one who needed help because she wanted to remember, not forget.

I must take time out to perform other duties besides those with my hands, he told himself. I need to administer to the whole person sometimes, not just his affected parts. I have been too much the European doctor, too little the human being.

When his last patient for the day was taken care of, he went to the office of Édouard Diallo in the front of the hospital. The hospital administrator had his desk cleared for the day and was reaching for his straw hat when the doctor came in. However, when Heinrich sat down and stretched out his legs as though he wanted to talk, Édouard was glad to join him.

Édouard was a tall, thin, fine-featured man with an elegant though passive air about him that to the Western mind would seem effeminate. He dressed in Western-style suits, his worn, white shirts always stiffly starched. Édouard was from a family, or tribe, of no social or political consequence, so every rung he climbed had to be done through his own efforts. His education, obtained in the Conakry Catholic Mission School, was less than enough to qualify him for important positions in the government, even assuming he could have secured an appointment. Yet he had kept doggedly working in the business office of the Conakry Catholic Hospital until this position of more prestige and responsibility had become available in up-country Siguirre as hospital administrator.

He purchased supplies, paid bills, and collected whatever he could from patients, managed the wages of employees, hired and fired the local workers. He was a steady, conscientious administrator, but easily diverted. He was all too often over at the Railway Club shooting billiards with his friends, or, since his position brought with it some prestige in the provincial town, out on social invitations and obligations which Madame Diallo compelled him to accept. Thus he was often absent from his desk.

Édouard had been curious about the white patient upstairs and there were plenty of rumors in the hospital that there was something strange about her, even some superstitious fears were uttered about the fact that she had walked out of the forest like an embodied spirit. He was glad now to have the doctor talk about it, and to have the official confirmation of her condition. He had a great trust in Doctor Heinrich's ability to handle events.

"Now, Édouard," the doctor was saying, "the commissioner has been unable to get any word from Conakry about a missing plane and our patient is in critical need of finding her family. We are going to invite her to start working here with the staff in such capacities as she is able, to help relieve the frustrations and tensions of her situation." And he went on to discuss with the administrator some of the details of Edythe's joining the hospital staff and how she would be paid.

"Now, Édouard, we must go further. We want you to journey to Conakry and make our own personal inquiries. The sisters and I feel this should be done."

Diallo bowed in his formal way. "I shall be happy to be of service, Doctor. Tell me what you think I should do."

So Heinrich explained to him what he must do, how he should talk personally with the Conakry airport control to see if they had sent messages to all large and small cities having airports on the West Coast. He should talk to the French, English, and American consuls. He should follow any leads they might suggest. He should urge them to contact other cities by cable or telephone. He should even examine the classifieds in the various newspapers available in the capital city. And lastly, of course, were the shopping lists for the hospital to be taken care of. His trip and all its duties would take at least two weeks, Heinrich knew. Maybe more. He was to leave the next day.

21

EDYTHE OPENED HER EYES to see a room that looked familiar. There was a painting of tree leaves where a window should be. The painting moved a little and became a window. The room moved back and forth. There was so much space. Something should be filling it, people maybe, she thought drowsily, people moving around. A deep lassitude drew her eyes closed again and she drifted in and out of sleep. She lay there trying to remember yesterday. Something had happened, something had shattered. She tried to get a hold of the memory. Yes, oh, God, I went to pieces. It was as though something snapped and shattered inside me. What did I do? And then she vaguely remembered the doctor being there and the feel of his body against hers. And then what? She opened her eyes again and all that she had felt yesterday—all that was so completely unbearable—came back. But that tension was gone now, dissipated, although nothing was changed. She was still in this room with the empty walls, by herself. Except that she did feel more lazy and relaxed and unstrung. Perhaps they gave me medicine, she thought.

After a long time she got out of bed and went into the tiny bathroom and mechanically prepared herself to face another day. When she came back to her room she got onto the bed again and pulled the sheet around her knees and sat there waiting. Waiting for something, for anything. She felt quite clear and calm now.

Down the hall, voices and the clatter of trays could be heard. Someone would be coming soon. How would they act toward her after the terrible things she had done yesterday? She noticed that there were no longer any books, papers, or glasses in her room. It was completely bare. Perhaps, she thought horrified, they will send me away to a place for the mentally disturbed and I will be lost forever. What if that is where I belong? Which is it, have I amnesia or have I gone mad?

But this train of thought was broken by Sister Hildegaard's stout, comfortable figure coming through the doorway with the breakfast tray. And the sister smiled at her and spoke in her natural way, in fact, with kindness and gentleness that seemed to Edythe to have a special quality.

"Eat well now, *ma chère,*" Sister Hildegaard said, as she arranged the tray on Edythe's lap. "The doctor is coming soon to see you."

"Sister," Edythe said, looking at her humbly, "I am truly sorry about yesterday. I just went to pieces. I didn't want to, but I just couldn't stop myself."

"There is no need to apologize to us, Edythe," said Sister Hildegaard. "Eat now, we will talk later." She sounded a little mysterious, as if she knew something she could not tell.

Soon after breakfast the doctor and Sister Caroline came in to see her. They both sat down, the doctor on the bed, the sister on the chair. They seemed in no hurry this time. The doctor did not try to make small talk to buoy up her spirits. The sister sat very still and her face was thoughtful.

Doctor Heinrich began by talking directly about Edythe's inability to remember her past and how this affected her ability to cope with the present. He told her that sending her to a psychologist would mean sending her away, and that they kept hoping to find out where she lived before sending her any place, and that they waited each day expecting to know something. Still they could get no word.

"You see, Edythe, we still believe that you survived the crash of a plane. You realize that whoever was

121

with you very likely did not survive. We would assume it was your husband or some member of your family, and probably a pilot, maybe a co-pilot, and others. Do you understand this is probably the situation?"

She looked at him, "Yes, Doctor. I have thought this myself. I know I may be quite alone."

Then he went on to tell her that she needed to get out of her room and to be busy. They had work in the hospital that needed to be done and if she would like to try it, she could work regular hours and make a small salary, perhaps thirty thousand Central African francs a month could be paid her. She could take her meals in the staff dining room.

Edythe's face brightened as she heard the plan. "Oh, I would like that very much," she exclaimed. "I'm tired of sitting here like so much baggage. The money doesn't matter. I only would like to do something."

"The money will matter," said the doctor, "for it will make you independent in a limited way. It is a small amount. Do you know the Central African exchange rate?" he asked.

She looked at him curiously. Why, yes, she knew that. One hundred CFA were like two French francs. Thirty thousand was indeed not much money, but it didn't matter. "Yes," she told him, slowly, "I do know CFA exchange. That says something about me, doesn't it!"

"It does," he answered. "It says you are no stranger to this part of the world. But then, we suspected that or else you wouldn't be flying around in a private plane, probably."

Sister Caroline was looking happier now and she smiled at Edythe, who asked, "When may I start to work? I am well. I would like to begin now."

"Easy, easy," said the doctor. "This afternoon would be the earliest. Let us say from three until five today."

Sister Caroline said, *"Bien,* Edythe. I am happy that this plan meets with your approval." Then she told

122

her about the laboratory work that Sister Gertrude needed done and asked if she would like to start with that much-needed reorganization. It sounded technical to Edythe and unfamiliar, but she agreed to try. They left soon, with Sister Caroline promising to come and accompany her down to the dining room for lunch.

Before lunch an aide arrived with a white laboratory coat for Edythe to wear. Pleased, she put on the white cotton coat. She felt good in it. It had deep pockets where she could thrust her uncertain, trembling hands. It came down a little over her knees. No longer did she feel either naked or strange. Sister Caroline came, more cheerful this time, and they went downstairs together. The sister showed her the rooms in the new wing, explaining the function of each. She showed her the kitchen where Bakary and Seitou, ladling out soup, smiled and nodded at the new hospital employee.

Sister Caroline ate lunch with Edythe and talked about the hospital—how Sister Hildegaard was considered chief housekeeper, even though she assisted with nursing duties also; how Sister Gertrude and herself had special tasks in addition to the nursing on the wards. The doctor came in when they were nearly finished. He spoke to Edythe as if she were always to be seen there. But when she was starting to leave he said to her in his doctor's tone of voice, "Edythe, even though you are up and about, I do insist that you rest after lunch until three each day. In this climate the siesta is a necessity. We all take one sometime during the day."

"Yes, Doctor," she answered obediently.

She noticed, as she went out of the dining room, the doctor's glance sliding over her figure. It was a good feeling, to be a woman now, and not a patient.

At three in the afternoon, feeling doubtful of her abilities, she found Sister Gertrude in the small laboratory. Sister began to explain the procedures to her. Soon Edythe was involved. It was not technical at all, much a matter of organizing things and being careful

123

and neat. Sister Gertrude was glad to find that although the names on the labeled bottles and jars and cans were probably completely new to Edythe, she did grasp their significance and the great need for caution and preciseness. She showed Edythe how to seal the freshly filled jars with paraffin to keep out the ants. The two worked together until five, when Sister Gertrude said, "That is enough for your first day. Now you must rest until dinner."

That evening, in her room, Edythe pulled open a fresh notebook she found on her bedside table and, with a ballpoint pen, began to write in French:

March 20: I know the date now because I have begun to work. Today I have been writing the date on labels for Sister Gertrude. I work in the hospital laboratory helping to clean, rearrange, relabel the many bottles and jars of drugs. It was a satisfying feeling.

I think I shall keep this journal in English. It will be more private.

Here the writing changed to English: *I feel like a new person with this job. I even feel a little important! I am beginning to use my mind (I have a brain that functions, don't I, in other normal ways?).*

I wonder about my age. Funny. The doctor thinks I am in my early thirties. What if he is completely wrong and I am forty or maybe twenty. Either, in a way, seems horrifying. I must be thirty or thirty-two or -three, for although my memories are empty I have a feeling of life lived, and of life ahead waiting to be lived. Sister Caroline is thirty-three and look at her hands, at the lines in her face. She has been taking life very seriously. I have the feeling I have been frivolous and idle. Still, I cannot dislike this person we call Edythe. My consciousness, my will to live, is this person. With or without a memory I am stuck with her. The thought this evening is not as desperate as it was before.

I like the doctor. I want to touch his face, trace his

mouth with my fingers. There is a heavy sadness about him I wish I could brush away.

I think of Paul Marion in that prison cell. I keep thinking I must do something for him, as if I were the one who had deserted him, almost.

22

THE SISTERS HAD DECIDED that they must look for a place for Edythe to live in the neighborhood of the hospital. The room upstairs was no longer suitable and, also, they needed it for other patients. Yet to find a place outside was no small problem. With Monsieur Diallo gone, Sy Kanadu, who otherwise would be delegated the task, had his hands full in the office. Sister Hildegaard took it upon herself, then, to look, and she went about the streets in the vicinity whenever she could steal a few moments from her work. It seemed a fruitless endeavor, looking for empty cottages to let. The small bungalows were all bursting with people already, the villas were much too large and, of course, they too were occupied by more well-to-do families.

It was Fatou, the receptionist, who found a place for Edythe to live. Her uncle's family lived in a villa just three blocks from the hospital and at the back of their lot, hidden from view of the street, was a two-room bungalow, probably originally built for a servant family. It had been used by family relatives more recently but now it sat vacant. Back of this small cottage was another building, a shack, really, where the present servants lived.

Fatou was friendly, eager, curious. Although she often exasperated the sisters with her flightiness, still she was loyal to the hospital staff and fulfilled her position adequately. It pleased her to be able to take Sister Hildegaard and Edythe to visit the cottage of her relatives. The little house was shaded by drooping casuarina trees and bougainvillea climbed over the broken screening of the porch and the nearby stone walls of the garden.

Many of the domestic chores for the family in the villa were performed in the back compound. Here chickens scratched and a thin dog scuttled, his tail between his legs, looking for food and a kindly word. As they entered the compound a woman was kneeling on the ground pounding yams in a stone mortar to make foo-foo. She left her work to come and stare at the nun and the white woman. Fatou spoke sharply to her, asking for her aunt, and the servant disappeared inside the villa.

Edythe pushed open the door to the small veranda and went into the cottage. The rooms were empty; in the first one was an iron sink and one built-in cupboard. A water closet took a small square out of the second room. The cottage was clean, odorless. Through the open windows sounds from the garden could be heard and voices from across the nearby wall. But here, inside, was a sense of waiting. As Edythe stood in the center of the second room, looking around, something tantalized her, wanting to be remembered. She could not quite get hold of it. The empty space seemed to be breathing softly, holding a sense of life. Was it her own heart that palpitated—her own life waiting to be lived? Sister Hildegaard came in and sniffed around the room contemptuously.

"It is not fit for you, Edythe," she announced.

"Nonsense, Sister," Edythe replied lightly. "I think I like it. It is kept cool by the trees, it is the right size. I wouldn't be afraid to be back here in this compound. We can cover the floors with mats, the walls with cottons."

"Well," said the sister, "first it needs a good scrubbing."

Fatou and her aunt appeared at the door. The aunt, an immense woman, her lustrous dark eyes ringed with antimony, wearing an orange-and-white *m'bou-*

bou and headscarf, smiled at the visitors, white teeth flashing.

"Bonjour, bonjour, mesdames," she said, and then paused, looking at Fatou for help. Fatou introduced her aunt to Sister Hildegaard and Edythe as Madame Kouakou, and explained the reason for their intrusion.

The aunt spread her ringed fingers before her. "It is only a servant's cottage," she apologized, "not good enough for the French lady."

"Non," replied Edythe, "it is exactly what I am looking for—small, comfortable, cozy."

The woman was pleased, she said, that the foreign lady liked her cottage, but insisted it was not good enough. Sister Hildegaard interrupted to ask about the water supply, and after being shown the pump in the kitchen sink and how it actually worked—with a great deal of effort, of course—Sister Hildegaard then launched into a description of what they needed in the way of furniture. Fatou's aunt insisted that all these things were available in the big house and could be brought out. They would furnish it the way madame wanted. But Edythe interrupted to ask about the rent. She remembered her small salary.

"Et le loyer, Madame Kouakou?" she asked.

The woman shrugged her plump shoulders helplessly, looking at Fatou. They conversed together in Malinké while the two women waited. Then Fatou turned away from the bargaining pretending indifference, and her aunt said to Edythe, "For the cottage, whatever the lady would like to pay. I leave it to you."

It was the polite way to begin to bargain. Sister Hildegaard took over and suggested a minimal rent, explaining that the cottage was small, the bathing facilities inadequate, it was too near the servants' quarters and the poultry in the back compound, mentioning every possible fault she could think of.

Madame Kouakou twisted her hands together, smiling all the time. She then mentioned that really perhaps they should have more than the amount suggested

128

since it was difficult to find a free cottage, every place was filled, their relatives clamored to come back, and they would have to give up some of their own furniture to furnish it. She suggested another figure, much higher.

Sister Hildegaard retorted by raising her first figure in a very offhand manner as though it couldn't matter less if they made a bargain or not. Fatou's aunt came down from her price and soon an amount was agreed upon and Edythe saw that she could afford it.

"D'accord, Madame. Excellent!" she said.

The woman, pleased with Edythe's attitude, was quite satisfied with the whole transaction. It was agreed that the following Saturday, three days hence, the house would be ready, although Sister Hildegaard knew that such precise dates meant little as time had other values in this country. It would take longer. But they all shook hands and with a light heart Edythe took Sister Hildegaard's arm as they walked back to the hospital. Fatou, elated that she had managed the transaction, skipped ahead to her post at the reception desk.

Although relieved that she had found a place of her own outside the hospital, yet Edythe was afraid, too. It seemed a big step to take. Was she ready? Could she manage? As she worked in the laboratory the picture of the cottage was in her thoughts, and that emotion she had felt on entering that second room still hung on the edge of her thoughts as an intangible something. If only she could think what it was!

In the dining room that evening she lingered over her coffee, hoping Doctor Heinrich would come in. But he did not. Perhaps he was in his own cottage, with Emma waiting on him. Disappointed, she went up to her room in the hospital. It was too early to sleep. She knelt on the floor by her window, idly watching the street. The muezzin in the mosque across the city began the evening call to prayer. She let the octaves of sound pour over her, enfolding her in their mystery.

A voice in the doorway spoke her name. "Edythe?"

"Oh, Doctor Heinrich!"

"I thought you were not here. I didn't see you at first." He came into the room, standing a little uncertainly in the dim light from the window.

"I was just watching the street," she said, getting up and turning on the little lamp by the bed. "I didn't feel sleepy yet."

They stood together in the lamplight and Edythe was aware of him as a man and herself as a woman. He had not come to see her as a patient. She wanted to reach out and touch him, but she did not.

"I heard Sister Hildegaard telling about the place you found to live," he said.

"Yes," she replied. "I think it will be all right."

"Are you sure?" he asked. "It sounds very humble."

"It will do," she said. "It's a good size, a good location."

He was observing her carefully. "It is important that you feel happy there," he said. "How do you feel about moving out of the hospital?"

She sat down on the edge of her bed. There was so much she would like to say to someone, to Doctor Heinrich, if only she could express these half-formed fears, inadequacies, and doubts about herself. The doctor sat on her chair.

"To tell you the truth," she said, "I am a little afraid and nervous. Yet I definitely want to live there. I think I lack confidence, as if I'm not sure yet of myself as a person."

"That is understandable. However, I don't think you should live alone. I've been thinking about it. What would you say to Emma's living with you?"

"Emma?" she asked, looking at him. The thought had not occurred to her. "Emma?" she said again.

"She lives in my cottage now," he said, "but I don't need her there. She needed a place when she was sent to us here, someone to look after her a bit. She would be as well off with you as with me, now."

"Oh, I couldn't take her from you," she said, embarrassed.

"Nonsense," he answered. "She can still come over and do whatever needs to be done to my place, but you would feel much better if someone else was sleeping there. So would I, for that matter. I'd feel you were in good hands. Emma is a dependable girl. At first, when she came she was—well, immature, a little like Fatou. But she's settled down."

A wave of pleasure swept over Edythe. She had the feeling of being taken care of, after all.

"Besides," added the doctor, a smile on his face, "the good sisters would feel much better if Emma lived with you instead of me."

"Since you put it that way," she said, smiling at him. "But do you think Emma will like it?"

"I think she will enjoy your company," he replied, "more than mine. I will talk to her about it. Now," he said, rising, "I haven't seen the patients on this floor yet. Why don't you come with me? You might learn something." He added the last teasingly.

Eagerly, Edythe joined him. They found Sister Gertrude at the end of the hall, and Edythe trailed behind them, watching and listening. Sister Gertrude gave her the tray of nighttime medications to carry. Edythe noticed the sympathetic, personal way the doctor treated each patient, placing his hands on them in some friendly gesture as he peered into throats, felt lumps, examined sutures, always giving them a word of encouragement.

When they had finished he said to her, "You have worked overtime today. Will you rest now, Edythe?"

"I will rest well," she answered, looking at him gravely. *"Bonne nuit, Doctor; à demain, Sister."*

23

THE SEASON OF THE YEAR that is spring in the Temperate Zone, in Guinea is one long yearning, *une maladie du pays,* for the rains to come. The rains fall on the plateaus in one season which may begin by the spring equinox, yet sometimes does not come until weeks later. Siguirre is on the plateaus in the midst of the belt of land called the savannas; there in the month of March they wait for the rain to begin, to come and relieve the parched earth, to fill the cracked gulleys and the wells, streams, and rivers, to wash away the accumulated dust that has settled upon the leaves of every growing plant. The wells have turned into mudholes, stock and wild life barely survive; people and wild fowl search the skies for signs of clouds that may hold water. Yet again and again the clouds gather and grow dark, the air becomes oppressively heavy and still. The heat lies close and intense. It seems certain this is the day that rain will come. And then the clouds roll on and disappear and the sun comes out again. It is impossible for life to go on, but continue it does. Once more the somnolent waiting; once more the hope that tomorrow it will rain.

Everyone is oppressed by the torpor. Tensions are high. People come down with sicknesses and fevers they have withstood the rest of the year. The hospital is at its busiest. The sisters, having experienced this season many times, know it will pass with the first torrential rain that will one day truly come. Yet they too drag themselves through their chores, searching the skies as they walk from their cottage to the hospital and back again.

Only Edythe was not obsessed with the weather. She was preoccupied by her new work in the laboratory and her constant inner search for the person she was. Also, she was preparing to move into her house. She had been to the market with Emma and Sister Hildegaard and had bought some necessities. Sister Hildegaard gave her linens and some kitchenware she was able to spare from the hospital.

The sisters had observed that the one product nearly always plentiful in the African marketplace was cloth —colorful cottons, broadcloths, French voiles and treviras. Emma offered the information that it took ten meters to make a complete *m'boubou* for a woman and Edythe, laughing, said, "That's enough to cover all my walls."

So from such plenty she purchased lengths of different colors to cover the walls, beads to hang at the doorway separating the two rooms, and woven papyrus to hang from the ceiling to make a partitioned closet and dressing area. Great rolls of soft woven reeds now covered the rough floors of both rooms.

On one of these hot, still days, Edythe and Sister Hildegaard sat sewing in the staff room. Edythe had reached a place in the laboratory where she could do no more until Sister Gertrude had time to help her. So she hemmed curtains for her cottage. She noticed as she worked that her fingers had long ago lost their manicure. Here and there she had a cut, and she could not avoid pricking herself from time to time with the sewing needle. It is obvious, she thought wryly, I had not done much manual work. I wonder if I had servants. Yet she did not mind her present condition; she felt an interest in and contentment with what she was doing. Her thoughts were positive these days; she felt alive. Everything seemed important—the food she ate, the rough cotton of her lab coat, the labels she copied for Sister Gertrude in a square, neat print. It was not that she was not trying to remember, not pushing at the walls that blanked her memory, yet sometimes there was a strange floating feeling as if part of her was disconnected from herself whenever she tried to reach into the past. The most troubling question was, Why had no one come to find her, to claim her? Did it mean there was no one out there who was bound to her at all?

The two women were sitting by an open window to try to catch any stray breezes. Sister Hildegaard was mending hospital linens. They had been working in silence, when Edythe looked up at the window and at that moment a stray gust of wind swept the last petals from an oleander bush in a quick shower of white past the window, and Edythe cried out, "Oh!", a look of wonder on her face. Sister Hildegaard looked up at her. Edythe was staring transfixed at the window, and then she turned toward Sister Hildegaard.

"Sister, I just remembered something," she said, her face alight.

Sister Hildegaard hardly dared breathe. "Yes?" she said, encouragement in the word.

Edythe continued, her eyes looking back into the distance. "I was sitting with grandmother," she said. "We were sewing and I looked up and it was snowing outside. Very suddenly the air was full of huge, swirling snowflakes and I can see grandmother and her kitchen. Somehow, I was waiting for someone to come, and seeing the snowflakes I thought of him, the the person I was waiting for. I don't know who. But I feel that emotion—that expectancy, that fear that maybe the snow . . ." she paused, looking into the past, and then continued. "Grandmother and I sat opposite each other. There was a round rag rug between us." Edythe's voice rose gradually with the excitement of remembering. "I remember the scrubbed linoleum floor, the table, the old-fashioned sink. It was a farm, see, and outside where the snow was falling were the fields and fences."

Sister Hildegaard watched Edythe, breathless herself. "Where was it?" she asked.

"Why, Grandmother lived in the country near Mason City, that's Iowa. The farm was about five miles out in the country."

"That is in the United States, then," said Sister Hildegaard.

"Why, yes," said Edythe.

"What was your grandmother's name?"

Edythe's face clouded. "I don't remember. I don't remember anything else at all. Her name, my name, whom I was expecting to come. Nothing. Only I was young then and I can remember how grandmother looked, and I know it was Iowa where she lived. Oh, how marvelous!" She suddenly jumped up in her excitement. "I remember something of my past! I had a past like everyone else, a childhood, a grandmother!"

"And you are an American," said Sister Hildegaard, "like the boy."

"Why, yes," repeated Edythe. "I suppose I am—or was. I remember grandmother's rosy cheeks, and the old-fashioned spectacles she wore, and her hair was gray and done up neatly in a bun. She taught me many things—to sew, to cook, to knit."

"I thought you knew something about sewing," remarked the sister. "Edythe, were your parents there, too?"

Edythe's face clouded. "I can't remember. There's nothing more."

"*Cela ne fait rien,*" said the sister. "You have regained a memory. It is a beginning."

Edythe put her work down on the chair. "I must tell the doctor. I must tell him I have remembered something."

"Of course, he will be very pleased indeed to hear this," said the nun. "Go ask Fatou if he is still in the hospital."

With light, quick steps Edythe walked through the halls up to the reception desk where Fatou was talking to a visitor. As Edythe came up, the man drifted away, and Edythe said, "Fatou, please, do you know where the doctor is?"

"He went home, Madame," answered Fatou, "about an hour ago. He will return later, he said."

Disappointed, Edythe looked around. She had so planned on telling him instantly. She had to find him. "Where is his bungalow, Fatou?" she asked.

The girl said, "Come, I show you the way to go." She went to the hospital entrance with Edythe and pointed a slim arm. "Down that street. The fourth house."

"Oh, that's easy. I shall go find him. *Merci,* Fatou. *À bientôt.*"

Edythe walked down the street Fatou had indicated. She knew she was being impulsive, possibly unwise, and yet the doctor was concerned for her recovery; he would want to know. She stood in front of a neat, sparse cottage, much like the others on the street—tin roof, square, screening around a veranda, built up off the ground, and no trees whatever around it. It was the African way, "trees for forest, man for town." She went up the two steps and knocked. No answer. She knocked again. A shuffling inside and then Emma opened the door, an Emma looking much less groomed and neat than usual, wearing a low, sleeveless blouse and wrap-around skirt, her pigtailed, dark head unturbaned. She greeted Edythe with a slow, shy smile and opened the screen door.

"Is the doctor here?" asked Edythe. "I want to talk to him, Emma, please."

"Come," said Emma.

Edythe followed as Emma led the way through a kitchen and into a sitting room. Shutters were partly closed to keep out the heat, and her eyes had to adjust to the dimness of the room. The doctor had not heard her. He was lying in a canvas lounge chair, his eyes closed, his shirt off, his bare feet propped on a wicker stool. In a languid hand he held a bottle of beer. On the floor nearby was a mat and a plate and some oranges. It looked as though it was the place where Emma had been sitting.

"Doctor," said Emma softly.

He jerked upright, wide-eyed in surprise. Edythe rubbed her perspiring hands against the sides of her lab coat.

"I'm sorry," she said. "I shouldn't have interrupted you, Doctor Heinrich." She was embarrassed to have come in upon his privacy. She should have waited. Yet the excitement of her message was still urgent.

The doctor got to his feet. "Edythe, *qu'y a-t-il?*"

"*Rien*, Doctor," she said. "It's just that—it's just that I've remembered something!"

As Heinrich looked at her he was aware of how beautiful she was when her eyes were alive and excited. The color in her face, the small pulse that beat at her temples, and hearing her words, he thought, I shall lose her—she will be leaving when it all comes back. Aloud he said, "Come, sit, tell me what you remembered."

He led her to the one overstuffed chair and sat down on the stool in front of her. The ceiling fan was circling slowly overhead. She sat, her hands on the chair arms, her eyes on his face.

"I didn't remember much, really," she began, and then she told him all. It was still there, her memory, one full cup out of that hidden lake.

When she concluded she added, "I don't remember grandmother's name, nor my parents, nor whom I was so intensely waiting for as it began to snow. Why can't I remember more! Why? Why?"

"Patience, patience. We are making progress. More will come now. I am pleased with this."

"It is so slow," she moaned, twisting her hands together. "I can't wait forever."

Heinrich took her hands in his and held them firmly. "Some people have to learn to walk all over again," he said, "a step at a time, some to talk again. For you, it is remembering."

"But when, when?"

"That we do not know. The mind is a strange land."

Suddenly Edythe noticed the doctor's bare forearm as he held her hands. Her eyes were transfixed by the dull purple numbers engraved in the skin of his arm, by the dull red triangle above them, and she knew what it meant. It meant the war, the concentration camps, Jewish people herded off like cattle, tortured, gassed, exterminated. This man had been in one of those places and survived. Where was she then? She had a feeling of the war, a knowledge of it, but herself —she must have been around twelve, fourteen. Her own troubles seemed petty in comparison. The doctor had noticed her rapt look and had withdrawn his hands and sat on his own chair again.

"Do you like music?" he asked, after a moment, his voice husky.

"Yes, I think so," she answered.

"Then listen with me. Emma, play that one over again."

Emma was sitting on the floor mat leaning against the wall. As he spoke, she leaned over to an old portable phonograph player nearby and unsteadily placed the needle on the record. The sounds of a Beethoven quartet filled the room.

Edythe relaxed. Yes, she liked music. The doctor smiled at her and leaned back in his canvas chair again. Emma clasped her hands around her knees, a little smile on her face. Suddenly the doctor sat up again and said, "Edythe, how old were you that time at your grandmother's?"

She looked inward, thinking. "I'm not sure, but it seems like I was quite young, maybe nine or ten. Why?"

"Only trying to fit together the pieces of the puzzle," he replied.

She leaned her head back and closed her eyes, listening to the sounds of the music. She was almost too excited to appreciate it. When the record was finished, she looked around and saw that Emma's place was empty. She and the doctor were alone. He was looking at her, studying her face.

"I didn't offer you anything to drink. Would you like one of these or a lemonade?"

138

Edythe started to rise from her chair. "I should probably go back and make myself useful."

He put a restraining hand on her arm. "Stay awhile. Have a drink with me.

"All right," she said, sinking back, "a beer then, I guess."

"Coming right up," he said, and went to the kitchen and she heard him opening and shutting the refrigerator. When he returned with her glass of foaming beer and another bottle for himself, he was wearing a shirt, and sandals on his feet. He turned the record over, started the machine again, and then sat down on the floor in front of her.

"Do you realize," he said, his voice relaxed, no longer the doctor ordering, advising, "that we now have quite a few facts about this person we call Edythe Clare Monsarrat?"

"No," she said, surprised, "it seems to me to be practically nothing."

"Not at all. Look. Now we know you are probably American, probably born there. But since your French is so fluent we gather you've lived many years in a French-speaking country. You probably married a Frenchman. Well, we don't know for sure that you are married. I would only assume you are or have been. You've been well cared for, haven't had a tough time —that we can tell from your hands, your looks, your fine rings, the quality of your one dress. You haven't been too unhappy, either. Your face doesn't show severe signs of ingrown unhappiness, self-pity, or frustration. You've had time to lie in the sun and play."

Edythe flushed and felt uncomfortable at this listing. What a useless life the doctor was picturing, and yet it sounded accurate as far as she could see. She didn't really care for that person, whoever she was.

Heinrich continued, "I don't think you've had children, through choice, or some other reason that we don't know. We also don't know your name, address, occupation, if any, or what family you may have, or where they are."

Edythe nodded her head sadly. "Yes, that's about it, isn't it."

"Not entirely," he said slowly. "No person is the statistics on his or her dossier." He paused a moment, his dark eyes sad and far away from the present. Then he spoke again, as with an effort. "After the war I was in a detention camp." He paused a moment, wondering what was prompting him to talk so much to this woman. But he continued. "An officer brought me a list of prisoners who had died en route from one of the concentration camps to our DP camp. He threw the list down in front of me, saying, 'Here is the information on these corpses. Please file it.' I looked down the list of the dead, not expecting to know any of the names, but a name jumped out at me, 'Augustus Teller, Marburg, age forty-five, religion Jew.' I knew him. He had lived down the street from us. I'd known him all my life until I went away to study medicine."

Again he paused and looked away. Outside could be heard the rumbling wheels of a peddler's cart, the singsong call of the peddler. Heinrich twisted the bottle in his hands and began again. "None of the thousand things I knew of him were represented in those statistics. I knew his devotion to his crippled sister. I knew his small dog named Hinkle who always followed him. I knew the leather breeches he wore year in, year out; the kindly way he had of stopping to talk to boys like me, sometimes giving us a pfennig or two. I knew he carried home bratwurst every Friday night and that he bought smoked fish on holdiays, that he took his vacations hiking in the Bernese Oberland, that he was fond of quoting Schiller." Heinrich paused and laughed a little at his own remembering.

"All these things together helped make up the person represented by those statistics. What I'm getting at, I guess, is that I'm beginning to know you, Edythe, without your vital statistics; to know the way you sit up on your bed with your knees drawn up and your hands locked around them. The neat way you walk across a room, the way you rumple your hair when you're disturbed."

In his mind, as he looked up at her flushed face, he thought, Yes, and that little pulse that throbs by your temples when you're excited and your skin I'd like to touch. Out loud he said,

"These things and others are more important than our bare statistics. You may regain your identity one of these days—you will, of course—but we already have part of it now. Do you understand?"

Edythe's eyes smarted with tears, not for the things he had said about her, but because his words were a counterpoint melody to the Beethoven quartet, word images were balanced against musical phrases, the past laid claims upon the present, the present was born of the past. Grandmother gave a memory of her kitchen and herself and the doctor's friend lives here in this room for him, too, just as when he walked the brick-paved streets of Marburg, and then died someplace between one displaced person camp and another. She nodded at him, blinking away the tears.

"I think I understand," she said. "We are the life we are living now, the person we are in this moment."

"Right," he said, "and Edythe, keep telling me that. I am the one who can't remember my own sermons." And he reached his arm, the one with the tattooed numbers on it, to touch her hand, and this time did not take it away.

The quartet finished its last perfect note. Next door a baby cried lustily, stopped, cried again, testing its power, and a woman's voice rose and fell in a clatter of Malinké. A screen door banged. They sat in their own pool of silence. Neither of them wanted to break the feeling that lay around them, a feeling that for a space of time they had experienced a special revelation of each other. Heinrich set down his beer bottle and got up. He offered Edythe his hand.

"Come, we shall go back to the hospital together."

24

MALINKÉ PROVINCE PRISON was a formidable structure; its ancient brick bulk loomed heavy against the
flat riverland. Long, open slits shielded in the ar-
chitecture of the walls were barred windows. The effect
was of no openings, of impregnability, of complete
incarceration.

At the back, facing the river, another level housed
offices and kitchens. At the river's edge, three or four
hundred meters away, the prison's grim predecessor
lay, a pile of crumbled brick, where in the days of
slave trading, a human cargo brought from the country
down the Niger were rehandled and then marched
overland to the coast to be sold. But this was history
now, its story untold except to the rare tourist.

The present prison stood for only a slightly less grim
purpose. In the old days tribal law took care of law-
breakers, but today the State took it upon itself to
separate them from society. Even so, tribal and family
influences were still strong as well as the influence of
Islam. The prison was now more populated with political prisoners sent to Siguirre from other areas than
with criminals. Beside it stood a guard tower and in
the back a great walled yard; beyond that were several
hectares of land devoted to ragged gardens which were
cultivated by the prisoners under the rifle's shadow.

It had seemed unlikely to Heinrich from the first
that Paul Marion could stand a long imprisonment.
He was not a robust person nor did he appear to have
the kind of ego that could withstand long deprivation.
He knew in the camps he had sometimes misjudged

men and he hoped he was wrong in Paul's case. The heat, the insects, the rodents, the presence of disease and rot in the prison, the corrosion of the mind, the whole claustrophobic quality of life there would take its toll on him. After the camps, Heinrich thought he would never again be touched by pity for the suffering of others. He thought his heart would refuse to arouse itself to more human anguish. But, in his self-examination, he found that if one is to be tortured at all by human suffering, it is a continuous, a life-long condition. Paul's case, of course, did not compare with the tragedies of the war years that were almost commonplace. Aside from unjust imprisonment, Paul was not mistreated, and there was the hope that he could survive his sentence, or perhaps be pardoned.

So Heinrich comforted himself as he waited in the great hall while the guard went to find Paul. A high iron gate barred the hall where he stood waiting from the prison yard. He could see Paul sitting on the ground in the shade of the wall, half dozing, half watching some prisoners playing volleyball. When the guard came up to him and spoke, he slowly drew himself up and came toward the building. The doctor noticed that his skin had a dingy, unwashed hue, the long hair was unkempt, he was barefoot, and his torso was bare, showing the too-prominent rib cage. The guard opened the gate and waved the two of them toward a bench at the side.

Paul shook hands with Heinrich, looking at him soberly. Stifling the impulse to reach out a hand and stroke the thin sad face with its stubble of beard, the doctor asked, "How are you feeling, Paul?"

The young man shrugged. "Okay."

They talked about his health first, and then Paul asked about the hospital people, and when he heard that Edythe had remembered a childhood spent in Iowa, he exclaimed, "Fellow Americanos! I thought she was! Imagine that, two of us." He was grinning, pleased with the news. "Do you think it will help you to find her folks?"

"I don't see how," Heinrich said, "with no names to go on. But we shall see. Our administrator is in Conakry now trying to find some leads."

"I wish I could go back to the hospital," the boy said wistfully. "But they even look at my shit these days. I can't pretend dysentery. Couldn't I have an emergency appendectomy?"

"Of course!" mocked Heinrich, "and how about the existing scar on your abdomen?"

"*Quel dommage!*" he said. "Maybe it grew back in. How about a hernia, then?"

"Not a chance," Heinrich said. "Just stay well. Get strong. Do you get the food?"

"Of course, and thanks a million. That's why I am so well. Of course, the prisoners who see Emma come with the basket hate me for it, but I don't care. It's really great. There's only twelve more days till the Pardon Board meets, Doctor. Monsieur Santillana did get all the papers in, didn't he?"

The doctor frowned. "I'm pretty sure he did, Paul, but, you know, it's only a chance. They probably only grant a handful of pardons each year for all the country."

"Hell, I know, Doctor. I won't get it." Paul kicked his bare toes at a clod of dirt on the floor.

"But we never know how things work here," the doctor put in, not wanting to discourage him either. "We have to hope for it."

When he got up to leave after a few minutes, Paul said, "I would sure like to see Edythe. Do you think she could visit me? Maybe I could help her remember something else about America."

"I'll see if I can get permission for her to come with Emma sometimes," Heinrich said. "Then you can talk together in your English, talk about the States." He kissed Paul's cheeks in the French way and shook his hand.

Looking back as the gate was slammed behind him, Heinrich saw Paul standing there, watching bleakly until the guard gave him a push toward the outside yard. Heinrich turned toward the outside gate. He wanted to escape the prison, the presence of mindless power, of crippling, crushing authority. It placed a fog over him that robbed him of his manhood; he only wanted to escape, to seek some retreat where they would never find him. Each time he left the prison after a visit to Paul he felt he would never go back. But outside, he regained the courage to go again.

Paul went back and sat in the shadow of the wall. In the mornings on their so-called free time or recreational time, the guards made everyone keep moving. But in the afternoons they let them sit if they wanted to. Paul thought of the doctor. He loved him with a rush of affection. He'd felt that same strong love for his father when he was small, but never after he'd grown up. He supposed the doctor had his faults. He didn't know what they were, though. Did he drink too much? White men who lived in the tropics often did. Did he fuck the black girls? Whatever the doctor did, he felt sure he'd do it discreetly and decently.

The whistle blew. The ballplayers let the ball roll away. Gathering themselves up from their siestas, other men stretched themselves. They slouched inside and stood in line to get water from the big drum. The smell of sweat was strong and sickly sweet. Paul padded down the corridor to his own cell, the guard behind him. The guard clanged the door shut and ground the bar down, the lock closed. Paul faced silence.

At least it was a cell of his own. He didn't have to live with an *indigène,* most of whom he would have had a hard time coping with. How come he had a cell to himself, a corner one, too, with tiny slits of windows high on two sides? He'd wondered that a thousand times. Didn't the blacks want him in with them? Privilege had to be paid for, or was this solitude, this privacy, a penalty? In the ethics of prisons that must be it.

It seemed, thinking of America, that back there

things were more clearly good or evil, at least in the world he knew. Here, there were no clear-cut distinctions, as far as he could see. Morality was an uneven, rainbow-hued color, something much more subtle. It must be a matter of belonging or not belonging to the culture.

He thought of Emma, who moved in two worlds, the black and the white. In the hospital she had seemed to always have a tentative air about her, as though she were not sure, as though she were holding back her real self. She might be different with only her own people around her, the same as he was different. Yet the Siguirre people were not Emma's people; he felt she was apart even from the blacks at the hospital. And in the prison, when she came in and out with the food basket, there was a disdain in her manner for everything to do with the place—disdain for the guards, the locking and unlocking of the gate, the authority symbols. He felt Emma hated the prison, that she was sympathetic to his plight. He liked her better than he had Barbette. Oh, he had been really smashed on that Barbette for awhile, though. Emma did not have her seductiveness, but there was more strength in Emma, more humanity, somehow. He knew that he was learning about people and how to judge them, too. But at the same time he had little confidence in himself. How could he ever have gotten himself into this mess? He had missed cues he should have caught. Well, he must get out. He knew if he was to survive, he must get out, pardon or no pardon.

But for now he was glad to be by himself. It wasn't like being in solitary. He was able to go out and work in the gardens and he had this time in the rec yard. He went to chow at noon and ate soup with the other prisoners. But breakfast and evening meals were brought by Emma.

In a moment of whimsey he wrote an imaginary letter home, "Dear Mom, life very good over here. Private room, good service, food brought in by beautiful girl. Sports and crafts. Scenery beyond description."

Shit. Paul kicked his latrine bucket and threw himself on his mat.

"Dear folks, damn lie. I'm dying by inches every day. Why doesn't someone get me out of this rotten prison! I exist. I exist."

He curled up in a ball and began to think of a dog he had before he went off to college. It was a beautiful German Shepherd named King. He could almost feel now King's fur when he buried his face against him, every hair of it alive, bristling, yet warm, giving. Oh King, oh long lost days, what am I to do? And then Paul wished that death could walk into the cell and claim him, for he could not bear to think of tomorrow. He sensed there would be no reprieve, neither by his calling to that black angel nor by the Pardon Board. Tomorrow would come, and another and another.

25

EMMA HAD BEEN HELPING Edythe decorate the cottage. They had been working for hours. Now the walls of the room were completely covered with panels of material tacked smoothly against the rough wood, alternating panels of plain forest green with a print of green, blue, and white animal figures. They had draped the rough ceilings with fishing nets and hung white curtains, held back with green ribbons, at the windows.

Decorating rooms was a new experience for Emma and she had been absorbed in the chore. When it was finished they both stood back, wiping off their perspiring faces and admiring their work.

"Very nice, indeed," exclaimed Edythe, picking up the shears, sewing materials, and tack hammer. "You've been wonderful help, Emma."

"Très jolie," murmured Emma, eyeing their work and thinking that she could not have chosen the different materials to all blend together in as beautiful a way as Edythe had done. "Are we finished now, madame?"

"Yes, Emma," Edythe replied, laughing a little, "for I must go to the hospital. But when are you going to call me Edythe? We are friends now, aren't we?"

"Yes, madame," said Emma, "we friends." She smiled and then giggled, with her hand at her mouth, realizing her mistake again. "I go to doctor's house now to wash—Edythe."

"D'accord," said Edythe. "I'll see you later." And she closed the screen door and went one way as Emma took another.

Emma went on to the doctor's cottage. She went through the familiar rooms, making things neat, picking up the clothes to be washed. At the bathroom mirror she paused to examine her image and straighten her turban. Then she took the soap powder and the clothes outside to the tubs at the back of the house. She found herself thinking, as she scrubbed, of the village of her childhood. She had not been back in many seasons—not since her mother and she had left when some unknown thing had happened to her father, some accident which vaguely she knew involved another village of Fulanis. After that her mother had, in anger, taken her and made their way to Conakry. There her mother had become sick and died, and the nuns had taken Emma in to live with them at the mission, eventually sending her to work for a French family. During that time a Peul whom she had met while shopping in the bazaar had gotten her with child, and the child was born in the Mission Hospital, and some kinsman of Emma's who was there in the same hospital had said to her, "Go home with your child, Emma, back to the village of our people."

But she did not. She stayed in the city, and the child grew sickly and finally died at the beginning of its second year, and Emma blamed herself for his death. And the nuns had said, "Go up to Siguirre. It is in the direction of your home. Work there for Doctor Heinrich until you are ready to go back."

The doctor had taken care of her, and she had helped him and had worked in the hospital and at his cottage. There had been times when he had asked her to his bed and she had gone, but he was always far away in spirit although he was as good to her as a husband, maybe better. Now she could see the doctor did not need her even in that way, and she thought more and more of her girlhood village life. Perhaps if she went back there she would find a husband who would breathe in and out the same air with her and sleep on the same pallet with her and drink from the same bowl, and give her children and the

149

children would live and flourish in the village, in the village of the ancestors.

With strong hands Emma wrung out the clean clothes and hung them on the line strung across the back of the cottage. She thought of Paul, to whom she carried the basket of food twice each day. She did not like to leave Paul. Why couldn't the important people, such as the doctor or the Italian scientist, manage to free him? He would die where he was. She did not want to think of the prison when she was back in her village.

She thought of the new move she was making into the cottage of the white woman—the woman they said walked out of the forest more like a spirit than a human—who did not know her own name or any of the things that had happened to her either in the forest or anywhere else, except for one grandmother. She had, or she remembered, an ancestor. That was the important thing. Emma did not feel any fear of this woman called Edythe. In fact, she was drawn to her. Somehow, in a way she could not understand, this move she was making into Edythe's cottage seemed a necessary step toward going back to her own home.

26

ON A SATURDAY, Edythe and Emma moved into the cottage. The sisters and Fatou were coming in the afternoon for a housewarming. At the careful coaching of Sister Hildegaard, Edythe had boiled water for drinking, and with this, still slightly warm, she and Emma made a fruit punch for the afternoon guests. Fatou had purchased sweet cakes.

The sisters arrived, carrying a gift, a luxuriant fern potted in a glazed ceramic bowl. "For the new house," said Sister Hildegaard, extending the plant.

Edythe was touched by the nuns' kindness. She set it on a low table in her room. "It's a plant from the jungle from whence I came," she said soberly and formally.

They all examined and admired the way Edythe and Emma had decorated the cottage. They stood around with their glasses of lukewarm punch. There were not enough chairs, so finally they all settled themselves on the clean floor mats, a low table in the middle.

"This Fulani style," said Emma.

They drank a toast to Edythe and her new home. When Edythe explained to the sisters how Emma would be staying there, too, she noticed a raising of Sister Hildegaard's eyebrows as she darted a quick look at Sister Gertrude, who nodded back smugly. The sisters were pleased, as the doctor had predicted. Sister Caroline applied herself to her sweet cake.

"You will be taking your meals at the hospital still, Edythe?" she said, more in a statement than a question.

151

"Yes, Sister. I don't plan to be domestic," replied Edythe. She looked about the room. "We've gone to so much trouble," she said. "What if tomorrow word comes that my family has been found—*if* I have a family, that is."

"It would be better for you to go where you belong, Edythe," answered Sister Gertrude.

"Maybe there is no one to go to," said Edythe.

"Don't say that. There is some family looking for you, waiting frantically for word of you."

Edythe sighed. "I like it here," she said. "I know it is temporary, but I would hate to leave it—and all of you."

The sisters didn't know what to say. Hospital patients always left. Sister Hildegaard held a romantic picture of Edythe and the doctor in her imagination, but Sister Gertrude, when the idea had been mentioned to her over lunch one day, had refused to entertain such a notion, even though she had admitted that it might be a good thing, that is, if Edythe were not already married. Of course, the sisters knew that Edythe must have a life elsewhere, a different kind of life, in more civilized surroundings. The doctor belonged to them and to the hospital. They all knew about Edythe's memory of her childhood. They supposed that gradually she would remember everything or someone would come and claim her and, like the Italian, she would go back to where she had lived before.

Finally, Sister Gertrude made the move to leave and the others got up too. Sister Caroline said a blessing on the new house and they all bowed their heads for a moment, murmuring a prayer for Edythe and her cottage. Work waited down the street at the hospital. Fatou hurried ahead to her duties and Emma went with her; the nuns followed more slowly, hating to end the unusual interlude.

When they were gone, Edythe cleared away the glasses and plates. Then she came again to her room, parted the bead curtains, and waited to see if the feeling was still there. Yes it was—something on the verge of taking shape. She waited, hoping the elusive memory would surface in her consciousness, but it refused to come. She lay on her bed and the afternoon torpor pressed on her eyes and she slept.

She awoke to hear a strong masculine voice saying, "Is anyone at home?"

Edythe jumped up and went through the beads to the outer door of the veranda. Doctor Heinrich stood in the shadows of the yard. He was wearing a blue shirt, open at the neck, and white trousers and sandals. He carried a small parcel wrapped in brown paper. He bowed to Edythe a little awkwardly.

"Doctor Heinrich," she said. "Come in. Don't stand out there in the yard."

"The good sisters said you would still be here," he said, looking around the cottage. "How nicely you've fixed it."

"Come," she said, leading the way through the beads. "This is the other room."

"Yes." He looked around. "Very comfortable and simple and cheerful."

Edythe smiled at his praise. *"C'est intime."*

She wanted to tell him about the feeling there, yet it seemed too gossamer.

Self-consciously, the doctor held out his parcel to her. "A housewarming gift. An old custom, I believe."

Pleased, Edythe opened the brown paper. A small, spread-eagled man-figure carved out of bone and hung on a narrow plaited-leather thong looked back at her.

"What is it?" she asked.

"It's a juju. A good luck charm. This one comes from a powerful marabout here in Guinea, so I am told."

"Good heavens! And what is a marabout?"

"You don't know that!" He sighed in mock despair. "I see you have not moved in the same circles as some of us. He is a holy man of Islam. I suppose he blesses

153

it or something. You hang the thing up over your doorway to bring you and everyone who lives here good luck."

"Ah!" said Edythe. "Emma wears something like this around her neck, a tiny horn. You don't think I should wear this—to get the most benefit from it?"

"No, when you have a home you should hang it over the doorway. I believe that is the proper thing."

"Well, then," Edythe said. "Let's put it up at once so the luck will start."

They inspected the top of her door frame and, sure enough, there was a nail there.

"See," said Heinrich. "Someone has hung one here before."

"I wonder if their luck was good," said Edythe.

Now the small figure protected her house. "We drank all the juice Emma and I made," she said. "I haven't anything left to offer you, not a lemon nor an orange."

"Never mind. I came to get you. That murderous sun is about to set. We could walk a while, if you feel up to it, and then stop at a little place I know on the quai where the fish is superb."

She looked at him, remembering how Alfoldi Santillana had mentioned the same thing. "I'd like that," she said, feeling the juju was already working. "Let's go."

Heinrich and Edythe stood at the railing which ran around the edge of the Lagoon restaurant. It was on a deck over the river, and the water licked softly against the wood pilings underneath.

"How would you like to go on an excursion with me to a native festival in the bush?" Heinrich asked. "Would it appeal to you?"

"Oh, yes," she replied. An invitation to go anyplace sounded exciting, and especially with the doctor. "Tell me about it."

"I've been going every year with D'jala Diop," he told her. "He has relatives who live in a village far up the Tinkisso. I've been twice—no, three times, actually. D'jala takes his family; youngsters and other relatives come along. It's a long and tiring day, but if you're up to that part of it, the change from the hospital would be good for both of us."

"It just seems a miserable time of year for a festival," said Edythe.

"Yes, that's what I thought at first. But you see, they pray for rain, they dance, they feast, and have story-telling. All in Malinké, of course. And this year it's a combination of the end-of-Ramadan feast and a pre-rainy season thing."

"I think I'd like to go," Edythe said. "When is it to be?"

"Some day this next week. Diop will let us know. He furnishes a vehicle, driver, and everything—always presuming we don't have a critical case at the hospital, of course."

"And if it has begun to rain by then?" asked Edythe.

"Oh, no, it won't," said Heinrich, "or the festival would have been called earlier." He was smiling a little.

Their dinner, steaming and pungent, was now on the table, and they went to it.

"I'll never understand," laughed Edythe. "How can they tell?"

"It's unscientific as hell; but nevertheless, their way works," Heinrich said, and he picked up his fork and began to eat.

Later, they sat back in their chairs with tiny cups of strong coffee in their hands, and watched the river. It was now a dark mass that pulsed and murmured in the dark, an anthropomorphic force, a being aware of its strength and its power, a third person with them. A comforting breeze blew across the water and whipped the flame of their candle. Clouds drifted across the sky, their dark forms dramatized by the crescent of moon which now and again revealed itself only to hide in the next herd of cloud shapes.

"Look, Doctor," Edythe said, pointing. "The moon —it moves so fast, playing games with the clouds."

"She is flirtatious tonight," said Heinrich, looking up at the moon and the clouds parting and meeting and parting again. He looked back at Edythe, who stared at the sky, her head back, her lips parted. He felt a yearning, a straining that began in his groin and raced through his torso to send a wave of warmth to his head. It was a stirring and pulling deeper than his sex drive; it felt on the edge of pain so that he wanted to close his eyes and will it back. He desired this woman, but through her he wanted fulfillment, something from life that was bigger and greater than either of them. He heard his voice as from a distance continuing the conversation.

"Do you know, Edythe, in the Mande tongues, of which Malinké is one, they use the same word, *carro*, for both moon and menstruation."

"They do?" she echoed thoughtfully. "Then does it mean they believe that we women came from the moon?"

"That is part of the mystery of the race, I suppose, back in the legends of time."

A lone star showed itself on the far horizon of the river above the outlines of palms on the opposite shore. Heinrich began to talk about Santillana's attempt to secure a pardon for Paul Marion.

"So, soon after the first of April we should hear whether or not we are successful. The board meets in Kankan, down the railway line to Conakry."

The thought of Paul disturbed Edythe's feeling of peace and contentment. "And if they refuse a pardon?" she asked.

The doctor shook his head as if to unload the unpleasant thought. "I cannot imagine," he said. "I hope Paul survives his sentence."

"But you will do something, won't you?" she asked.

He looked at her. "What can I do, Edythe?" he asked.

"I don't know," she said, helplessly, "but surely

something. You have great influence here. I already can see that."

He was silent, and she went on, "Couldn't you pressure people who are in authority—pressure them for a pardon or a parole, or even a retrial?"

"I am a doctor, Edythe," he replied sternly. "I am here to work, not to play political games."

"Of course," she said, her ardor collapsing. "I just was thinking of Paul, that he must be saved."

Heinrich was silent. He shifted in his chair, and then said, "We must not be too negative. We must wait and see what happens. He wants to see you, you know. He asked. How would you feel about going there sometime with Emma?"

With a start, Edythe realized that she felt a strong reluctance and fear at the thought of visiting the prison and had been trying to push away the fact that Paul was there and that she should go to visit him.

"I'll go," she said, stifling her fears.

"Good," he said. "I'll make a call or send a note to the commissioner to see if he will let you in as a visitor."

As they walked home a few rain drops fell. But it was a false alarm. The clouds drifted westward to the Fouta-Djallon and disappeared. The doctor left Edythe at the door where, inside, Emma slept on her mat.

In her room, Edythe lit a candle and opened her notebook and began to write.

March 25: A memorable day! (What a word to choose!) I moved into my cottage with Emma, so I am no longer a hospital patient. The sisters had a housewarming for me and brought me a plant. There is a memory trying to come, yet it refuses to break through. It is like seeing something unrecognizable in the distance when one is traveling. One keeps expecting it to take shape, to become familiar as one moves closer, but it remains indistinct, too vague to recognize. It is a scary feeling. What will it be? Is it anything at all? I stay away from the abyss. It gets easier to do all the time.

The doctor is a strong man, I think. When I look in his face I tend to lose myself, to fall—is it to fall in love? Yet I feel there is a rigidity about him. Or could it be something to do with his abyss (understandable, knowing a little of his background). Did he lose a wife or a sweetheart during the war, I wonder? There is so much sadness in him.

Anyway, I was happy all evening. The river, the moon (carro), *his hand touching mine now and then as we walked through the dark streets.*

She paused in her writing and pushed a small bug out of the candle wax with her ballpoint pen, thinking of the evening. Then she went on, *I am going to visit Paul in prison. I am frightened of this, yet somehow I feel compelled to go to him. I feel I must.*

She closed her notebook and got into bed, and moving cloudshapes guided her into sleep.

27

IN THE STILL, gray dawn, Sister Hildegaard said her prayers over her beads and read from her daily missal in the dim light, her spectacles perched on the edge of her nose. She read for Monday after the Fifth Sunday, the epistle, the psalms, and the gospel. As working nuns, their celebration of the Lent and Easter events had to be a personal celebration. In truth, the season being what it was, it was difficult to properly observe their fasting as they had been trained. It was an added burden to bear, but the nuns knew the importance of a good diet in this climate, and in this regard, the doctor watched them sharply.

Sister Hildegaard rose from her knees slowly and stiffly. The knowledge of all the work waiting to be done in the hospital kept her from lingering any longer than necessary in the chapel. Her bones ached as she stumbled through the cottage. She was tired and the day was just beginning. She heard the other sisters beginning to stir as she went out the door.

As she stepped outside, she sensed immediately that it would be another hard day. The close, stifling atmosphere had not changed. A savage sun, muted orange behind the dust and haze, had already emerged from the horizon and begun its journey. A climate unfit for human life, thought Sister Hildegaard. Wouldn't the rains ever come?

Her glance slid over the dried-up garden as she passed, pitying its plight, for it was far beyond her ability to help. Sister Hildegaard was bone-tired. The hospital was full and the doctor had told them to be prepared to put up extra beds. Soon patients would be in the halls. The prolonged dry season brought out all the diseases the province could possibly produce. It was becoming a matter of forcing herself to move ahead and perform the familiar duties automatically. She was still strong, yet at fifty and with twelve years spent in the tropics, she needed more rest.

As she entered the silent kitchen she thought of Edythe, and then of herself as a young woman—younger, actually, than Edythe. She prepared the coffee, thinking of the farm in Alsace-Lorraine. Life there had been hard, especially after her brothers were conscripted for military service. She had had to help her father with the barnyard chores. She remembered sloughing through the thick mud of the barnyard carrying pails of slops to the pigs, and hay to the horses, and pails of foaming milk back from the milking sheds. She remembered the sounds of the village church bells heard across the fields, so clear and lovely and beckoning. It was a great day when she was accepted for her novitiate and a troop of people came across the fields from the village to get her. In the midst of these memories she heard the door open and shut and, looking across the kitchen, she thought she saw her father's bent figure, his hands, gnarled with the rheumatism, trembling, his expression bewildered, unable to believe that she had been chosen for the Church, that she, too, was being taken away from him. Dear God, dear father! But it was Bakary, the cook. He was shuffling over to get his apron. He, too, was tired and must have had a hard time getting himself up and to work. She called to him to hurry and get the porridge going.

There was a great clatter and banging as Seitou and the assistant cook, Moussa, came in and started their work for the patients' breakfast. With the coffee on the fire and two huge pots of water set to boil, Sister Hildegaard went to check on the laundry. Dirty linens were piled in great heaped baskets. The laundry staff, a young man named Balomo and an older woman, Diagoma, were there, half awake, and beginning to fill the iron sinks with water. Sister Hildegaard checked

160

their soap, bleach, and disinfectant supplies, and then went back to get her breakfast.

Immediately after breakfast she went to the sterilization room for her own work. Noticing Sister Gertrude pass, she called to her.

"Sister, is Edythe finished in the laboratory?"

"Well," said Sister Gertrude, coming to the door. "There is certainly more work there if I could work with her, but, of course, I have to be on the floor so I can't show her the work. I can only be in one place at a time."

Sister Gertrude's voice held a querulous note. Her face looked drawn and pale. Sister Hildegaard did not notice, for she kept putting cloths into the autoclave as she talked.

"I could use her here," she said. "She could wrap sterile packs. It takes so long to do, and I have dozens of things to see about. The kitchen staff keep needing me—if they don't know what to do they just stand by their mixing bowls and sleep. Then there are the extra beds to get ready, and I'm expected to work on the wards . . ." She had to control her voice to keep it from breaking, the immensity of her tasks overwhelming her.

"Well," said Sister Gertrude sharply, "we all have more to do than we can manage, all of us." She stressed the "all." "And you know the plan was not to use Edythe as regular labor. After all, she isn't really hired help in the way of the others."

"But she's willing," broke in Sister Hildegaard, "and the work needs willing hands. I work as fast as I can but . . ."

They both drew their breath in sharply as Edythe slipped in between them, placing an arm about the shoulders of each sister.

"*Bonjour,* Sisters," she said. "Here I am, breakfasted and ready for work. What shall I do?"

The sisters were embarrassed. Sister Hildegaard closed the autoclave door, set the timer, and pushed the switch.

Sensing the strain between them, Edythe said, "I thought I'd ask if I could do other work, too, since you haven't the time to train me now in more lab work, Sister Gertrude."

Sister Gertrude warmed to Edythe's cheerful offer and said, "Sister Hildegaard does need help, Edythe. If you don't mind this kind of work, perhaps for part of the day . . ."

"Bien sûr," she replied. "Show me what I should do, Sister Hildegaard."

Sister Gertrude hurried off to the wards.

In the forenoon, two cholera cases were brought to the hospital and put in isolation. This immensely increased everyone's load. Cholera vaccinations were given to every hospital patient and worker by noontime. In addition to the cholera vaccine, Edythe was given a typhus shot as well.

When she met the doctor in the dining room at lunchtime, she said, "Doctor, this is the first day I've been as busy as the rest of you."

He put a hand against her cheek. She was glowing and taut.

"Go slow, Edythe. Rest two hours this afternoon. The germs thrive better than we do."

She rested her cheek lightly against his hand. It was the nearest they had come to a caress.

"I'll rest," she promised. "But will you let me work with the nurses? They need help badly. I think I could learn how to be useful."

"It's not pleasant work; it's something you have to get used to gradually." He was wondering if she could ever tolerate the odors, the sickening sights, the strange habits of many of the patients. Yet perhaps she could relieve someone in the women's and children's ward.

"We do need you," he said, "if you want to give it a try. If it gets to be too much for you, will you promise to say so and find other work?"

"Yes."

"Then go to Sister Caroline when you come back from siesta. Tell her I said to teach you."

Sister Hildegaard and Sister Caroline came in for their lunch just after Edythe left, and Doctor Heinrich told Sister Caroline to expect Edythe at the women's ward in the afternoon. "She is eager to help," he said. "Perhaps we should give her a chance."

"Can she do anything that the Malinké aides cannot do better, though?" asked Sister Caroline, and then thought to herself that she did not speak with love and charity.

Doctor Heinrich gave her a questioning look, for it did not sound like Sister Caroline. "We can use as much help as we can find," he replied gently. "And I believe Edythe learns very fast, perhaps quicker than the girls you have been training. More than that, there is the benefit it will have on her own recovery."

Sister Gertrude came to take the doctor to the examining room for an emergency case, and Sister Caroline looked after him, aware that what he had said was true. She sat down at the dining table where Sister Hildegaard waited, as Seitou brought in the lunch for both of them. She sat looking at the plate of food without picking up her fork.

Sister Hildegaard began to eat. "Is something wrong, Sister?" she said. "Is it the food?"

"I would like to fast this noon," said Sister Caroline, still looking down at her plate.

"You cannot," said Sister Hildegaard. "You know what the doctor has told us. How would you be by four o'clock this afternoon? God understands." She said the last more gently, realizing that Sister Caroline was troubled.

Slowly, Sister Caroline picked up her fork and unwillingly put a bite into her mouth. Rigidly she chewed the food.

"Perhaps, you could give up your dessert," Sister Hildegaard said, eyeing the pudding that waited for them in separate saucedishes.

Then she said, hoping to distract her companion from whatever was bothering her, "I understand the doctor took Edythe out to dinner the other night. To that Lagoon restaurant."

As there was no reply from Sister Caroline, she went on. "If you ask me, she is getting to be more than a patient to him. Not that I blame him, poor, dear man; he's no priest, and I expect he's starved for a woman's company, a woman like Edythe."

Sister Caroline forced herself to look up at Sister Hildegaard and try to converse. "I just hope he doesn't get too involved before he knows whether or not she —she's free. She may have a family, a husband."

Sister Hildegaard shook her head sympathetically. "I know what you mean," she said. "It's risky, isn't it, with an amnesic patient. Though she's not a patient, really. But, of course, it's time the doctor married."

"Marry a patient!" exclaimed Sister Caroline. "I doubt that."

"A former patient," said Sister Hildegaard calmly. "Doctors usually marry nurses or rich women or patients."

Sister Caroline laughed a little. "How do you know, Sister?" she asked.

Sister Hildegaard shrugged her broad shoulders. "I've noticed," she said. "Tell me, Sister Caroline, why has he buried himself up here all this time? He could be making piles of money like the rest of them back in Paris or Strasbourg or any of those places."

"He was sickened by the war," said Sister Caroline. "I doubt if we could ever really understand how it was with him. I have thought he wanted to use Africa as a wall between himself and—and his own world."

Sister Hildegaard looked at her, trying to understand. Then she gave up. "Well, Edythe seems to be good for him. I've never seen him so—so perky."

She had finished her own pudding and waited, watching to see if Sister Caroline was going to eat hers. But the nun left and went out through the kitchen to their cottage. Sister Hildegaard hurriedly ate up the second dessert, stacked her dishes and carried them to the kitchen, and then followed Sister Caroline, longing for the brief siesta that awaited her.

28

AT FIRST EDYTHE could not sleep. She thought of her meeting with Doctor Heinrich in the staff dining room, and of his touch on her cheek, but then, remembering all the unanswered questions of her life, she thrust the thought away and concentrated on resting her weary body. When she opened her eyes the curtains of her room had been drawn. She sensed it was mid-afternoon. The cottage was perfectly quiet. Emma must have been in while she slept. From the compound she heard a low murmur of women's voices and the pounding of pestle against mortar, scrape and pound, scrape and pound, as they worked manioc into a paste, and then the sound would stop and voices would take up again in a drowsy murmur, punctuated by light-hearted laughter.

Edythe closed her eyes again and then something prompted her to sit up. She looked around the room and suddenly that elusive feeling came to her, that tantalizing half-knowledge. She had had a playhouse. Not as big as this cottage, but nearly so. It had had two rooms also. How long ago it must have been. She and her father had been living in France. Her father! She saw him in memory. She felt a rush of affection for him. Where was he? Was he still alive? No memory of this at all, not even his name. What was his name? Her name? She saw in her mind's eye the big villa where they lived and, behind it, hidden in the back underneath overgrown pines, was the small house which had been filled with storage items when she first discovered it. She remembered coming into the second

165

room, which was empty, and exclaiming that she had found her own special, private place. She felt again the emotion of that time long ago, that sense of discovery, delight, and secretiveness. She was in the *lycée* then. She must have been around fourteen and it had been difficult, the studies all in French, the French girls in their little coteries that didn't include a stranger, an American who spoke with such an atrocious accent. She remembered going into the playhouse, the storage things had been taken away. It had been cleaned, dusted, and furnished with cast-off bric-a-brac from the big house.

It was in that little house she went to cry over her frustrations and loneliness, and to write love letters to people who never received them. Her father seemed to be away often on business trips, and there was a housekeeper, a French woman, who looked after her. She had been terribly strict and not always easy to understand. She seemed to remember screaming and throwing things at the woman, and the calm, strict way she was taken by the arm and led out of the big house over to the playhouse and pushed inside, where the door was firmly closed behind her.

I must have been a brat, Edythe thought, rolling over on her stomach. Why can't I remember her name, that housekeeper—she was really good to me. And my father's name, dear father! There was no mother in the memory, nothing else came back.

Edythe went to the hospital. Fatou, at the reception desk, was doing copywork to help Sy Kanadu. Edythe asked where to find Sister Caroline, and Fatou, preoccupied, pointed her pencil toward the women's ward. Edythe went to report for work. Sister Caroline, seeing her, came into the hall and she listened as Edythe told her the story of the new recollection.

"Soon it will all come," Sister Caroline said. "It is the work, the activity, that does it. It frees your mind so it can find its way back."

Sister Caroline regarded the woman beside her, noticing the confidence she gained with each new memory and the sense of what she must have been like before.

"Are you sure you want to work with the patients?" she asked, uncertainly.

"Of course," replied Edythe. "I want to. I can't bear for all of you to be working so hard and not be doing my share."

Sister Caroline began to explain the procedure of taking temperatures, and encouraging the patients to take as much water and juices as possible. She taught Edythe to say, "Drink, please" in Malinké. Soon Edythe was absorbed in her new tasks.

But the work was not easy. The children, who interested her the most, were the most difficult. They vomited often or made other messes in their beds, and although the aides were usually there to clean up, Edythe tried not to shrink from her share. Yet she found herself gagging often and was ashamed before the young Malinké aides who worked calmly and efficiently through each crisis. Edythe brought cool cloths for the children's faces and hands, and clean bed cloths to place over the scrubbed mats. Somehow the afternoon ended, and when she heard the clatter of the supper trays in the hall she knew she could go. Her first experience in the wards was finished.

As she was leaving the hospital she passed the doctor. He stopped and said, "I saw you working. You make a good nurse."

"Oh," Edythe said, pleased at his praise. "I'm really terribly ignorant about it all."

"You learn quickly," he said, "and the patients liked you. I could tell."

She started to tell him about her recall of memory after her siesta, but he was in a hurry and did not notice, and went on to the wards above. Edythe went out, thinking to herself, It was really so little, anyway; it hardly told me anything new.

That night she wrote in her journal: *I have had another recall, but it was such a small window into my* past, I could see very little—a house we lived in once and a playhouse in the back. It was a small, dark place, like a womb, perhaps, where I crawled away from everyone to cry over adolescent tragedies. It seems irrelevant now and I don't see the connection to this cottage, which is bright and open. Here I feel the stirrings of something—something tremendous. Of what I don't know yet.

I worked in the wards with Sister Caroline and she taught me nurses' duties. I held a small, squirming black baby in my arms and loved him, he was so precious, he felt so comfortable fitting into my arms. I'm tired to death, but almost happy—I—Edythe Clare Monsarrat!

What, oh what was my father's name—our name?

29

HEINRICH ROSE from his brief siesta. He stood in his shower, letting the sting of the cool water clear out the grogginess that always resulted from a rest that was too short. Then he filled his sink with water for shaving. It had been another hectic morning, with another cholera patient and several dysenteries coming in. The outpatients would be waiting for him, God knows how many lined up in the corridors. He had overlooked an important architectural detail when he laid out the plans for the new wing. There should have been a door coming directly in from the outside to the examining room and another exit at the back. He had been so obsessed with keeping the new wing away from the heavy traffic, keeping it clean and quiet, that he had not planned carefully enough for the outpatients. Well, some day they could add on again.

He knew he was at his best in a busy hospital. He organized his time and went methodically from one duty to another and nearly always came out at the right time with everything accomplished. He had even found time in that morning to send Sy Kanadu to the commissioner with the request that permission be given Edythe to visit Paul Marion. Equilbecq had signed the request and sent word that no news had come yet concerning the white woman. Heinrich wondered again about the passengers of the unknown airplane. It would seem that they were the kind of people who could disappear for days without being missed. Edythe, too. He could not understand it.

As his razor cut through the foamy soap, Heinrich

wondered if he should try to put in a call to Conakry himself to see what had happened to Édouard Diallo. He was missed and needed. But he came to no decision and let the idea fall away. His thoughts flew over the rest of the day. Edythe would again be assisting Sister Caroline in the women's and children's ward. He would try to talk with her after she was finished about going with Emma to visit Paul, now that the way was clear with the authorities. He thought of her slim, graceful figure moving between beds in the ward. It must have taken a lot of fortitude on her part to work with the *indigènes* that way. He had suspected her of having been too protected back wherever she came from to be able to see it through.

He rinsed off his cheeks and patted them dry with a thin towel. He was remembering another slim, graceful woman moving about in a garden cutting roses and dropping them in a basket. Only this woman was dark and a little smaller, more delicate perhaps, than Edythe —younger, too. Adrienne, whom he had planned to marry when he finished his training and could afford a wife. Over her shoulder she flashed him a smile, innocently coquettish. He followed her through the paths of her father's garden, obsessed in his adoration.

Sighing, Heinrich pulled clean trousers out of a drawer, shook them out, and then stepped into them. He had turned off the picture from the dead past. Once more feeling refreshed and vigorous, he went to the hospital, reminding himself to seek out Edythe later that afternoon.

He found her in the staff dining room. She was sitting on the bench, leaning against the table and drinking a glass of juice. Her damp, light hair curled around her ears where she had brushed it away from her face. Her face was rosy from the heat. Heinrich could hear Emma talking to the cooks in the kitchen. She was probably fixing Paul's basket.

"Would you like to go with Emma tonight?" he asked. "I've arranged it with the commissioner. We'll

170

find a taxi for you, as you've been on your feet enough."

"You mean I should go there without you?" Edythe sat upright, the prison looming grim and dreadful in her imagination. Somehow she had thought the doctor would be with her.

Heinrich spread his hands helplessly, "I don't have the time, Edythe. I must make the rounds again."

"Of course," she answered. She was disappointed but tried not to show it.

Watching her Heinrich thought, she expects me to go and I really don't want to; I'm tired, and the prison depresses me. He heard himself saying, "Edythe, it's no place for you and there is no necessity for you to go. Stay here."

"Oh, no," she said, "I want to see Paul. I shall go with Emma."

"If you insist on going, then I will come, too." He sighed, knowing at that moment that if this woman, through some chance, were to remain part of his life, he must not succumb to the lethargy he felt, or the distaste he held for so much of "the world out there."

They ate a light supper and, leaving Emma free of her usual chore, set out with the basket. Heinrich hailed a taxi and they sank back against the shabby seat. The hot wind blew through the open windows. As they rode, Edythe described to Heinrich the memory that had come to her the day before. Her green eyes shone and the vein in her temple pulsed with her emotion as she told the story of the house in France. As he listened, he recognized that Edythe pulled him out of himself and revitalized his spirits.

Strange, he thought, in remembering that playhouse she could not remember what French city they were living in. Retrograde amnesia left so many gaps when the memories began coming back, as though willfully certain details were left in obscurity. As Edythe told him her story she suddenly remembered the housekeeper's name was Juliet, yet still she could not remember her father's name.

In the prison a guard led the way down a dark corridor to Paul's cell. He was standing at the gate, his hands gripped around the bars, a gaunt young man with long ragged hair, rumpled dirty clothes, and loosened sandals. He grinned a welcome as he saw Heinrich and Edythe approach. The guard unlocked a padlock, drew back a heavy iron bar, and opened the cell gate. Paul stood a moment with his head against Heinrich's shoulder without speaking. The other prisoners had long since eaten in the dining hall and had returned to their cells. He had stood waiting for Emma. It was not the hunger that made him faint, but the loneliness, the feeling of being abandoned by the world. The doctor gave him a comradely hug and then pushed him back, saying, "Look, Paul, Edythe has come to see you."

Paul smiled at her, but he seemed embarrassed and he did not offer a hand. "Hello, Edythe," he said in English. "It's good of you. I've—it's just been a long day."

Edythe had glanced around the cell, shuddering at its bleakness. Putting more cheer into her voice than she felt, she began to tell Paul of her new duties in the hospital and about the cottage where she and Emma now lived. Then Paul probed her for more details of her childhood in Iowa, but she could produce nothing more than he had already heard.

The guard rattled the gate. He was anxious to leave.

"Only a few days until the Pardon Board meets," Heinrich said as they stood watching the guard secure the gate, and then he wondered why he had even mentioned it.

"Don't plan on it, Doctor," Paul said, as though Heinrich were the one to be comforted. "They won't give it to me."

They followed the guard down the corridor. Edythe had the feeling of deserting Paul, that she should go back, do something about his confinement. It was a terrible feeling. With an effort she kept walking ahead with the doctor. In the big hall they turned and looked back to where Paul stood against his gate, watching them. Edythe lifted an arm stiffly to wave, but he did not move.

After they had been riding in the taxi for a few minutes, Edythe said, "Someone should appear in person before that Pardon Board on Paul's behalf. A personal appeal sometimes carries more weight than a dozen forms in sextuplicate. Something more must be done."

Heinrich, depressed as he usually was after a visit to the prison, merely grunted at first, and then he said in dismissal of her remark, "There is no one to do that, Edythe. There's nothing more we can do."

When their taxi drew up to the portico of the hospital entrance, a Land Rover was parked in front and a driver who looked familiar to Heinrich was waiting by the machine. He pointed inside when they got out of the taxi, saying, *"Monsieur l'Italien."*

Heinrich looked at Edythe. "Alfoldi. I wonder why he's back."

Inside they were met by Sister Gertrude. "Thank God you're back," she said to the doctor. "The good scientist is ill, very ill. We've put him in Edythe's old room."

The doctor hurried away, and Edythe wandered back to the staff dining room, not wanting to leave until she knew what had happened. It was a long time before anyone came. The doctor and Sister Gertrude came in together, and Heinrich was talking.

"There must be someone with him all night, but it's out of the question for any of you. You've been at it since early morning."

"What is it?" asked Edythe, feeling a premonition of dread.

"Alfoldi is very sick," he said. "He's running a high fever."

"Is it cholera?" she asked.

"No, it doesn't seem to be, but we're running tests."

Sister Gertrude already was heading for her laboratory. "I'll send someone for Monsieur Paques," she

173

said, "in case we need him when I've finished these."

Paques was the apothecary who came on call. Edythe caught Heinrich's arm. "Please let me help with Monsieur Santillana tonight. I owe him my life, and I want to help. I couldn't sleep anyhow."

"How can I take chances with your health?" he asked, though tempted to use her, "when you're not even a nurse and you've worked all day?"

"So have the rest of you. Please, let me stay with him. There will be a nurse on the floor nearby, if I need help."

"That's true," he said. "I'll let you take a part of the night, but I'll be in and out myself. It is already ten o'clock. Can you stay until one?"

"As long as I can stay awake," she answered. "Show me what I should do."

The night seemed endless. Santillana, who had been fighting the fever alone for some days, was dehydrated and weak. At midnight the fever mounted to such a dangerous level that the doctor came in with Sister Gertrude and they took a spinal tap, thinking it might be meningitis. Edythe could see the relief on both their faces when the fluid they examined was clear. The doctor gave Alfoldi massive injections of quinine, and went to get some rest.

In the early morning, as Edythe sat watching the patient in his fitful sleep, her thoughts suddenly moved outward and a clear picture flashed into her mind and she saw herself opening a door and entering a bedroom by the sea. Glass doors opened to a balcony that looked over beach and water, and on a building off to the right was printed in black letters the words *"Motores Cap d'Antibes."* There was a man sleeping on a bed, and she saw herself dropping her purse onto a chair, and taking off her clothes quickly and going to the bed and waking the man, hearing the name "Nicki" uttered, and they had sex together. She saw the two of them moving about the room in many different positions, her memory's eye following their naked bodies outlined against the sun-drenched sand and sea and the white sheets in disarray. There was a feeling in the room of something single-minded, something determined, almost violent, and then the picture was gone, and only the name—Nicki—and the sign—*Motores Cap d'Antibes*—remained. And she thought, Who was that man? But she had not seen his face and had no memory to tell if he was her husband, if he was her lover, or who. But the few spoken words were in French and she could remember the man's powerful physique and she saw again his tanned arm reaching to pick up a pack of Gauloise cigarettes.

She sat looking at the flushed face of the Italian. Nicki. Was that her name? She covered her face with her hands. Did I love the man I did all that with? Oh, God in heaven, I need to know! She reached over and touched the hand of Alfoldi Santillana. How involved she was now in the lives of the people around her. What would regained memory give her to make up for all of these friends? And this vignette she could share with no one, no one at all.

30

HEINRICH COULD NOT DEFINITELY diagnose Alfoldi's illness. A microbiologist could perhaps separate the organism that was at work. He treated his friend with quinine and a fever-reducing medicine. The symptoms resembled malaria, and Alfoldi had been in a malaria area. Yet, in his own mind he was not convinced. It was one of the times that Heinrich wished he worked with a team—where, if one did not know the answer, another did. Another cholera victim had been brought to the hospital and died. The first three were better. They would survive. There was never any doubt about the symptoms of that disease.

That morning Heinrich received a cable from Conakry from Édouard Diallo. He carried it around all day in his hospital coat pocket without telling anyone else about it. It said only, "Information woman in hand return soon." Heinrich knew that soon in Édouard's terms might mean several days yet or even more. It had already been two weeks since he left. The arrival of the cable left him with a feeling of disappointment. Didn't he want to have Édouard's news? Why did he dread his return? He had to admit it probably meant he would lose Edythe. Soon he would know the facts of her life, the names of people in another place who claimed her in one way or another. Soon she would have another name.

There was no denying life had been more interesting since her arrival. He remembered the night at the hospital when he had stood by her bedside watching her sleep, and the feeling he had had then that this woman

176

symbolized the mystical, the feminine, and the beautiful. He was in no hurry for the outside world to claim this person. He knew she was becoming too much a part of his life. He looked for her each time he passed through the hospital and whenever he came to eat his meals. He thought of the boring hours he had spent at the Railway Club, idling away his free time with drinking, tennis, and billiards with companions who did not interest him. He had not been there since Edythe came.

He went often to the bedside of Alfoldi in the corner room on the second floor. Sometimes he sent the nurse in charge downstairs for a break while he sat in the chair by the bed. He would sit and look at the high dry flush on the tanned face and think of Alfoldi's life in Rome to which he would soon return. He, like Edythe, would leave. He would return to the wife, Laura, whose letters always came in packets, written in a neat, vertical script. Back to the university chair that waited for him in the earth sciences department. He would be in demand as a lecturer after this long African stint. Heinrich felt a little jealous of Alfoldi's life in the Eternal City—Although, he thought, it's not for me. It's too civilized. He must have to wear a tie, pay dues to professional societies, attend many meetings, make formal calls on university deans.

The sisters took their turns at the Italian's bedside. Edythe was on duty every night, sleeping now in the daytime. She was earning the respect of the staff, for she worked as hard as the rest of them.

And then Alfoldi Santillana's fever dropped. Whether it was the quinine or that the fever had simply run its course, the doctor could not be sure. But it was gone, and Alfoldi opened his eyes one early morning and smiled weakly at the woman by his bed.

"Buon giorno," he said in Italian without thinking.

"Monsieur Santillana!" exclaimed Edythe. "You are better. You are cool this morning. Here, let us measure and see."

She popped the thermometer into his mouth, and then cheerfully recorded a normal temperature on the bedside chart.

Santillana said, "Our positions are reversed, young woman. I seem to remember when you were my patient."

"Oh, but I'm so glad you're better. We've all been so worried. Doctor Heinrich has been in and out of this room a thousand times in the past four days."

"Mon Dieu, has it been that long! Well, I am finished with being a nuisance. It was not my time to die, as it was not yours back there in the forest."

"You are no trouble, Monsieur Santillana. Will you be still now while I go downstairs and spread the good news?"

"Of course, and then you rest, *mon petit chou.* I won't need anyone here."

Edythe went to find the doctor to tell him that his friend was going to recover.

Santillana continued to improve, although the doctor kept him in bed for three more days.

"I still don't know what you picked up, Alfoldi," he told him on the day he was released. "We tried every test we could think of, but nothing was positive. I was worried for a while."

"C'est à vivre dans le tropique," said Alfoldi, shrugging his shoulders. "That's life in the tropics. And now I have to get to work, Heinrich. I must go over my notes before leaving to be sure I haven't missed anything essential."

"As long as you are not running around and you eat heartily," said Heinrich.

"Bien sûr. I'll just sit at l'Hôtel l'Ivoire and work in my room. It's fortunate I had the presence of mind to bring all my notes and books in with me."

"You'd never forget them, my friend; your book is your child."

"The only one I have, I'm afraid," remarked the

Italian. "And speaking of children, isn't it about the first of April?"

"Yes, tomorrow."

"Then the Pardon Board meets, doesn't it?"

"It does, Alfoldi, and you'll be pleased to know Edythe has been going to the prison to visit Paul. She goes when Emma takes his food basket."

"Buonissimo. It may help him over a bad time. In case the board turns him down. But they can't, of course. I think they realize by this time the true picture. *On l'a pris au collet*. He was really framed."

"Oh, I don't know," replied Heinrich cautiously. "There was never any proof found of a conspiracy, even though we feel certain it was a jealous suitor. They are going on the facts in the case, Alfoldi, and there Paul hasn't a chance from a legal point of view, as I see it."

"The boy has suffered enough for his audacity in wooing the governor's daughter," said Santillana testily. "I can't leave this country in peace with him rotting in that jail. They must pay some attention to justice." He spoke passionately, sitting up in bed, thumping his fist up and down on his own bony knee.

Heinrich turned toward the window. He looked gloomily down on the street where a team of oxen lumbered slowly past pulling a load of firewood. A little boy walked along, rapping them smartly with a long switch. Heinrich said over his shoulder, his voice harsh, "We don't live in a just world, my friend. Don't you know that yet? And suffering is not equally divided nor the innocent delivered. Don't you understand this?"

Gently, Alfoldi replied, "Dear friend, forgive me for letting my foolish tongue rattle on. I should tend to my plants. Would it not be an excellent remedy for both of us to go your illustrious villa? There we can offer libations to the rain gods and pray that they look favorably upon this poor earth."

Heinrich found he was able to pick up his friend's light banter. *"D'accord!* As our Lenten duty we shall partake of the wine and offer our pagan prayers. Come on, Alfoldi, out of bed!"

"How my Catholic ancestors must grieve for me," said Santillana, climbing out of the bed. "Hand me my trousers, Heinrich."

31

PAUL MARION SAT ON HIS BUNK, leaning against the cool brick. The morning light threw a bar of gold onto his prison floor from the high slit in the wall. Another day faced him. Nothing to do. There was no more work in the prison gardens until after the rains. That was all anyone could talk about, the rains, and when they would begin. He, too, searched the skies for clouds when he was taken to the compound for exercise. He had the feeling that the heat was a monster who held them all in its viselike grip and was squeezing them, day after day. When it rained, finally, it would set them down again and melt away.

Paul thought of spring at home. He remembered the redbud and the dogwood, pink and white among the dark trees on the hills, followed by the tender green shoots bursting out on everything, the sweet smell of the new earth when his father plowed the garden for his mother. It was his mother's garden, the only thing his father did to it was to plow and cultivate it, from then on his mother did everything. He pictured her sturdy, middle-aged figure in old blue jeans, stooped over the rows, pushing seeds into the soft, red earth. This was his father's busy time at the big farm where he worked, getting the equipment ready for the new growing season. Paul spent hours thinking of such things, remembering his childhood, incidents he had not thought of in years. He could bring them out when he concentrated on it.

For some time, Paul had been thinking of death, of ending his own life. He did not really think the pardon would be granted, no matter what Santillana said. He considered how it would be to die and how it could be managed. It would have to be by hanging, he thought calmly. There was a hook high on one wall of his cell. He had no idea what it was for. It was impossible to reach, but if he had a rope he might be able to make a loop and, by throwing repeatedly, eventually catch it on that hook. He lay on his mat and stared at the hook and considered himself dying that way. The thing was, he didn't really want to die. He just wanted to get out, desperately. No, escape was what he really wanted. He had been turning it over in his mind nearly as long as he had been in prison, watching, listening, trying to find some way it might work. He had been surprised to hear of the prisoner who had managed to get as far as the river but was shot in his small boat. It must have been a poorly planned attempt. He would do better than that.

He went over all the plans he had dreamed up, discarding some, considering others, going through all the intricacies of each idea, what he would need, where he might get it. He had decided he must have confederates, prisoners or someone on the outside. Yet he had found no prisoner he could trust. He was afraid they would rat, or might chicken-out at the last minute. Most of them seemed content to wait out their terms. So someone on the outside must help him. The doctor? Ah, he would not even consider asking him, too much at stake there, although the doctor would have been the perfect confederate. Santillana? Emma said he was at the hospital very sick with the fever. Perhaps he would die. Paul hoped not, for the Italian had been a friend to him. No, men that age usually didn't risk going against law and order. They had their careers and families to think of. The woman, Edythe? Ah, maybe. Perhaps she was his chance. But what could she do? He would hate to involve her in his desperate plans, she had such troubles of her own. Yet she was a fellow American, and he had to have someone. He could not afford to be big-hearted when it came to escaping. He would ask Emma when Edythe would come again. They could talk English together and then no one could understand them. If he talked to Emma the guard would understand every word. So Edythe must be his chance.

Now he must think of a plan that could work. He began to think of the first steps. Would it be a break from his cell or from the rec yard? It couldn't be in daylight, no chance there but a rifle shot in the back. However, he'd take that risk if all else failed. He must plan an escape from his cell or the corridor. It must be at night. Maybe when the rains came. A heavy rain—in fact, the first one, and with everyone thinking about the break in the drought, the excitement of the new season, they might be careless. Filled with ecstasy at his ideas, Paul jumped off his mat and began to exercise. He must get in shape. Only the strong survive. He sparred a phantom punching bag; he did push-ups until he sank onto the brick floor exhausted.

32

THE LAND ROVER JOLTED through the tall, dry grasses of the savanna. Edythe clung tightly to the handrail. She looked down at Nhoti, the young son of Doctor Diop, and he, a nerve-bundle of excitement, anticipation, delight, flashed her a brilliant smile, white teeth flashing in the shining, velvet face. Heinrich looked happy, too, Edythe thought, turning to look at the doctor. The three shared the back seat of the open vehicle; a driver and the brother-in-law of Doctor Diop were in front.

"Un jour à la compagne," said Edythe gaily, echoing a phrase she seemed to know from the past.

"Here we say *'à la brousse,'* " Heinrich replied smiling. "To the bush. What do you think of it?" He indicated the panorama of savanna before them.

Reaching up a hand to adjust the straw hat she had bought especially for the trip, a worker's hat which she had adorned with a blue ribbon, her eyes traveled across the yellow sea of grass. It was broken occasionally by the gnarled, misshapen outlines of the baobab tree, its few leaves sparse as an ancient's tuft of hair. She could see now a stunted mimosa tree in the midst of the high grasses, and underneath its shade a lone herder rested. With the approach of the holiday caravan—a truck crowded with people, two Land Rovers, and a sedan—he came running and shouting, waving his arm. But as they rolled on unheeding, he stood staring after them, watching the vehicles disappear through the grass.

Edythe had glimpsed the Tinkisso River on her left,

but it had been disappointing, more sand than water, a narrow stream like a creek in other countries. To her right as they rolled along there appeared the 'bush'— a dense tangle of undergrowth, some few high trees, but for the most part scrub bushes and gnarled, twisted trees entangled with each other forming a perfect haven for the wild life of the savannas.

The expedition had begun in the early gray dawn when the doctor picked her up at her cottage. They were taken to the modest villa of the Diops, where a breakfast of hot, thick, black coffee, hard rolls, and fresh papaya and pineapple was served to the friends and relatives who gathered to travel to the feast site out on the plateau. Edythe met Madame Diop, called Line. She moved among her guests smiling and friendly, interspersing hospitable comments with good-natured scoldings at the children and orders to the servants, her flat nose and high cheekbones glowing with a rosiness beneath the rich brown. The children clustered about her, pulling at her *m'boubou* in their shyness, hiding their faces against her plump thighs, their hands caressing the maternal figure with the richness of child-love. The servants swooped in and out with the platters of fruit and bread, their bare feet silent on the floors. Many curious, interested glances were directed toward Edythe and the doctor. They were the only whites there and she the only stranger. She felt an excitement at being coupled with Heinrich in their glances, and she felt like an actress playing the part of a woman named Madame Monsarrat. The children darted about the room, shiny from their scrubbings, dressed in clean, cotton garments, radiating energy and excitement. Finally they had been delegated to a vehicle for the trip, and Edythe felt a sense of adventure, for the children's enthusiasm was contagious.

As they bounced along in the heat of the morning, Edythe answered Heinrich, "Yes, I like it. I love it."

"It will be a long day," he warned. "Are you all right? Do you need to stop?"

She shook her head, smiling. They sat so close, her legs often jounced against his and her arm rubbed against his hairy forearm, and the touch each time caused her flesh to tingle. Their faces, moving with the up and down of the vehicle, passed each other's with the motion, the heat from their bodies rising and mingling. The little boy sat on the edge of his seat cool and whole, undisturbed by anything outside his own completeness.

When they arrived at their destination, the village of Missidougou, Edythe was disappointed. It was only a collection of grass huts with thatched, conical roofs, great conical storage vats made of mud and thatch, and one dusty street through its center. But there were many people, and they came swarming out of the huts, picking themselves up from all around the village in the bits of shade, calling and shouting. They surrounded the vehicles. Everyone chattered; there was a great shaking of hands, a gleeful lifting out of the baskets. The talk flowed over all like waterfalls of cacophonous sound.

The doctor got down from the Land Rover and helped Edythe. People surrounded them, staring openly. Most of them knew the doctor and insisted on shaking his hand many times. The women touched Edythe's white dress; they shrieked with laughter at the straw hat and its gay ribbon. It had all the appearance and sound of rudeness yet she sensed it was not; they were just curious and innocent of offense. The sea of faces moved over her, engulfing her with its waves of welcome.

The village sat on a slight rise. There was not a tree near it, Edythe noticed, with dismay. To the south she could see the banks of the river. Around the village was an area showing signs of agriculture.

There was a set pattern to these occasions. Business was first. That meant the two doctors must examine the people waiting to see them. A rough table and a couple of wooden chairs had been set up. The doctors set their bags on the table. The first patient was already seated, his mouth wide open. He was obviously suffering from an infected tooth. His cheek was swollen, his face contorted with the pain. Heinrich stood aside. This was D'jala's kind of work. He was used to it in his clinic. After a brief examination, D'jala took an instrument from his bag and in a few moments had jerked out the rotten tooth. The patient had not movd nor uttered a sound. Edythe had turned away.

After this was over, Heinrich asked if she would act as his assistant and hand him the things he needed from his bag. So she became one of the team, feeling a kind of professionalism as she obeyed Heinrich's orders. The cases consisted of phagedenic ulcers, old wounds that had refused to heal, abscesses, sores and rashes of various kinds, people complaining of pains in their stomachs. Doctor Diop examined the women in one of the huts, his wife assisting. But there were no serious diseases among the villagers, no leprosy, frambesia, or malnutrition. There were two men whom Doctor Heinrich advised to go into the hospital for hernia operations, a common ailment among the *indigène* men. When the medical work was finished, the air of gaiety returned, voices grew lighter and happier. It was time for the feast the women had prepared.

Mats were laid on the ground and a protection from the sun made with cloths stretched and tied to poles. The people of the village supplied roasted wild river birds, outarde, and duck, succulent and delicious even though served cold. There was mutton cooked with rice and peanut sauce. Fruits and sweets were brought by the townspeople, a real treat for these village folk, for at this time of year they had no fruit. But there were honey and nuts found by the children.

People spoke to Edythe in Malinké, and always there was a Diop child nearby who translated it into French for her. A woman of the village was apologizing to her that there was no fish. A child gravely translated. "She say no fish now, fish later after rains. River fish dirty, fish die." They pressed food upon her, and finally she had to walk away to keep from eating more.

187

She was stuffed, but the rest ate on, the bellies of the children becoming round, the men laughing and licking their fingers, the women moving back and forth with baskets of food. It was truly a happy, uninhibited feast.

The doctor touched Edythe's elbow as she stood by a pole, half leaning.

"Come," he said, taking her arm. "Let's walk off this mountain of food. We can go down to the river."

They walked on a well-worn path. Several children followed, talking softly. The riverbed was nearly dry, a mere trickle flowing through, and here and there, in a deeper depression, stood a stagnant pool.

"In the rainy season this whole area is a lake," Heinrich said, gesturing in a circle. "That's why the village is built on the rise."

The children saw a snake and chased after it, waving sticks. Heinrich and Edythe sat on the riverbank in some shade. They dangled their feet where some day soon the water would be flowing again. They could see on the other side of the riverbed a pool of standing water. Tree branches drooped over it, and a lively population of birds flew in and out of the grove— snipe, water hen, *paauw* and egret—and the ducks splashed and played in the mud.

"How lovely this must be when the river is full," said Edythe, thinking of the village in a new way.

"I've been here once when it was full," Heinrich said. "It's amazing how quickly it fills up during the first rain. You can see it entering the Niger just above Siguirre. It is powerful for a while and an equally powerful force in these people's lives."

"You have a rich life here in Guinea," said Edythe. "One would never imagine it was so without coming here."

"Ah, but I miss a lot, too, Edythe."

"How often do you go out, to Europe?" she asked.

"Never," he replied firmly. "I haven't been back since I came, ten years ago."

"Heavens!" exclaimed Edythe, staring at him. "But

surely you go to Conakry, to Dakar, or Nairobi, someplace like that?"

"Not often," he said, laughing a little. "To Conakry two or three times. They have nothing I need."

"But you said you miss a lot, being here," Edythe countered.

"I meant, there is a lot we don't have, but actually I get along very well without civilization," Heinrich answered.

She was quiet a minute, thinking. "But you do get the papers, books, and magazines from other places, don't you?" she asked, knowing that she had not seen any around the hospital or the doctor's cottage. "So much goes on—so much happens. A lot of it is bad, I know, yet there is good, too—new ideas, new movements, new leaders."

He resisted her enthusiasm. "My time is filled here, my life is filled." He paused suddenly, realizing himself in what isolation he had been living. "I seldom examine my life," he admitted.

"Since I came here I have done nothing else," she said simply. "Before that, of course, I do not know."

They were quiet, swinging their feet gently against the bank. Edythe looked across the river to the south, a great expanse of savanna.

"I seem to know that African countries are in motion, there are new independent nations being born all the time. There is fighting, too, in many parts of the world, new ways of thinking about things."

"Well," said the doctor, "there is always fighting. And I want none of it."

"The refugees from the lands in the south, from the Congo, pour into the cities and live in misery," she said. "Of course, I am sure I have done nothing useful to help. I can tell that I am not used to working. But I am aware that it is going on." Then she turned to him, her eyes bright, "I envy you, Heinrich."

It seemed right to say his name in this place instead of "doctor." "I envy you because you seem so full

189

whereas I—I am such an empty, worthless thing, with nothing, with little inside."

"You feel that way because you can't remember. You are far from worthless or empty. I am amazed at your growing competence, impressed with your willingness. You will begin to feel confidence in *what* you are, no matter *who* you are."

"You are not only kind, but you are wise," she said, looking at him mischievously, "and you're not all that old—not old enough to be a sage."

"Now you're teasing me. But if I have any wisdom, it came from adversity," he replied, "and misery."

They did not speak for a few moments. Edythe wished she dared to question him about his former life. Then she said, "Everything I have is the here and now, and the part of me that you people can know and see. It's a naked feeling. I am not hiding anything; there's nothing to carry around with me except the isolated snatches I have remembered. I feel as though a gust of wind might send me up into the atmosphere." She laughed.

He watched her, trying to understand what she was feeling. It was impossible to imagine himself divorced from his past life. He envied what she had been given. He realized too that when he was with her he didn't feel the weight of his past. That didn't occur when he was with the sisters, or Alfoldi.

Finally he turned to her, "You are doing good things to me, Edythe Clare."

They heard children's voices coming closer and knew they were not alone any longer. Several excited little boys appeared, their eyes shining. The eldest held up a snake they had killed to show them. Edythe screamed, shrinking back against Heinrich, aware of the feel of his solid body. He caught her, laughing, and when they got to their feet, their hands lingered in each others'.

They could now hear the sound of drums from the village.

"Do they dance now?" asked Edythe.

"No, first the *griot*, the storyteller, then the dancing. The musicians warm up the atmosphere a little, gather people around."

"And what shall we do while the *griot* recites?" she asked. "I wouldn't understand a word of it, would you?"

"My Malinké is not too good, either. I catch a few words, but his gestures are enough if one can understand some words here and there. You may be sure there will be a seat for us in a central place of honor."

"Oh, dear, so that means I won't be able to sleep while it goes on."

"Yes, you can, if you wish," Heinrich said. "Put your straw hat over your face, and I shall listen carefully enough for both of us," he added pompously.

"Oh, *Herr Doktor*," teased Edythe, "wear your sun helmet and we shall have another Doctor Schweitzer at Missidougou on the Tinkisso."

"Come, now, don't try to get at me," he said, giving her a push off the path. She gave a scream and reached for him, for she was terrified of what might lay hidden in the tall grasses. His hand pulled her back. The children came racing past them, laughing and shouting, the drums calling them like a command. They followed after the children.

At the village edge, Heinrich said, "Go find Line and ask her what the women do about a restroom. We may be sitting a long time." And he left her to go with the men.

The remains of the feast had been taken away from beneath the cloth sunshade and now the villagers were arranging themselves in a circle on the ground, preparing for the important event of the day. For their special guests there were reed mats. The children jostled around, and Heinrich began to wrestle with Nhoti and his brother, for the storyteller had not put in his appearance yet. Edythe watched as the doctor tumbled in the dust with the two boys. He ended by pinning them both down, holding them with his legs and his

191

arms while they wriggled and squirmed and giggled.

Edythe thought, I am falling in love with him. Have I ever known men before like this man? She had vague thoughts of childhood summer days and men tumbling with children in the summer grass, but no faces would come into focus. Was it at grandmother's house, our house—wherever it was? Was it my father, my grandfather?

And then the *griot* came, creating awe and excitement. He was a small, thin man, gray and ancient, with a tiny gray beard, wearing only the *kenbe,* or full pantaloons. With a sense of ease he sat in the dust at the exact center of the circle and folded his feet underneath him. Small boys tried to fold their legs exactly as he had done. The storyteller looked around solemnly. He put his hands together as if in prayer and lifted them up above his head. Then he let them fall and began to speak. He began slowly in a level tone of voice, but as the story went on his voice rose and fell, his hands gestured, his body moved. The audience, even the smallest of them, sat entranced, their eyes on the teller of stories. The stories were about their own ancestors and their adventures. They chronicled the history of Karamoko Alfa who conquered the Fouta-Djallon many centuries ago.

Edythe felt her eyelids becoming heavy and caught herself swaying in a light doze. The doctor gently took hold of her and pulled her onto his knees.

"Sleep a while," he whispered. "No one will mind."

She closed her eyes. She felt the doctor's firm legs beneath her, his hand lying against her hair. She wanted to turn to him, pull him into her arms. The voice droned on, no one moved except to sometimes brush away the flies. Edythe fell asleep on Heinrich's lap.

When the story was finished the *griot* rose to his feet, and with a dramatic flourish he stamped around the circle, imitating the hero chieftain after the great battle. The crowd then stood and stretched themselves and moved about. Small boys followed the storyteller,

192

stamping their feet, churning their arms. The circle dissolved. Drinks were served. They had been brought from town in the truck that morning, soft drinks for the children, palm wine and beer for the grownups. Edythe awoke and, a little embarrassed, got to her feet.

Line came and teased her for the nap, but not unkindly for she knew Edythe could not understand the story.

"And now we have music and the people dance. You dance, too," she added, a twinkle in her brown eyes.

Edythe took the warm beer and drank it from the bottle. It was late afternoon now and the worst of the heat was over. The musicians were in place—two drums, a small violin-type of instrument with a miniature bow, and the kora, which was made from a gourd and had strings like a mandolin.

The tent apparatus was taken away, for the open skies made a better roof. While the women were busy with the babies and children, the men began to dance. Edythe found a group of children playing a game with small shiny stones which they dropped into rounded recesses dug out of the ground, and they let her play with them, and she became absorbed in the game.

Suddenly they heard someone shouting at the dancers in Malinké and everyone, even the musicians, stopped immediately. They were pointing across the bush, and Edythe saw orange streaks flaring up and rolls of black smoke rising from behind the bush.

A little boy shouted at her in French as he ran, *"Feux à la brousse!"* A bush fire! It was perhaps a kilometer away, but moving rapidly. There were shouts and people ran about looking for stray goats or oxen, to be sure they were in a safe area.

Heinrich appeared at Edythe's side. "Bush fires are all too common this time of year," he said.

"What starts them?" she asked.

"I don't know—a careless herder, or a spark from a hoof against a stone in the wrong place, a stray bolt

193

of freak lightning. But it often comes like ·this and spreads quickly, kilometer after kilometer."

"Will it come this way?"

"We are safe here because there is no grass on these fields. But still, it is a loss to have the countryside seared."

As they stood watching, they saw antelope leaping and running away from the sweeping flames, and the rippling of the tall grasses told them that other smaller animals were fleeing, also.

The men were worried that it might block their drive back to Siguirre. The crowd settled down to watch. Darkness crept around them and clouds obscured the sunset across the Tinkisso, but now the burning of the bush lit the late evening sky. The children were quiet, sitting with their mothers, touching them for comfort.

After some time it was evident that the fire was moving north and not east, and it was decided that it was safe to travel back to town. The children were asleep all around the village. The visiting children were picked up one by one and taken to the vehicles. Most of them slept in the back of the truck, empty now except for the baskets. Nhoti was with his brothers and cousins in the truck, and Edythe and Heinrich had the back of the Land Rover to themselves. It was a long, jolting ride back, but Edythe was stimulated after the events of the day and not sleepy at all.

She and the doctor were left off on the street by her cottage. They walked hand in hand through the dark compound to her door, the dogs sniffing quietly at their heels. They stood by the door, not wanting to part.

"Come inside," Edythe said.

They went into the first room, accustoming their eyes to the dark.

"Emma isn't here. She must be with Fatou," said Edythe. "She doesn't like to be alone at night."

They stood close together in the dark room.

"Two adults," said Heinrich, his arm around Edythe, "and we are awkward and afraid. At least I am."

"No," said Edythe, turning to stand against him, "I'm not afraid, never when I'm with you."

"But I am a lonely, blundering bachelor. I want to make love to you, Edythe. I feel we both need this, yet I'm so conscious of my inadequacies for someone like you."

"What nonsense you talk, Heinrich," Edythe said, rubbing her cheek against his neck. "We are both displaced lovers."

"I cannot even make that claim. You may be my teacher, lovely woman."

"Come," said Edythe. She took his hand and drew him through the curtain of beads into her room. A strip of light from the moon lay across the floor mats and against the beads that still swung gently behind them. Edythe reached her lips to find the doctor's, and she unbuttoned his shirt, caressed his chest, reached her hands around his body, feeling the firm muscles of his back and his thighs, for the first time feeling that she was leading him, not he leading her, yet it seemed right, for he acted as though he were in unfamiliar territory, shy in love, and still when he did not touch her as she wanted to be touched he murmured in her ear, "Edythe, are you sure enough of yourself, sure enough of me?"

"There is no such thing as being sure, Heinrich," she whispered, as if they needed to be quiet. "There is only now, and you and I wanting each other."

"But when you remember, Edythe, remember your other life, perhaps you will regret."

"Never, Heinrich," she answered. "This is our world, here and now."

"Good," he said, and his hand reached to unfasten her dress.

Their coupling was a measured, unhurried pleasure in each other, like youth discovering the body for the first time, except with less fear and with more knowledge of themselves. And in the act of love Edythe thought of the fire on the bush, its flames leaping skyward, and she found herself borne aloft on the points

195

of those flames and she entered a familiar private room and from there fell into an abyss of pure sensation, and when she became aware of Heinrich again she heard him repeating her name over and over and over, "Edythe, Edythe, Edythe."

"I love you, Heinrich," she whispered, her lips against his ear.

"And I you, Edythe. I love you very, very much."

When Heinrich awoke at dawn, he bent over the sleeping form beside him. He watched Edythe's face, relaxed and peaceful in her sleep; he looked down at her breasts, gently moving with her breath, and he leaned down and kissed them, the soft sleep smell of her body drifting up to his nostrils like perfume. He could hardly believe it was he, Heinrich Fink. He thought of yesterday and of their conversation on the banks of the Tinkisso. I must go out for a few months, he told himself—perhaps Paris, or even Berlin—hear good music, go to some university seminars, read, talk to people, visit the theater. How insular I have become. Edythe knows, or feels it, too. He felt a new sense of elation and enthusiasm. He kissed Edythe's forehead, but still she did not awaken. How he longed to make love again. His organ swelled and yearned. Edythe turned in her sleep, smiling faintly. Quietly, Heinrich got up and dressed and went to his own cottage.

An hour later Edythe opened her eyes and found sun patterns lying across the mats where moonlight had been. For a moment she thought she had been dreaming of the doctor, and then she knew that it had not been a dream. She turned quickly, seeing only the place where he had lain, and she flung her arms out to embrace the invisible form. Then she lay back, letting contentment flow over her, and in a few moments she was dressing in her lab coat. As she brushed her hair and observed how her face seemed to glow, she wondered, Will the sisters be able to tell?

33

ON APRIL SECOND it still had not begun to rain, though there was a slight change in the air, a slight lifting of the heaviness and heat that stretched itself across the plateau. It was as if somewhere far over the forests, over the distant purple hills, it was raining, and soon relief would reach Malinké Province, too. But today the plateau people dragged themselves about their tasks or sat with glazed and dull expressions. Their gaunt cattle stood by the useless wells, suffering from hunger, thirst, and festering bites, their tails swinging listlessly. They refused to move, looking upon their masters with great, sorrowful eyes.

Alfoldi Santillana went to Heinrich's cottage in the late afternoon, and finding the door unlocked, entered and sat slumped in his friend's chair without turning on the ceiling fan or removing his shoes. So the doctor found him when he arrived from the hospital. Alfoldi had brought a bottle of whisky, which still sat on the kitchen table wrapped in newspaper.

Paul's pardon had been denied. Alfoldi had gone to the prison to get the news, one of his first excursions away from his hotel since his illness. Now, in Heinrich's presence, he became emotional over his experience. He told his friend that he had been treated badly by Warden Naby, made to stand and wait an unendurably long time, his legs nearly turning to jelly. Naby had been brusque and preoccupied, almost rude. Santillana still smarted from the treatment he had received, but his indignation was over Paul's loss.

"Four more years," he exclaimed. "Can you imagine!

Four years more in that prison! My book will long since have been published, Laura and I will have taken the trip we've been planning to Buenos Aires to visit her sister, I will have been teaching at the university, driving my Fiat back and forth from Colonna into the city, tending our garden weekends, season in and season out, taking summer trips into the Provence, up to the mountains every winter to ski, and, Heinrich, that young man, that boy, in the beautiful years of his young manhood, will still be in that stinking prison, that murderous, infested cell, that strangulating atmosphere of menacing guards—move on there, get going, push, shove, slam down the bars, lock the padlock—and who knows how they're treated when no one's around to see. No, he'll never make it, Heinrich. I give him one more year at the most."

Heinrich had been pouring their drinks in the kitchen and he brought them in and handed his friend the scotch and ice. Alfoldi, exhausted with his tirade, drank most of the whisky and leaned his head against the overstuffed chair. Heinrich sat in his lounge chair and looked at him while he lifted his glass to let the whisky roll into his mouth and find its way slowly down his throat. He was exhausted from his day at the hospital, and now he felt depressed by this news, although he was not surprised, nor was he indignant. His experience had taught him not to expect anything but the worst when it came to the police. He remembered, too, that Alfoldi's departure was imminent and he and Edythe would be the only ones left who cared about Paul, except for the sisters.

The two men spent the evening in desultory conversation and drinking. When the bottle was quite empty, Alfoldi got to his feet unsteadily.

"I must go find a taxi," he said, "before they all go home to bed."

"That is strange," said the doctor. "I always thought they did not sleep."

"Wrong, my friend, they must sleep. They disappear, don't they, just when I want to get home?"

"They don't sleep," persisted Heinrich. "Maybe they roost, like chickens."

Heinrich walked with his friend to the corner of Rue de Jean Jauré and they stood there talking nonsense together until a taxi came limping past. Alfoldi stumbled into the vehicle and it took off with a lurch. Heinrich made his way back to his cottage.

He dropped into his chair and automatically switched on his shortwave radio, but he did not listen. Instead, his tired thoughts drifted to Edythe. All day he had sailed through his work so debonair and buoyant that when he caught Sister Caroline looking at him, he felt that she could see into his mind and know why he was light of heart. Now, after the evening drinking with Alfoldi and commiserating on the bad news, combined with his utter weariness, he felt melancholy. He asked himself if he had gone mad to fall in love, mad to think he could make a woman even reasonably happy—he, Heinrich Lange—and to fall in love with an amnesic patient—he should have his head examined. More than that, he was depressed by the weight of the world's troubles, soured by the pardon denied Paul. The commissioner evidently had given little weight to his and Alfoldi's plea on Paul's behalf. Equilbecq had not lifted a finger to help the young man. Of course, there must be hundreds of Paul Marions suffering in prisons around the world. He had no business feeling involved in this particular case. Damn it, he would not feel involved! He had felt a touch of happiness like forgotten spring. Did everything have to change?

His reverie was interrupted by a knock on his door. His first thought was of Edythe, but he dismissed it, knowing she would be asleep. No, someone needing him at the hospital. He opened his door and found Édouard Diallo standing there.

"*Mon Dieu,* Édouard!" he exclaimed. "You are home! Come in, come in."

"Pardon, *Monsieur le Médecin,*" said Édouard, coming in. "It is a late hour, I know, but I thought perhaps to make my report tonight privately might be better than at the hospital tomorrow."

"Excellent!" said Heinrich. "Come."

He led the way to the sitting room. Now that Édouard was back with his news of Edythe, he dreaded knowing. He was like a patient waiting for a diagnosis when he already suspects the results are bad.

"You got in on the seven o'clock?" he asked Diallo.

"Yes, but I went home first, Doctor."

"Bien sûr, as you should have. Sit, Édouard." The doctor waved him to a chair.

Édouard looked tired and strained. Heinrich wondered if the strong-minded Madame Diallo had given him a bad time for staying so long in the capital. On the other hand, the journey on the train from Conakry was long and exhausting. Édouard did not have his usual meticulous appearance. His white shirt was not fresh, he wore no tie, his black shoes were dusty. Still, he wore the eternal suitcoat.

"How is your family, Édouard, both here and your relatives in Conakry?"

"All well, Doctor," was the reply. "All well, thank you. It is very hot here in Siguirre. Conakry is much cooler."

"We look for the rains every day, Édouard," said the doctor. "Every day the skies torment us with signs of rain, and then the clouds drift away toward the Fouta-Djallon."

"It is on the other side of the mountains they get the rain," said Édouard. "Tonight when I walked here there were a few drops. Enough to tease."

"A drink, Édouard?"

Édouard touched his stomach lightly. "No, Doctor. Too much in Conakry. You know how it is when you go there. Everyone must wine and dine the visitor. It gets to be too much."

Heinrich agreed and waited for the kernel of Édouard's visit.

"Bien, Doctor, I found the information we sought,"

he began. "Concerning the white woman. There *was* a plane crash—that is, there must have been, as two persons and a British twin-engine Dove are missing out of Dakar."

"Out of Dakar!" exclaimed the doctor. *"Mein Gott!* Why didn't the authorities have this information right away? Why has it taken them over a month to realize a plane was missing?"

"Well," said Édouard, uncrossing one leg and crossing the other. "It is not too impossible, Doctor. Your patient is no doubt a woman called Nicole Cordrey—a woman, they say, with a husband she does not live with, a woman who drifts about with various men, with some money, few morals, many friends among the people of the discotheques and the beaches."

Heinrich listened, thinking this was his Edythe that Édouard was talking about. The voice droned on, reciting his catalog of information.

"She was—is—I am not sure which—married to a French businessman, Felix Cordrey, of Dakar, Casablanca, and Marseilles. He travels much of the time. The pilot of the plane was a very young chap, Adnan Bouché-Leclerq—what they call a sportsman, some say a playboy, you know. He has the plane, a boat, and automobiles. He takes out safaris for the boar and duck shooting. He often hops from one city to another in his plane or takes his cruiser up and down the coast wherever they find the gay life of the beaches, so his absence was not unexpected or out of the ordinary. Now, on this occasion they told us that Madame Cordrey left with Bouché-Leclerq to go, they thought, to a boat regatta in Las Palmas in the Canaries. That is how the plane was signed out at the airport in Dakar. When they didn't show up at Las Palmas, the Dakar authorities checked with friends of the pilot and they said they thought he was going to Monrovia. But this wasn't anything so unusual for these people—to take off for one place and end up at another. They live as though they had a hundred lives to fritter away and his friends were more or less just waiting to hear where

201

he had perched or to see him when the whim brought him back to Dakar."

Édouard paused and wiped his face with his handkerchief. He glanced up at the slowly revolving ceiling fan as if to ask why it couldn't produce more cooling breezes.

"And Madame Cordrey, were there no friends, no one who knew where she had gone or when she would be back?" asked Heinrich.

"The consul talked to her friends, yes, Doctor, and they said she had been waterskiing all that morning and she came into the Harbor Bar where these friends were and said, 'I want to go away, I must go away!'— something like that—and they said to her, 'Go find Bouché-Leclerq, get him to take you. He always wants to go someplace.' And she went off to find that person and that was the last they saw of her."

"But the husband," put in Heinrich, "did he never inquire?"

"He has been in France, Doctor, on a business trip, and now he is back in Dakar, but they told us the couple live in separate establishments."

"And Equilbecq's inquiries—I should think that would have indicated to someone that the plane was down."

"Indeed," said Édouard, "but it's taken this long for them to decide that this really was Bouché-Leclerq's plane. I think they really doubted there was a plane up there in the jungle. It's very far off course, you know—destination Las Palmas, plane supposedly down in upper Guinea forest and no wreckage to prove it."

"Yes," breathed Heinrich, as if to himself. "I see. Anything can happen in Africa, and this seems to prove it."

He was thinking that Edythe's husband was alive after all, if, indeed, this man was a husband to her still. No, he must think of her as Nicole, Nicole Cordrey, married to Felix Cordrey, French businessman.

202

"And the pilot's family—was there one in Dakar?"

"No, no family in West Africa, they said. His father is in Paris. A family lawyer, though. I have his name on this paper." Édouard drew out a folded piece of notepaper from his suit pocket. "And Madame Cordrey, she also has a lawyer. See—Monsieur Buffier, SIFA Building, 4-D, Dakar. And Monsieur Verdurin, also SIFA Building, 5-A, for the Frenchman. Oh, Madame Cordrey, they call her Nicki, not Nicole. Even the French consul up there, he knew her. He referred to her as Nicki. He said she was a swinger." Édouard laughed. "I do not know that word, Doctor."

Heinrich said, "To us, Édouard, she is a dependable, generous, wholesome woman who works as hard as the nurses in the wards. We have no cause to question her morals or refer to her in slang terms."

"Yes, Doctor," said Édouard, "I am only reporting to you what I have been told."

"I understand. And you have done your job well, Édouard. No one could have done it better."

"Thank you, Doctor. The French consul in Conakry, he made several calls to Dakar, back and forth, very cooperative. I had to go to his office many trips. It took a long time to do everything. All the things we needed too—I have bought them all."

"Good. But now what are they going to do about Edythe—about Madame Cordrey? She still is amnesic. She still needs help. Is the husband going to take responsibility for her? Is he coming to get her?"

"No, Doctor. The consul in Dakar reported that her lawyer, Monsieur Buffier, would come to meet her in Conakry, if you wish. Whenever you think she is well enough to travel you are to let him know."

"My God!" exclaimed the doctor. "Cordrey is not coming himself?"

Édouard slapped his hands down on the chair arms. "This is what they tell me. I don't know how white folks in Dakar do these things. Perhaps they send lawyers for wives who walk out of a plane crash by

203

some miracle. If it were Madame Diallo, I would go myself, even though she is not beautiful nor young anymore. Still I would go to get her."

"I am sure you would, Édouard," said Heinrich, thinking of Edythe's plight from a new point of view. "As for Madame Cordrey, we shall keep her here awhile. The thing is, Édouard, she has begun to remember. Bits and pieces of her life are coming back, mostly from her childhood days. I'm hoping she will remember everything one of these days. It would be better for her if it happened that way. I think I'd like to wait a few days to see. Could we keep this information private, just between us—and the sisters, of course?"

Édouard agreed readily enough, and left soon after that. The doctor put out his light and sat for a while in the darkness, thinking. He knew he would have to tell the sisters about Edythe, at least something about her, about Nicole. As for his feelings for her, nothing was changed, he knew that.

34

WHEN PAUL WAS GIVEN the news that he had been
denied a pardon, he took it stoically. He had really
not expected any other answer. True, hope had existed in spite of his better judgment, but now that it
was settled he accepted the news in a matter-of-fact
way. Four more years of prison faced him. He knew
his life was degenerating. He knew he had only one
recourse now. Escape. Escape or die in the attempt. It
came to that.

If he was going to escape, he told himself, he must
plan it with more cunning and more daring than he
had ever done anything in his life. He must have help.
He would have to ask Edythe. She had been with
Emma several times now, standing slim and straight
inside his miserable cell as Emma unloaded his basket.
She usually talked in English, telling him little things
about life at the hospital. Sometimes she just chattered
on to take his mind away from his surroundings.

"What do you miss the most from the States?" she
had asked yesterday.

And he had answered as he glanced at the farina
and papaya and goat's milk, "A hamburger and french
fries, a chocolate milkshake, strawberry shortcake,
pecan pie à la mode."

She had laughed. "I'd forgotten such things existed,
but I remember now when you say them. What else
besides food?"

"Oh," he had said, "I miss driving a car, football in
the fall, and Christmastime—you know, the carols at
church and the stores full of Christmas junk and the

Salvation Army Santa Claus going ting-a-ling with the bell and kettle, and everybody in a good mood and the snowflakes settling cold on my face."

Then the homesickness swept over him in such a wave of longing that he turned his head away, and Edythe looked sad as she followed Emma out the gate of his cell.

He must hope that Edythe did not leave Siguirre before he was able to use her help. For he was going to escape; he was going to make it work. He began laying plans. Oh, if only she wouldn't disappoint him! He was planning so much on her willingness.

When Emma brought his supper basket that evening he told her to bring Edythe the next time if she could. He had to seem careless and cheerful as he asked, for the guard was always present, listening and watching. The guard peered into the basket under the napkin. If there was something there that particularly appealed to him he would try to talk Emma into giving it to him. Paul had never seen her give him more than a contemptuous glance. She was allowed to either set the food down in its bowls and plastic containers or to hand it to him.

This evening he could see compassion for him in her large, dark eyes. She must have heard the news. "Madame coming morning," she said, as she followed the guard out the door.

With Edythe he could speak English and the guard would not understand. Paul rehearsed everything he needed to say to her.

She came the next morning with Emma and the breakfast basket. She was wearing native dress—probably, he thought, one of Emma's—and she had a piece of green material tied around her hair, fastened at one side. The guard stared at her, fascinated.

Edythe had heard that Paul's pardon was denied and her own joy was deflated. She stood just inside the iron gate and Paul, standing in the middle of the cell, his bare feet planted firmly, hands in his trouser pockets, spoke to her in English. Although his voice was level and casual, almost languid, his words stunned her.

"Edythe, I have to ask you to help me. I'm going to crash out of here."

She felt her facial muscles tighten, was aware of the guard standing beside her, his hand on the gate.

"He cannot understand and please don't look that way. Pretend I'm talking about a picnic in the park. Relax, smile at me. That's better, Yankee. Okay, I need your help. You are the only one I can ask. This is my plan."

Edythe tried to compose her face, not to look as tense or as vulnerable as she felt. For, after all, she reminded herself, she was only standing there, his words falling upon her like someone tossing pebbles.

"I shall leave the night of the first torrential rain, whenever that is, when everyone is all hyped up on the change in seasons. I'll waltz out dressed as a woman of this country. I need a boat, for I'll travel down the river toward the capital of the next country. I can't say these names aloud even in pig-latin. Do you follow me, Edythe? I need women's clothes—like you have on, only the complete outfit—a good boat with plenty of gasoline, a tool to pick the lock here or a key. Those things. Don't forget the head scarf."

The talk, even though incomprehensible to the guard and even though they usually spoke in English, for some reason made him feel uneasy, and he prodded the visitors to leave.

"Vite, vite!" he said.

At first Edythe, listening to Paul, wondered if he had gone mad, but his face looked normal, serious, intent, intelligent.

"Maybe the Italian will help you, Edythe, I don't know. I know it's a lot to ask. We must move fast so as to be ready. Just get the things to me somehow. I'll take care of them until the right time. Will you do it?"

Edythe had only time to say quickly, "Yes, yes, I'll try, Paul, I'll try."

They had to leave, and she had the picture of him staring after them, doubtful, anxious. Could he be serious, asking all that of her? Yet she knew the answer. He was desperately serious. And he was asking her to do all those impossible things, smuggle in the costume of a woman, a tool for his lock, to get a boat!

She and Emma walked back to the hospital. Emma, in her usual way, was silent, and Edythe's thoughts were buzzing with Paul's plea. She wished she could tell Emma, but she wasn't sure she should. She was the one Paul had appealed to, a fellow American. Yet she was helpless herself, a stranger in Siguirre, and a woman. Someone may as well have asked her for, well, for her memory suddenly delivered on a platter! Could Paul really expect to escape as a woman dressed in a *m'boubou*? If it was night, if it was raining, yes, all that would help, but what would a woman be doing walking out of the prison at night? And the boat! God's heavens, a motorboat!

She seemed to feel a familiarity with boats, as if she had handled them before. Why should she feel that way? Does it mean I've had experience with boating in my life, she wondered. Oh, lost and hidden life, help me now, she prayed. It would take money to help Paul. She had so little. And the tool that would open that padlock on the iron gate which the guard clattered shut behind them! She would have no idea how to find such a tool or key.

Paul must be mad. Paul had fallen into his abyss. Yet the more she thought of it, the more it all began to seem possible. Daring, chancy, but possible—that is, *if* she had someone to help her. He had mentioned Santillana. But Alfoldi was leaving any day to return to Italy. Her inclination was to go to Heinrich. The urgency of her thoughts made her walk fast, and Emma dragged behind. She slowed down and waited for Emma and took her hand.

Edythe was back on day duty now and the workload increased every day. In the hospital the two parted, and Edythe went to work with Sister Hildegaard, making sterile packs for dressings. As she worked, her mind worried over the plea Paul had made to her. To help a prisoner escape was a serious thing. One became guilty of a crime, she knew that. But in Paul's case, the imprisonment was wrong, *it* became the crime. Could she say No to him, turn her back, leave him there, abandon him? He was like herself, a prisoner of circumstance, living a life in limbo, disconnected from his past, and worse off than she for his was a true prison. If he tried to climb a wall and run, he would be shot, and she would never forgive herself then.

Supposing they failed—supposing he did not escape? Supposing she said No right now? Paul was young, maybe four more years of his sentence were not so much when one considered all of a man's life. Most people survived prison sentences. But, in spite of all that, she knew she couldn't turn her back on him. She would talk to the doctor, ask his help. Surely he would join her and want to help Paul, he who had been a prisoner, too. He would feel the same urgency, the same responsibility. She would try to get a word with him and arrange to talk later on.

35

WHEN HEINRICH ARRIVED at the hospital that morning, he decided that he would talk to the sisters about Diallo's trip. It was their right to know and he would ask their opinion about telling Edythe right away. He asked them to meet in his office after lunch.

He had hoped to see Edythe when he went to the dining room, to look at her and adjust himself to thinking of her as Nicki Cordrey. But she had gone to the prison with Emma. He had a full day ahead and after his tea went about his duties.

The sisters were waiting when he came to the office after a hurried lunch. They waited expectantly to hear what news Édouard Diallo had brought back with him. The doctor told them Édouard's story.

"So you see," he concluded, "Edythe does have a husband, another name, a place she belongs, yet it seems to me there is no one there very concerned about her."

He waited for their comments, examining his hands, rubbing his thumb back and forth against a fingernail.

"When will you tell her?" asked Sister Gertrude.

"That is what I wanted to talk to you about," he said. "My feeling is that since no one else is in a hurry to get Edythe—I mean Madame Cordrey—back, then perhaps we should not be in a hurry to send her off. She seems happy here. She has had two recalls of memory. I am hoping that soon she will remember everything. It seems a burden to put on her right now, especially since there is this negative reaction from the husband and, if what Édouard says is true, they are separated."

"Maybe the husband isn't negative," said Sister Gertrude. "Perhaps he really cannot come."

Heinrich looked at her soberly. He could not imagine she could be right. "I am more inclined to think it may have a lot to do with Edythe's amnesic state," he said, "Perhaps she was feeling like a lost person when she left on the plane trip. We cannot tell, of course."

He glanced toward Sister Caroline, whose intent yet sympathetic eyes watched him. She spoke then.

"There is much to what you say, Doctor. I think we should wait—say, until after Easter, anyway. Perhaps another week. I believe her work here is the best treatment. I wish she could stay longer, for it's as if she is taking hold of life in areas quite unrecognized and neglected before."

"I want her to stay, too, of course," put in Sister Hildegaard. "I've grown terribly fond of Edythe. She brightens up our life here. Yet if we know who she is, it doesn't seem right, somehow, that she shouldn't know, too."

"Yes," added Sister Gertrude. "We don't know how these facts would affect her. Perhaps she would remember everything at once."

Heinrich looked doubtful. "No, Sister, I believe the mind remembers when it is ready, when something trips the lock and opens the door. And it isn't necessarily the knowledge of facts that does this, although she would accept, I am sure, what we told her of the facts." He paused, and then added, "From what Édouard said, she sounded so alone in Dakar."

"I wouldn't send her back to that ungrateful man, nor let him come for her," said Sister Hildegaard. "If Edythe left him—that is, if she doesn't live with him —there must be good reason. Let's keep her a few days longer."

After their talk they knew they had not reached a good conclusion, but they knew too that Edythe would stay with them for a while longer. It was as if that too were waiting for the rains. As if no decisions could be made before the rains, no changes.

As they got up to go back to work, Heinrich said, "When it is time for her to leave, one of you must accompany her to Conakry to meet this lawyer."

He went slowly out of the hospital, avoiding the outpatients who were already gathering for the afternoon clinic in the shade of the pepper tree. He was wondering how much his own feelings were interfering with his professional judgment. Perhaps Edythe should be sent immediately to her home in Dakar and be put under the care of a physician there. But he knew he would not decide to do that.

The sisters went away thoughtfully, aware that Edythe really was another person, a Madame Cordrey of Dakar. Edythe was a stranger named Nicki, a sophisticated, hard sort of name.

When Heinrich opened the door of his cottage he found Edythe sitting by his kitchen table.

"Edythe!" He reached out his arms to her and she went into them. For a moment they stood locked together. "It seems a month since the other night," he said against her hair.

Edythe leaned back in his arms, looking at him. "More than that, an eternity," she said. "It's because we keep so busy, so many things happen."

"Come," he said, "this is siesta time. Lie down with me. You will be more than rest to me and I shall fill you with energy for the afternoon." He pulled her toward his room.

But she held back. "Heinrich, I came to talk to you. I must talk first."

"Very well, we will talk."

He took her to the sitting room where they sat opposite each other as they had the first time she came to his cottage, but he did not let go of her hands. Perhaps it has come, he thought; perhaps she remembers all now and has to tell me.

"Now what is it? Have you had another recollection?"

"No, I came about Paul."

"About Paul?"

"Paul did not get his pardon, you know, and he is going to try to escape."

"From that bastion! That is suicide! How do you know this?"

"We spoke in English when I went with Emma with the food this morning. He has a plan—it's very audacious, of course, Heinrich—and he has to have help. He plans to escape dressed as a woman of this country. He says at night, the first night that the rains come. He needs a tool or key to open the lock on his cell, the woman's clothes, and a boat for the river, a motorboat. He will go to Mali, to Bamako. He asked me to get those things for him."

"Crazy, crazy!" Heinrich said. "Have nothing to do with it, Edythe."

She sighed. "I have to, Heinrich. He has to have help. He will die in prison otherwise. Didn't you say so?"

"You cannot be involved. You will be leaving the country soon. You must not get into trouble with the police."

She shook her head. "I can find a way to get things to him, I think. Except for a motorboat—I don't know where to find that. I want you to help, Heinrich." She looked at him, pleading.

Heinrich withdrew his hands and sat back in his chair. "I am a doctor, Edythe, here to cure the sick, not help prisoners escape from their jails. I have the whole hospital to think of, not one person." His own voice speaking to Equilbecq echoed in his ears.

She was silent, twisting her ring around. Then she said, "The tool for the lock, not even that?" The reality of this man was suddenly clear. She should have known he would say exactly what he had said. She had been dreaming to think he would help in such a wild scheme.

213

Heinrich was quiet, staring at her, angry with the whole situation. He loved this woman, he wanted to keep her. And she was forcing him to deny her first request of him.

"Edythe, I love you, but I cannot risk my whole work," he gestured toward the hospital. He had almost said, "my whole world," and then realized that she would think, What a small world you have, Heinrich. "I am aware of Paul's need, believe me," he continued, "but he is one person. He is young."

"But you said he would die there if he had to stay, and I know he will, too. He's not hard enough. And if none of us helps him, he may attempt an escape and get killed in the process."

"Perhaps he will be all right," Heinrich was pleading with her now. "Next year they may give him the pardon."

Edythe did not reply. They were not going to agree on helping Paul. She could see that now. She felt bereft of confidence, of the sense of being loved completely, of the exaltation that had followed her the last two days. She got up. "I must let you get some rest now, Heinrich."

The doctor got up, too. "Edythe, I forbid either you or Emma to get involved in this."

"I won't involve you, Heinrich," she said, "but you can't forbid me, you know." She turned and her green eyes seemed to be reproaching him. He followed her to the door and put his hand on the knob, not letting her leave. They looked at each other in misery. Edythe found her eyes on his mouth, tight and unhappy, and she thought, What has happened between us?

"You must understand," he told her.

"Oh, I do. I think I do. But I have nothing important to lose by helping Paul."

"You have your whole future," he said.

"Ah," she said, thinking, It is only the present that has any meaning, the present I want to keep. "That's a chancy thing, the future," she said aloud, and took

214

his hand from the doorknob, kissed it on the palm, and then went out quickly.

When she had gone, Heinrich threw himself on his bed and tried to rest, although he knew it was useless. Strange, he had never once thought of her as Nicole Cordrey when she was there. She was Edythe, his Edythe. And he had let her down. He had had to. Now she must despise what had happened between them. He thought of Paul and groaned.

36

EDYTHE MET ALFOLDI SANTILLANA the same day completely by chance. Leaving the hospital after work she walked down the long street that led past the prison and joined the quai by the river. She was resolutely trying to put the doctor out of mind. All afternoon she had thought of him, feeling at one moment guilty for having asked him to become involved in such a hare-brained scheme, and the next moment feeling resentful of his quick dismissal of Paul's plan. She had decided to go ahead on her own, to do what she could, and now she was looking for a boat.

When she reached the quai she noticed a dusty road that followed the riverbank away from the town. She followed it, the wide shallow river on her left. A short distance past a copse of oil palms were a couple of rickety wharves where a few boats were docked. Most of them were pirogues, dug-out native canoes. Nearby, spread out on an overturned hulk, fishing nets were drying. A couple of outboards, a slim sailboat, and a runabout rocked gently on the soft river currents. All of them were fastened with chains to the wharf, locked with padlocks. A fisherman was just pulling out toward mid-river in his pirogue, his figure dark against the setting sun.

Hesitantly, Edythe walked out on a pier and looked at the anchored boats. She felt the stirring of memories, a familiarity with her surroundings. She examined the runabout. "It's a Viking," she said to herself, peering at it closely. "Just the size Paul should have."

Nearby was a smaller dock and there was a fine outboard carefully covered with canvas. She could see its name, *The Patience,* printed in wavering, hand-blocked black letters on the side, and on the mooring post the owner's name, Johnny. Patience, that was what Heinrich said to me, she thought. I wonder why I am here. A lot of good it is doing! These boats all have owners, of course, and I can't just steal one for Paul. It is so hopeless!

She was turning to follow the road back to the quai when a familiar figure came trudging toward her, his gaze intent on the road.

"Monsieur Santillana!" Edythe cried out, delighted to see a friend. "What are you doing here?"

The Italian stopped in his tracks amazed. *"Ma chère* Edythe," he said, taking off his straw hat. "I might ask the same of you. I am out for a stroll before taking my dinner at the Lagoon."

"And I have been looking at boats," Edythe confessed, feeling that this chance meeting must surely have significance for Paul's cause.

"Boats!" he exclaimed, looking around at the two docks. "Are you planning an outing or an escape?"

She looked at him, startled. "Ask me to dinner with you and I shall tell you," she said lightly.

"By all means," the scientist said, looking amused. He took her by the arm. "Off we go. It seems to me I asked you once before, didn't I?"

They walked back along the quai. The sun was setting across the river in an unearthly blaze of colors. The Niger was a dark star opal, the fires of the sun shimmering through it. Children played along the shore, their cries carefree in a world without the consuming heat of the day. The tall, thin black women stood in the shallow river, their skirts tucked around their waists, washing clothes. They bent over their scrubbing, like black egrets outlined against the evening sky. Round gourds holding clothes floated around them. Solitary bathers stood here and there, half mesmerized by the interplay of sky and water as they

217

splashed water up on their shining bodies and let it fall again. Near the shore the seared leaves on the ragged palm trees moved gently in the slight air currents.

At the Lagoon, Edythe told about Paul's plan for the second time that day, and Alfoldi put down his fork and stared at her.

"It is insane," he exploded at last.

"Perhaps. It is desperate, but so is Paul."

"Do not get involved in it, my dear Edythe. We will all end up in that bastion."

She sighed, finding her appetite lost for the fresh fish and the spicy sauce swimming around her mound of rice.

"I don't know how the women's clothes would help," she said. "Why would a woman be there— leaving the prison late at night?"

"Oh, that part is believable," Santillana said. "Paul has been observing. Someone in the prison has been having late-night visitors. It could be Dumezil; he used to be second only to the President, but he is now under arrest in Malinké Province Prison. He well may have a mistress in the town."

"I never thought of that," said Edythe. "Well, Emma and I can manage the clothes and perhaps smuggle them in to him, but the tool for the lock and a boat—I feel so helpless."

"You would feel more helpless in jail yourself, my dear," Santillana said earnestly. "And so would I. I've struggled to get Paul out by legal means, but when it comes to an escape, do not count on this old professor. I want to get home to my wife and my garden and my book. I'm sorry. I strongly urge you to stay out of it too."

So Paul had been wrong, thinking Santillana would help. And why do I think of Emma as helping me? She, too, may be afraid.

Alfoldi walked her home through the dusky streets. There was little to talk about on the way. Edythe said goodnight and started in her door when he said,

"There's one thing, Edythe. You might ask Sister Caroline about a boat. That is, if you persist in this folly."

Then he said, *"Ciao,"* and strode away in the dusk.

That was strange advice, Edythe thought, as she went into the cottage. She labored over her journal that night, trying to express her confused feelings.

The night after the trip to Missidougou, Heinrich and I swam toward each other across channels of desire and need. When we met I thought, perhaps this is it. Perhaps the abyss is filled now. Maybe I shall not feel such a need to find the person I was. But I was naive to think the love of even someone like Heinrich could be everything. Here I am, caught up in the urgency of Paul's needs, and I find also I must seek that woman in the forest, that woman "Nicki." Heinrich will not help Paul. He is cautious. For his own reasons he wants to stay in control of things. I am willing to be spun around by fate and take the consequences. But I do love him, nevertheless.

Edythe's sleep was broken by restless turnings and confused dreams. It seemed that she dreamed all night of sailing in a boat, a sailboat with the rudder broken. She kept trying to repair it, hopelessly, and she bobbed about on a sea overhung with plants and foliage. They hung down over her floundering boat—blooming plants, tropical plants, flowers and vines, feathery ferns. In the morning she lay awake, thinking of the dream and listening to the sounds from the compound—the hens clucking and scratching in their contented way, the squeaking and twittering of the weaverbirds—and she remembered suddenly as if the memory had always been there, walking into the familiar red-carpeted lounge of the Harbor Club (in what city was it—where?) and her friends were sitting around in comfortable chairs with drinks in their hands. They had been sailing and waterskiing. She recognized faces, but no names came to her except one, that of a brunette in a long, flowered chiffon thing worn over her bikini, Giselle Lelong. Why, they were hardly friends. Why should she remember Giselle's name and not the others? Everyone was looking toward her and saying, "Nicki, Nicki, where have you been? All these days and nights! You rogue, you!"

She heard her own voice answering, "Oh, we just cruised up to Tangiers to the casino. And Alain won a packet! I lost, of course."

Behind her, Alain himself appeared amidst shouts and greetings, and he was certainly not the one in the other memory—he was fair and slight. Well, her own name was Nicki. But Nicki who? And what a scatty life she must have led! Oh, dear, she thought, everything is so awful. I must have been some dreadful person named Nicki. I remember Alain. I didn't really like him much. Why did I go away with him? None of those people would fit into my life here. No one I have remembered except grandmother, and I suppose she is gone now. I am Edythe, not Nicki. Was that really I walking into the Harbor Club? I can't see myself, I can only remember moving across the red carpet, hearing those voices, seeing those faces!

Depressed, she got up and prepared herself to go to the hospital. She glimpsed Emma stirring in the other room. Later, she thought, she must talk to Emma. She must get that settled. So, letting the memory sink at last into its place along with the *Motores Cap d'Antibes* and the lover whose face she could not see, she let the day ahead unfold its routine. Sister Caroline. Yes, she must talk to Sister Caroline.

37

SISTER WAS TOO BUSY during the morning. Edythe met her in the hospital chapel during her siesta hour where Sister Caroline listened as Edythe told her of Paul's plan. When she had finished the nun sat without speaking. Her first impulse was to say, "No, Edythe, No! No, Nicole Cordrey, have nothing to do with this." But she didn't. However, she did say, "You know, Edythe, if Paul Marion carries out this plan, if it is discovered or even suspected that you were involved, they could make things very difficult for you."

"I have thought of that, Sister," Edythe replied. "But I decided to go ahead."

Sister Caroline sighed. "Well, Edythe, I will think about this thing. I cannot give you an answer in a hurry. It can wait until morning, can't it—this business of the boat?"

"Yes, Sister. Of course. I shall wait."

"About the rest, I would advise you to take Emma into your confidence. She's the only way to get the necessary articles to him. She will figure out how to outwit the guard."

"Yes, Sister."

"Very well, and let us meet here again after breakfast tomorrow. I will give you my decision then."

And Sister Caroline rose and hurried away. Edythe wondered what she had meant. How could the sister help? Yet she had not been indignant nor upset nor fearful as Heinrich and Alfoldi had been. Edythe was learning so much about the people she lived and worked with. And it seemed as though all of them knew so much about each other that she was not yet aware of. There were catalogs of knowledge, layers of perception around each person, and she was only an initiate into this society. For some reason the Italian had known Sister Caroline might help them, a thing Edythe in her conception of the nun would not have suspected. And Sister Caroline suggested that she take Emma into the plot.

The sick people continued to pour into the hospital. Sister Hildegaard had extra beds in the halls now, but no more cholera cases were brought. For that they were thankful. Edythe was working regularly in the women's ward. When she and the doctor passed, their glances caught, held, and then let go. He looked sad, she thought, but her own spirits were far from light.

That afternoon, as usual, the doctor and Sister Gertrude worked in the outpatient clinic. The line of sick and hurt seemed endless. Heinrich knew his mind was only half on his work, for the sister had to remind him of things several times, things he usually noticed or remembered himself. When the last *indigène* was treated and sent on his way, Heinrich suddenly slapped his hand on his desk and said, "It's got to be!"

Sister Gertrude, putting cards away in the file, said, "What, Doctor? What has to be?"

And he laughed a little, and said, "Never mind, Sister. But please find me the card of that man they call Baba, who comes sometimes with malaria."

"Oh, yes," said Sister Gertrude, "I remember that one, I think. Yes, Baba, the lock artisan."

"I believe that is the one," Heinrich said carelessly, and he took the card she handed him and read it carefully. "All right, put it away again."

He took off his white coat and hung it up and went to his supper.

38

IT WAS THE NEXT DAY that Heinrich found an hour to
spare from the hospital. He went to the Rue des Ar-
tisans, in the old part of the city. The street, closed to
vehicular traffic, swarmed with pedestrians. Both sides
were solidly lined with tiny shops, or rather enclosed
spaces, where skilled workers toiled and their prod-
ucts or services could be purchased. There were cob-
blers, and others who worked great iron sewing
machines doing intricate embroidery; others made
arms and agricultural implements; there were masters
of keys and locks, carvers of great oxen yokes from
mahogany, and many other tradesmen.

Heinrich had been there before and he easily found
where the locksmiths worked, and the shop of the
man, Baba, who, from time to time, came to the hospital trembling and burning with malarial fever. Customers were thick about the man's stall, and after
giving a nod of greeting to Baba, Heinrich strolled
away. In another place he found some small bronze
figures—acrobats, wrestlers, kings sitting on thrones
—all made with great imagination and skill, and
which, in ancient times, were used as weights in the
measuring of gold. Heinrich turned them in his
hands, thinking how much Edythe would appreciate
such artful work, and he bought several. At another
place he found plaited leather. He had passed the
stall a hundred times before without noticing it, but
this time he stopped to admire and then buy some for
Edythe. He could not remember when he had bought
pretty things for a woman before.

When he returned to the locksmith's booth the man
was alone and he motioned the doctor inside, holding

up the counter so he could come through and drawing aside the cotton curtain at the back. Inside was a small room where two boys sat on low stools filing on metal. A low forge held glowing charcoal. The walls of the room were hung with locks and keys.

"Tell me, *Monsieur le Médecin*," the man said, "what can I do for you? You need something."

"Yes, Baba," Heinrich said, looking around the walls of the shop. "I have a friend who has a storage room, and the huge lock on this door was accidentally closed, and he cannot find the key."

"I see," said the man, and he went to the wall and picked up a large lock. "Is your friend's lock anything like this?"

Heinrich recognized its similarity to the prison locks. "Yes," he said, "I think it may resemble that."

"Sit, Doctor, and I shall make a tool for you that will work on such a lock."

The locksmith rummaged about on a workbench and brought out a tool, which he inserted into the lock. Then he withdrew the tool and held it on the forge and one of the boys took up the bellows and pumped so the fire glowed red-hot. The steel lying on the coals gradually grew cherry-red. Then, taking it out with tongs, the locksmith hammered and pounded, turning it quickly and deftly as he worked. Again the fire, again the hammer, then he thrust it sizzling into a can of water. Then, taking the lock, he inserted the piece of steel from a different angle than a key would enter and turned it this way and that, and the lock snapped open.

"Is this what you seek?"

"That should serve my friend well," said Heinrich. The tool was wrapped in sheets of an old Arabic newspaper and handed to him, and he said, "How much, Baba?"

The locksmith hesitated, and then he said, "If I do not give a price there has been no transaction. Only a gift passing between friends."

"You are a good man, Baba," Heinrich said.

"Come to me when you have need." They shook hands and he went back to the hospital.

Later in the day, when the afternoon patients were gone, Heinrich took the parcel and went to Edythe's cottage. He intended to place it inside for her to find, but Emma was there. She opened the door.

"Come in, Doctor," she said in her soft voice. "Edythe not here now."

He went into the room. The package felt like a burning weight and he laid it down on the table. The paper fell open. Emma picked up the tool.

"For Paul?" she asked.

Heinrich glanced at her sharply. "Has Edythe talked to you?" he asked.

"Not yet," she said, "but I know."

"Yes," said Heinrich. He was aware that Emma understood many things without their being put into words. She was turning the tool in her hands, her fingers examining its strength. Then she reached to the cupboard behind her and brought out a banana and, working skillfully, she soon had the tool inserted in the depths of the banana. An ordinary glance could not perceive its entrance. The fruit looked perfect. Heinrich breathed deeply.

"*Parfait,* Emma!"

She smiled at his praise, pleased, knowing her own skill. "I put it in basket tonight," she said quietly.

"Tell Edythe I brought it, Emma, and that if she has other needs still, to come to me. And give her these."

Heinrich took the gifts which he had bought from his pocket and laid them on the table. Then he touched Emma's cheek with his hand, and went out. As he walked home he was both worried and exhilarated by what he had done. At any rate, he told himself, the risk had to be taken. The thought of losing Edythe could not be borne.

39

EDYTHE WAS THE FIRST of the staff in the dining room. She sat toying with the food Seitou had placed in front of her, her thoughts elsewhere. The evening heat was so enervating she was without appetite, and she was also disturbed. She had been upset since her meeting with Heinrich and had kept her feelings hidden. She had to be cheerful and efficient in the wards, but now that she was alone and tired, she let her misery engulf her. In addition, she felt burdened and apprehensive over the whole business of Paul's request. It was too much to do alone; each thing he needed was too difficult to get. This evening she would talk to Emma, to see if she would help her. Strange, how one moment her life seemed filled with joy and purpose and the next there was nothing but despair.

One by one the sisters came in and sat at the supper table. If Edythe had been less engrossed, she might have noticed a different atmosphere, a shade of deference in the way they spoke to her. They did not intend this to happen, yet they thought of her as another person now. She was not the woman they had nursed, the woman they had named, not the former patient now working with them. They knew now she belonged to a different world, a sophisticated world of pleasure, money, and leisure. And soon she would return to it.

Edythe lingered at the table with the sisters, watching the door from time to time. When the doctor came in, he sat down next to Sister Gertrude, and he looked at her in a calm and loving way, and Edythe won-

dered how he could look so content when they had
disagreed over something that seemed to her to be
fundamental, and had parted in disagreement. She
forced herself to eat the fruit placed before her, but it
would hardly pass the tightness in her throat. The
sisters watched Edythe and Heinrich, trying to inter-
pret what was between them.

And Heinrich, as he ate, thought of Edythe as
Nicole Cordrey and tried to link that hard-working,
determined person with the playgirl in Dakar who had
been described to him. She had a husband who was
alive, yet it was questionable whether or not he wel-
comed his wife's return from her miraculous brush
with death and her amnesic state. And Edythe's feelings, when she remembered, what would they be?
Would she want to be with the man? Yet she had left
him, left his house, gone with other men. She must
have been unhappy in spite of the gay life she led;
somehow he was convinced of that, nearly convinced
it had had something to do with her amnesia. He
thought of her returning to her cottage and Emma
telling her what he had brought. Would her face light
up, look radiant again as she had looked after *le jour
à la brousse?*

The desultory conversation at the table touched
upon the events of the day, the chores to be done in
the evening. Edythe stayed long enough in the hospital to help Sister Caroline do nighttime medications.
As they were putting away the pill glasses, syringes,
and trays, working in silent harmony, Sister Caroline
said as if to herself, "Another strange Good Friday."

Edythe glanced at her. *"Mon Dieu,* Sister. This is
Good Friday?"

"It is hard to remember here, isn't it?" Sister
Caroline replied evenly.

Edythe said goodnight and went to her cottage,
thinking how the sisters must miss having their Church
and the activities of the Easter season. She found herself remembering Good Friday parades someplace in

227

Europe, with long, colorful processions, singing, and the holy statues carried aloft by the people.

She found Emma sitting in the near dark on her mat.

"Emma," Edythe said, coming in softly. "Are you all right? Is anything the matter?"

Emma's luminous eyes looked up at her and she smiled. "I just rest, Madame," she said.

She got up and lit two candles. Then she put some water on the small kerosene stove to make tea. Edythe took off her lab coat and put on a cotton wrap-around garment. She and Emma sat on the floor in the second room with the clay mugs of tea in their hands. The candlelight made shadows on their faces. There was silence around the cottage. Even the dogs did not bark. The night air was heavy and warm.

Emma wiped at the side of her face and said, "Too hot for tea."

"I know, and for the candles, too, but I need both," said Edythe.

"Doctor come, bring things for madame," Emma said, and got up and lifted down from a shelf the gifts Heinrich had brought.

Edythe looked with pleasure at the small brass figures. She turned the plaited leather over and over in her hands. Heinrich had brought gifts. Somehow, although touched by them, they did not seem to heal the hurt, the disappointment of their disagreement. Then she heard Emma telling her about a tool, a tool to open the lock, and she grasped Emma's words; she was telling how the doctor had brought it and she had hidden it in a banana and had taken it to Paul in the supper basket.

"The doctor did that!" she said, "and you . . ."

Emma then knew about Paul's plan! Emma had already smuggled the tool for the lock to him, and Heinrich had brought it. Oh, my dear one, she thought to herself, I do love you, and now the gifts he had given seemed like jewels, and she thought he had opened to her a new dimension of his love.

"Emma," she exclaimed, reaching over to catch the girl's hand, "I was going to talk to you about Paul tonight. You are far ahead of me. How did you know what Paul is planning? You didn't understand his English, did you?"

Emma gave a little shrug, and Edythe wondered, Why do I even need to ask? She intuits things, she has special senses that I don't have. Then Edythe talked about the other things that Paul wanted—the boat and the *m'boubou*.

"We'll hide the *m'boubou* in the food basket somehow. Perhaps if we do it two different times it will not be so bulky, but will only seem like the towel that is there around the food. I will send him the *m'boubou* you loaned me, if you don't mind."

"That not good one," Emma said scornfully. "I have better *m'boubou* for this thing, dark." She went to the box that held her things and rummaged. She came back with a navy-blue, thin material with dark red figures. "At night this very dark," she said.

"It's perfect, Emma. If we can use this for Paul, I shall buy you a new one."

"*De rien,*" Emma said, sitting down again. "Now I show you how to hide *m'boubou.*"

Skillfully, she laid it out and very carefully she rolled it up, pressing down hard all the time with her strong hands until when it was finished the entire four-piece outfit was folded into two thin rolls of material. Then Emma took a bowl such as food might be served in and she wrapped one roll around the base of the bowl. It would not be noticed.

"Guard never see," said Emma confidently. "*Jamais.*"

"Emma, you are wonderful," said Edythe. "Now if anyone ever asks you anything about it, you know nothing, nothing; everything was done by me without your knowledge."

Emma did not understand this at all. "No, madame, I do. I know better how to do."

Edythe sighed. "Yes, truly you do. But only if anyone asks, if they should find out—the guards, the police—tell them you know nothing. Tell them it's the white woman's doing."

Then Emma understood, and she looked disgusted and dropped the subject. It was decided that the first part of the *m'boubou* would be taken in the morning in the breakfast basket.

When they stood up and took their teacups to the other room, their arms went around each other and Edythe tried to remember a fragment of poetry she had known once about how brotherhood is not by the blood but by the life lived and the danger. And sisterhood, too.

40

IN THE MORNING, Emma smuggled the first part of the *m'boubou* to Paul. It was not difficult because Édouard Diallo had sent with her a book for Paul, bought at the doctor's request, in Conakry. It was a collection of poetry in English and had just come to the surface among other new hospital supplies. Emma handed the book to the guard to inspect as she laid out the breakfast for Paul. The guard passed the book to Paul and ushered Emma out of the cell.

After breakfast, Edythe went into the chapel to wait for Sister Caroline. She sat with her hands in her lap, her eyes fixed on the altar where the candles burned. The chapel did not have the scent of incense and melting wax, the stale scent of arid space, of other churches she had visited. Actually, there lingered in the air the strong odor of pharmaceuticals, as if to remind one that this was a hospital where patients had priority over worship.

Through the open door came the soft swish of garments as Sister Caroline came in. She went directly to the altar, where she knelt. Watching her, feeling removed from the nun's piety, Edythe thought, it must be that I do not believe anymore. It seems like something I have lost long ago. If I could believe, she thought, I would pray that Paul escape the prison, that Heinrich and I can be together, that there is no one between us. Yet isn't it possible that someone else prays that prison bars remain strong, and someone prays that I return to another life? That is why I look for faith outside the church, even though Sister Caroline's faith gives her that strength and calm I admire in her. Then Edythe thought of her grandmother's face, a strong, yet gentle face, looking down through the years at her, an anchor, a center. Perhaps faith is a kind of family or racial feeling of belonging, she thought, remembering the quiet centeredness about Emma as though she, too, were anchored securely to some place or some people. Heinrich seemed centered in his work, as did Alfoldi. Paul seemed to float in a sea of uprootedness. As I did, she thought. But I am finding myself slowly.

It seemed a long time before Sister Caroline rose to her feet, genuflected, and came to the bench where Edythe waited. The two women faced each other. Edythe smiled at the sister's stern face, but after murmuring, "Sister," she waited. Something momentous hung on what Sister Caroline might say.

"Edythe," the nun spoke at last. "Most of the night I have thought about this request of a boat for Paul. You see, we have a boat."

Edythe gave a gasp of surprise. "Who do you mean, Sister? Who has a boat?"

"It belongs to the Mission. It is only an outboard motorboat; most of the time it is just moored, almost never used. It was purchased for Father Donnegan to go down the river and minister to the *indigènes* who live far from town and can best be reached by water. But Father Donnegan has not been well. He has not been here in many months, and I don't know if he will come again. I decided that if a boat is needed so badly to save a life, and I have heard the doctor talk as though Paul cannot survive his imprisonment, that I would take this responsibility. I am the one with the key. It is I who lets you take it."

She was breathless after the long speech. Mutely, she opened her hands to show the key.

"Sister," began Edythe, but she was interrupted.

"I have not told the other sisters nor asked their advice," Sister Caroline continued. "If there is trouble, if the police should trace the boat, then it will only be I who have to take the blame." Her clear gray eyes that looked at Edythe were calm.

"The boat is docked beyond the private marinas on the river road. It has a small broken-down dock of its own, but the motor itself is on the veranda of the cottage where we sisters live. It is very heavy and I don't know how you can manage it."

"Emma," breathed Edythe. "She and I can do it."

"So," said the sister, "and does the doctor know, Edythe?"

"Yes," Edythe said reluctantly, "but he does not approve. He is worried over it."

"Ah," Sister Caroline sighed.

"I am sorry, Sister," Edythe said, "but I could not leave Paul with no help. He appealed to me. I had to try. He doesn't belong in that prison. Doctor Heinrich knows that, too."

"The doctor is thinking about the hospital," said Sister Caroline, and then she added, "and about you, of course."

"Do you know what horsepower the motor is, Sister, and how big the boat is?"

"I seem to remember that the motor is ten horsepower; it is a good one. I went with Father Donnegan one time. The boat is, oh, about four meters long, I would say. It is called the *Father George* after the priest who was here before, but the name is hardly legible."

She smiled, remembering past times. She handed the key to Edythe then.

"This key unlocks the padlock chaining the boat to the wharf. I would rather you come and get the motor before lunch. The sisters will be busy in the hospital. I could arrange to be there when you come."

Edythe considered the physical job of getting the motor to the boat. "It will have to be by taxi," she said. "I shall try to find Emma and a taxi and be back here around ten o'clock."

"Very well, then. I shall expect you. And, Edythe, I suggest you let Emma hire the taxi for this adventure. Run along now."

Edythe went out quickly to do her errands, leaving the nun in the chapel.

41

THE DEED was almost miraculously accomplished. The outboard motor, heavily oiled for protection, was wrapped in a greasy, tattered canvas in a corner of the cottage porch. Edythe and Emma transported it to the waiting taxi and thus to the river road. There they let the taxi go, and staggering with the burden together, they transported it until they found the wharf where the *Father George* sat in its solitary mooring. They took off the canvas top and lifted the motor into the hull of the boat, and Edythe tightened the bolts, fastening it securely. It was not much of a craft, in need of paint and poorly outfitted for anything beyond basic transportation. But it seemed water-tight, which was the important thing, and there was a floating cushion, an empty gas can, and a pair of oars. Edythe felt a familiarity with what she was doing, and as she worked checking everything, she kept trying to will the memories that tugged at her to tell her where she had been in motorboats before and who had taught her to handle them.

There was some gas in the tank. Edythe put the engine into neutral and pulled the recoil starter. The motor sputtered and after a few attempts it finally took hold. She revved it up, tried the shift lever and the throttle control. She checked the exhaust port to see if water was spitting out properly. Everything seemed to be in order. There was not too much vibration; the motor had a good roll to it.

Emma stood on the dock watching Edythe admiringly.

"It doesn't sound too bad," Edythe called up to her. She sat in the boat for a few minutes thinking of Paul and his desperate journey—if he ever reached as far as this wharf. He must have this tank full and an extra can of gas, she thought.

"We are going to try boat on river, madame?" Emma was leaning down from the wharf, her eyes shining.

"I'd like to, Emma. I wish we could," she said. "But I must get back to the hospital. They need me in the sterilizing room this morning."

She got out of the boat and they covered it again with the canvas. Carrying the empty can, they walked off the dock and up toward the quai.

"Could you buy gas, Emma?" Edythe asked, bringing out money from her lab-coat pocket. "You would need to bring one can and put it in the tank and return to buy another full can." Emma's buying fuel would cause no speculation, for it was often purchased in cans for taxis, cars, and such uses. "You remember the place in the boat where I said the gas belongs?"

"Yes, madame, I remember," Emma replied.

The two parted, Emma heading toward the shops on the quai and Edythe to the hospital. She planned to go with Emma in the evening when it was time to take Paul's supper. The key and the directions for finding the boat must be hidden in the food, the rest of the *m'boubou* under the dishes. That would be the end of their contribution. She had never believed it could be accomplished. Now when would Paul make a break? It was noon and the skies were cloudless. It was unbearable to look toward the sun, yet the atmosphere had a tautness that foreboded change.

When Edythe went to the staff dining room for her lunch, hungering not for food but for a glimpse of the doctor, only Fatou and Sy Kanadu were there. They seemed very friendly these days, laughing and talking secretively as if they shared a private world, drifting together whenever there was a chance. Fatou was changing from a giddy girl to a blossoming woman.

236

They moved over to make room for Edythe when she brought her tray to the table.

"Do you know if Doctor Heinrich has eaten?" Edythe asked Fatou.

"Yes, he finished and went out," replied Fatou, "and he asked me if I knew if Edythe had eaten." She laughed, looking at Sy, sharing thoughts.

Edythe sighed. She had wanted to thank him for the gifts, and more than that, for coming in with her to help Paul. She could not begin to analyze his change of heart—whether it was for her or for Paul, or for something in his own past—but he had done it, probably against his good judgment. As she left the hospital to go to her cottage for a siesta, she met Alfoldi Santillana coming up the steps. He turned around and walked with her.

"We are still friends, my dear Edythe?" he asked, his brown eyes twinkling a little.

"Monsieur Santillana," she exclaimed, "of course. It was really presumptuous of me to ask what I did."

"Not in the least. And let me tell you, you have my deepest admiration, young woman, as well as my real concern. Does Heinrich know of this escapade?"

Edythe nodded. "I think he felt the same as you, Professor." She let it go at that. There was no need to tell that Heinrich had changed his mind.

"Yes, age and experience tend to harden the arteries of impetuosity and risk," he said. "But I have found a way I could help Paul more anonymously. I have some leftover West African francs. Is there any way they could be smuggled to him or left for him outside? They could be very useful if he should actually manage to get out of that bastion."

Edythe was overwhelmed. "Indeed, monsieur, they would be invaluable. Emma and I will manage to get them to him, somehow."

Santillana stuffed a handful of bills into Edythe's pocket and then, bidding her goodbye with a cheerful handshake, he turned around and left her, saying he was off to his prescribed siesta and that she should do the same.

In her cottage Edythe threw herself down on her bed and pulled her journal toward her.

I go deeper and deeper into Paul's escape plans, drawing more people into it, feeling quite frightened; at the same time I am exhilarated by the generosity of others. I am amazed at myself, and I feel other people's amazement at me. It is as if I am compelled to do this whole thing as well as I can. Am I trying to prove something? Am I trying to prove that I am not such a worthless person as I suspect I am—or was before?

After writing and re-reading, she slowly tore the page out of her notebook, and the entry from the day before, and shredded them. It is unwise to put these things about Paul on paper, she thought. I must wait.

42

THE AFTERNOON FOLLOWED its usual routine of work. The chores of a crowded hospital kept them busy. Edythe carried glasses of juice to each patient, often holding the glass, encouraging a child or an ill woman to drink. She assisted Sister Caroline by holding the tray of bandages, scissors, and medications as the nun administered to the patients, and sometimes she was called upon to help unbandage a sore or wound. I am an apprentice to Sister Caroline, she thought, as she worked, realizing she was learning a profession. She made countless trips to the storerooms, kitchens, and laboratory for supplies. She assisted weak patients to the toilets, and helped those recuperating to walk about again. The aide who usually worked with them had succumbed to a fever, and the two women worked alone.

Edythe paused finally to wash her hot face at the sink and noticed for the first time how dark the hospital ward had become. Suddenly a great peal of thunder rolled through the skies in the distance. Everyone who was on his feet went to the windows to look. Sure enough—heavy, dark clouds were moving overhead. The air was fresh. The smell of moist earth drifted over the town, coming from across the savannas. Excited chattering broke out from everyone.

"Is it really going to rain at last?" Edythe asked Sister Caroline as they stood side by side at the window.

"It looks like it, this time," said the sister. "When the rains start, Edythe, many of our patients get miraculously well, and they just leave the hospital and disappear."

"They do! But why, Sister?"

"I don't know, really. It's as if something very primitive and strong calls them back to their homes and villages when the rains begin. That is where they feel they must be. And those who are able to walk, go. Perhaps it is part of what the black poets call *'negritude'*—a sensitivity to all things and their rightful place, an intense emotion."

Awed and thoughtful, Edythe turned back to her duties. As she worked she thought of Paul, wondering if this night would be his night. Once she and Emma delivered this basket of food to him, he would have all the things he had asked for. She suspected he would act as soon as he could after that. A tremor of fear for herself and what might happen when Paul escaped went through her thoughts.

When she had a moment to spare, she wrote Paul a note in English saying that *Father George* was fueled and waiting, and describing in as brief a way as she could the boat's location. She mentioned the francs, saying to use the money where necessary, hoping that in a tight spot, Paul could bribe his way out. She felt like a conspirator and marveled at how quickly one learned the ways of intrigue and deceit. Perhaps, it occurred to her, we know all the time and practice deceit more often than we realize, in ways that are part of our normal behavior.

Before the afternoon was over, rain began to fall. It came suddenly, as if the heavens had opened the gates at last. The clouds were really rain clouds, with no signs of passing away. It was settling into a steady downfall. Everyone in the hospital was excited. The atmosphere was electric. To her amazement, Edythe saw patients get up off their mats quietly, gather together their few belongings, wrap their *m'boubous* around them and, without a word to anyone, walk out of the hospital. No one made any move to stop them.

Sister Caroline looked at Edythe and smiled, almost

240

laughed a little, making a funny "I-told-you-so" expression which made her face look very youthful.

The doctor stood in the hospital foyer, the office help, orderlies, and some patients clustered about him. They were all exhilarated by the breaking of the dry spell. They talked in voices half an octave higher than usual, their hands moved, their bodies moved, jokes were passed around, good wishes and blessing were offered for the season. Heinrich's eyes watched for Edythe to come from the women's ward. He was feeling refreshed. He wanted to share the moment with her. When he saw her, he broke away from the group and called to her. She reached out a hand to him.

"How can I thank you?" she said to him in a low voice.

"We do not need to speak of thanking each other," he answered. "Are you finished in the ward? Can you come home with me? This is a good time."

Disappointed, she had to say, "Heinrich, I have to go with Emma to the prison. This is the last, you see."

He understood, and questions rose to his lips, but he said only, "In this rain, Edythe? Must you go?"

"I have to," she said. "It may be tonight, you know." She backed away from him as if he might keep her from going.

"Come to me later," he said, "as soon as you get back."

"Yes," she said, and left him to go to the hospital kitchen.

43

IN THEIR COTTAGE, Edythe and Emma studied the food basket to decide on a plan. They pocketed the note and the key deep inside the hard roll. Santillana's money was more difficult. They worried over it for some time, and finally decided to take the corn pudding out of its bowl entirely. Then they placed the money in the bottom of the bowl and carefully put the pudding back over the money.

"Paul can wash the francs in the river," Edythe said.

"Guard never see," said Emma, satisfied.

Now they had the second half of the *m'boubou* to conceal. Emma worried over this. The roll of material was essential to Paul, yet most easily could trip up the whole escape.

"Tonight I play coquette," she said finally, placing the material around the bottom of the bowl as before.

"To distract the guard," said Edythe, understanding. She felt it was the first thing they had done or planned that would go against Emma's principles.

"Yes," said Emma. "It can be done tonight."

"I think we should take a taxi, Emma," Edythe said firmly. It was an extravagance that would come from her own pocket.

"Tonight we never find taxi," corrected Emma. She went to her box and brought out an old umbrella.

It was dark when they arrived at the prison. They stood at the heavy gate, waiting for the guard to come and let them in. Contrary to the exuberant mood at the hospital, the guard was in a surly mood. Perhaps because he had to be on duty instead of celebrating at home with his family and friends. He refused to let Edythe enter, after allowing Emma to come in with the basket. Abruptly, he closed the heavy gate in her face, saying that she could wait outside. Disappointed at not getting to see Paul, Edythe turned and found a place to wait under the slight protection of the arched entrance. At least Emma alone would have a better opportunity to distract the guard's attention. It would take some doing to flirt with that guard.

She stood leaning against the wall, with her arms locked around her damp lab coat. She was full of worries—worry for Emma, worry for Paul trying to break out of this impregnable place, worry that he might not ever find the *Father George* in the dark and the rain, afraid, in fact, he would be detected before he ever got that far. She stood looking at a streetlamp in front of the prison that cut a circle of light silver-shafted with the rain. From the guard tower a bright stream of light swept mechanically around and around the prison area.

Suddenly lightning cracked sharply, throwing a white canyon across the rooftops of the town, followed by a great rolling crash of thunder. In that instant, Edythe was back in an airplane feeling a shock of terror as the plane brushed the tops of trees, and an agony in her rigid limbs realizing the plane was going to crash, and then the tearing and the splintering and the impact with earth that tore her consciousness into shattered splinters, blocking out shock and pain and thought and memory.

"Oh, Ohhhhh," she moaned, shaking her head back and forth. Yet here she was, whole and strong, standing in a strange town, a town called Siguirre, against the dark wall of a prison, watching a tropical rainstorm and feeling the length and breadth of her own life. Feeling a newborn, a reborn, person. It was a bitter-tasting remembering, remembering herself— Nicole Armitage Cordrey of Dakar, Senegal, formerly, well, of a number of places—Rabat, Lyon, Washing-

243

ton, Des Moines, Mason City. She thought of her pink villa on the Corniche in Dakar, which she had rented when she left Felix; remembered telling her maid to watch the house and water the plants as she left that day—that last day in Dakar. She had felt so desperate to get away from there, from her friends and from the life she was living. How long ago was that? It must be about six weeks! Was that all? It seemed years ago in time. Now she knew Heinrich, there was the hospital and her job where she had learned to do useful new things, and the sisters, and her little cottage hidden in the Kouakous' back compound, and Emma—and Paul! Paul! That was why she was here, she and Emma were helping him to escape this prison—to "crash out," as he put it. Good Heavens! She, Nicole Cordrey, doing this!

Why, her name was different now. It was Edythe Clare Monsarrat, a name made up by Sister Caroline, that devout, unpredictable, intelligent, old-young nun beside whom she had been working all afternoon. She must tell Heinrich who she really was—tell him that now she knew that she did have a husband, Felix, and about their ill-matched, unhappy marriage—explain to him how she had tried to work things out, but the fact was she didn't love Felix, and couldn't tolerate the abrasions of their loveless marriage. It had been a year ago last Christmas that she had moved out. Luckily, her father had left her a modest income—she didn't have to be dependent upon Felix. She must tell Heinrich how she had applied for a divorce but a technicality about her citizenship had ham-strung the proceedings, so the papers were stalled in the local court and her lawyer awaited a brief from Lyon. She had not pushed the matter; it hadn't seemed important then.

She remembered now that day of her ill-fated journey, and remembered how she had walked across the strip of concrete at the airport toward Ad's plane, carrying her bag, feeling as if she were walking on some other planet, unrelated to everything, everywhere. It was not boredom so much as not knowing how to deal with the pain, with the lost feeling of having missed some road originally there and originally unique and important. She had been concealing it too long from herself, using pleasure as a drug, and now the drug didn't work any longer.

The amnesia—Heinrich called it retrograde amnesia, induced by trauma—had finally blocked everything neatly. Would the amnesia come back again, now that she didn't feel the pain anymore, now that she was happy, even here in the rain, against this prison waiting for Emma? Because, in spite of worries, it was happiness. She was alive and in love with living. Poor Ad Bouché-Leclerq, he must lie in the forest where they crashed. She remembered finding him that day in Dakar and persuading him to take her away. He had been planning a fishing trip, but she had stood there beside his cruiser where he sat lounging against the leather cushions, and she had said, "Come on, Ad, there's a regatta in Las Palmas. Let's go. I want to go. Please take me."

She saw the young face, tanned and healthy, looking up at her, the long brown hair, "hippy" style, they called it, the tawny lazy eyes. And he had come, under her persuasion, or perhaps through not caring whether he fished or flew, but he had come, and now he was dead in the jungle. Was it her fault? The crash wasn't. That was partly because of the radio equipment's breaking down. Did she need to feel the weight of his death as her responsibility—as she felt Paul's prison escape? Paul—Ad. Both youngsters, really. Different, of course, yet something about them was so alike, and now she could see the link she had felt to Paul may have come from Ad, whom she had left in the jungle.

She remembered the flight again. The radio equipment malfunctioned soon after they were airborne, but Ad had laughed as he gave up fiddling with it, saying they could do without it on such a clear day. But then he had wanted to change course and go to

Monrovia instead of Las Palmas, insisting that they could have more fun there, and someone would be there who owed him money. She had kept insisting on Las Palmas, and when she finally wavered, he changed course and they flew south again. Clouds had gathered and obscured the coastline, but still they hadn't realized they were in danger until the gauge on the fuel tanks forced Ad to face hard facts. The storm had engulfed them suddenly. Would she ever forget that one look Ad had sent toward her—a look of open fear, begging her to do something to save them, perform some miracle, say some word!

She heard footsteps, the gate grating on its lock, the opening and the clang of the gate, and then Emma's voice saying, "Madame?"

"Emma!" Edythe clutched Emma's arm in relief. They ran down the steps and into the rain. They ran until the prison was behind them, and then they paused under the protection of a shop's portico to catch their breath.

"Emma, tell me, how did it go? Did you manage all right?"

Emma made an unpleasant face. *"Oui, madame, très bien.* Paul has everything now. Guard not see."

"Bless you, Emma."

"I think tonight Paul go, madame."

Then Edythe said, "Emma, go on home. I'm going down where the boats are to wait for Paul. I'm afraid he will never find that third dock in the darkness and rain, and every moment will count. I'll crawl under the canvas of one of the big boats and wait for him."

"No, madame, I come too. We both go."

They retraced their steps and turned off from the quai to the dirt road, now wet and slippery, its dust turned to mud. Sliding and slipping, they made their way to the first wharf and crawled under the tarpaulin of the runabout anchored there, and curled up together to wait. They were both trembling with the wet and the excitement, but gradually their trembling stopped with the warmth from each other's bodies.

They tried to relax and endure the long wait ahead.

Edythe whispered to Emma, although no one was within a half kilometer of where they lay. "What if we never hear Paul—the rain makes so much noise, and the river?"

And Emma replied, "I will hear." And Edythe believed her.

Edythe put her head down on her arms and thought of Heinrich. Heinrich, her thoughts whispered, I am Nicki Cordrey. I know now, I know.

He would be waiting for her to come. At what hour would it ever be?

44

WHEN THE RAINS BEGAN, Paul felt his tension mount-
ing. This was the night he should make his escape. Yet
there were too many loose ends. He paced his floor,
waiting for Emma to come with his supper, his thoughts
disjointed and pessimistic. What if for some reason to
do with the storm she doesn't come? They had not
found a boat. It had been too much to hope for. He
should never have planned on such a thing. Yet now
he could open the lock, and he had part of the
m'boubou. Would they bring the rest of it? With the
rains maybe the woman would not come to the prison.

Since Paul's cell was directly at the end of the corridor, he often stood at his gate watching who passed
in the hall at the far end, and he had many times
seen a woman enter late at night and leave an hour
or so later. His plan, when she came, was to wait as
long as he dared, thirty minutes or forty, and then
leave shrouded in the *m'boubou,* hoping the guard
would not peer too closely. He had heard some words
spoken to her as she entered, and her muffled reply.
He hoped in the rain any conventional phrase flung
up from a muffled face would suffice as he walked
out. He knew it was risky, but his whole plan was that.

Paul picked up the book of poetry the doctor
had sent him. It was really too dark to read, for
only a dim bulb burned in the corridor. He could
say one or two of the poems by heart now. He threw
the book down again. Would he ever see the doctor
again? He felt that an end stood before him—an end

to this awful episode. When would Emma come? Would Edythe be with her? She was something, Edythe! No memory, maybe, but she knew how to manage the present.

He heard the guard coming, joking with someone, and he stepped back into his cell, waiting. Footsteps came down the corridor and they were at the gate, the lock clanged, the bar was drawn, and Emma stood in his cell lifting out the food, paying no attention to him, joking with the guard in a way unusual for her. She set down bread, corn pudding, goat's milk, and fruit. A healthy, balanced diet for a desperate journey. Then Emma's eyes met his in a mute message and he telegraphed back to her, I read you, Emma, bless you, Emma girl, may your tribe increase. She was gone and the gate was locked, and he heard the guard talking in the corridor, giving Emma some kind of wisecracks, and she very flirtatious and gay with him.

Paul waited until the corridor was quiet and he was alone. The guard would not come back for the dishes for half an hour. He unwrapped the garment from the pudding dish. In the hard roll he found the key. My passport to Mali, to Bamako, to the world beyond, he thought. There are Peace Corps kids in Bamako; they'll hide me, help me. I'll make out if I ever get that far. He held the key tightly in his hand. His mind raced as he found Edythe's note, and he praised her silently for the boat *Father George*. With difficulty, he read her neat script, and he memorized the words and then chewed up the note. Would he ever be able to follow those directions? To wash away the sour taste of the paper, he drank his milk. Don't think I can possibly eat that corn pudding tonight, he thought. My stomach is seasick already. But then, it might be a long time before I eat another meal. Paul ate the food, and Santillana's money lay there, messy with clabbered milk and corn.

My God, all these bills! I'll make it now, I will, oh, Christ, which one of them sent the money? It has to be the Italian! He cleaned it as well as he could, folded it, and then tore a piece of his old T-shirt off and folded it around the money and used the rest of the shirt to make a belt around his waist to hold the packet next to his skin.

He finished the scraps of his supper and set the dishes neatly on the bench and lay down, pretending sleep. He listened, every sense alert. With the rains it was harder to hear ordinary things. Down the hall he heard the guards' voices loud and boisterous. The prisoners, talking among themselves, sounded different tonight as the line marched back from the chow room. There was an excited pitch to their voices. Gradually, the evening quieted down. The guard took away his dishes. Then Paul went to work on the lock. He had practiced the night before, spending what seemed like hours figuring out how to undo the strong, old lock, and he had finally succeeded. It had opened in his hand like a toy. Now, tonight, would it work again?

Try it now, he told himself. Then close it again so as not to take any chances. The more times I try, the safer it is. He stood by the cell door and felt for the lock, which he could not see but only feel by reaching. Working with his hard, sharp tool he explored the vulva and then the vagina of the lock until suddenly, in one random thrust, a magic touch of steel on iron, it opened again in his hands.

Good! He locked it again. The *m'boubou* he practiced in the dark. No problem with that, and with the rain no one would question wearing the turban draped over the face and neck to protect them from the elements. Now, he thought, I must watch and wait and hope that woman comes to whomever it is can afford to have a lay in prison.

The night dragged on. The rain increased the tempo of its beat against the prison walls. Paul thought of the river out beyond the prison, of the rain falling into it, adding to it, mixing with it, joining in its long trek to the sea. Would it be hard going out there in a boat? Was the motor of the *Father George* up to it? Did they fill the tank and put in extra gasoline? How much did the tank hold? Could he find the boat? He repeated Edythe's directions to himself. Sounded easy, yet there was the dark and the rain and unfamiliar surroundings. What if they challenged him as he left the prison? Would he run? Of course, they would shoot. Yes, but it wouldn't matter. It would be all up anyhow. Pray that they shot to kill. He was sure if he got outside unchallenged he had it made. They wouldn't discover the mistake until the woman came out. So he figured he had a possible half-hour advantage if he found the boat promptly, and if he could start the motor. A search might not get organized for ten to fifteen minutes. They had to find who was missing. They would search on the river, not easy this night. Figuring his odds, he reasoned he would have a good head start, but then he told himself he was a fool to be so optimistic.

Every muscle, every nerve in his body was alive and quivering. He stood by his gate watching the hall, his eyes accustomed now to the dim light. A flash of lightning sent a momentary clarity across his cell and the corridor, and a clap of thunder shook the skies, and the bulb in the hall went out. Looking down the corridor he could no longer see any light at all. A power failure, what luck! It happened often in Guinea, especially during the rains. Tonight must be his night! He watched and listened. He heard the guards shouting back and forth, verifying the reason for the lights' going off. He saw a torch and the wavering light it threw in the far end of the corridor.

Then he heard the clang of a gate, and he saw, in the flickering light of the torch, the dark figure of a woman passing through the hall. She disappeared in the other direction. Paul immediately dressed himself in the *m'boubou*. His hands trembled. Blouse, skirt, wrap, and tie. Now the outer garment over the head and shoulders, and then the turban. He wrapped it about his head and neck, covered his face to the eyes. There. He was dressed. Now the lock. His fingers trembled so he could not get the lock. It wouldn't work like it had before. He stopped. He took a few deep breaths, lectured himself. It's not been five minutes, you fool. You can't go yet, anyhow. Take your time. He wiped the sweat from his palms. He tried again. Another bolt of lightning—like the light of day, that one. He had jumped quickly back from his gate, hoping he had not been seen in that brilliance. Oh, God, if it does that when I leave through the gate I haven't got a chance, he thought. He worked, sweating, his tool searching the spot. Gentle it, he told himself. Make love to it. Sing to it. The spot was touched. The lock fell open. He stood motionless a few seconds, breathing hard. Then carefully he removed the lock, using two hands so he wouldn't drop it. He slipped back the bar inch by inch until the gate swung free. Okay. Get ready. He kept the tool, sticking it in the top of his trousers. It could prove useful, and he couldn't leave it behind to incriminate anyone. He considered that he had used twenty minutes' time. Another ten before he dared leave, the hardest time of all to wait. He counted the seconds, one thousand, two thousand . . .

Paul left the cell, moved silently up the corridor, hoping no other prisoners were listening as keenly as he had been. Now he was in the great hall. To his left a torch was stuck in a holder on the wall, its wavering thrust of flame cutting a circle of light at the gate. The guard sat on his stool, a shapeless bundle, drowsing, leaning with his head against the wall. Now Paul changed the angle of his approach and began to walk as much as he could like a local woman, erect, one hand under the cloth drawing the material up over his face to the eyes. He had to make enough noise so he didn't need to speak to ask for the gate to be opened. His sandals flapped solidly against the stone floor.

The guard jerked up and looked toward him. Paul stared back. The guard got up and started to unlock the gate. Paul murmured indistinctly the Malinké word of thanks. He wondered suddenly if the woman handed the guard money when she left. He walked through the gate. To his horror the guard spoke some words he didn't understand, and reached behind a pillar and handed out an umbrella. The woman must have left it with him as she entered. Watch it, Paul warned himself, don't show your white hand! He reached his hand from under the voile of the *m'bou-bou,* grasped the handle and, with his back turned to the guard, he put up the umbrella and stepped out into the rain and down the steps of the prison. The gate clanged shut behind him.

Christ, he was out! He walked quickly through the rain and crossed under the darkened streetlamp, turning toward the quai. How dark the streets were. He glanced back. No one was in pursuit. He folded the umbrella, tossed it as far as he could and, running, tore off the garments as he ran. At the quai he turned right as he had been told, the soft, slippery road under his feet now. All the garments were off; he wore only his trousers. He rolled the *m'boubou* into a wet ball and thrust it under his arm. He felt and heard the river but could not see it yet. He came to where the boats should be. Still no siren. He stood trying to get his bearings, trying to see a dock. Maybe it was ahead farther. Calm down. Don't panic, he told himself. He walked slowly ahead. He could make out a dock and boats bobbing violently up and down on the water and another smaller dock beside it. He was supposed to find a third dock for the *Father George,* a small, rickety one. Oh, God, where was it, where was it?

Two dark forms moved toward him, silhouetted against the river. Paul jumped back, but he heard his name spoken.

"Paul?"

"Emma, Edythe! Christ, you scared me! What are you doing here?"

Grabbing his hand, Edythe said, "Paul, come quick. We were afraid you'd never find it by yourself, not in time."

He held to her hand and followed the two of them another fifteen meters along the river. There was the small dock, one boat, nearly hidden by the undulation of the bank. The motorboat! They pulled off the canvas and Paul threw it on the bottom of the boat along with the *m'boubou* and the tool he pulled from his trousers. Edythe and Emma stood on the wharf. The river swirled around it. The river was flowing with power now and a sense of urgency, of mission, already changed from what they had known. Paul, standing in the boat, fumbled with the motor, tried to find the ignition, the starter cord. He knew he was nervous, and he tried to calm himself. The truth was, he had not been in any motorboat for many years, not since a fishing trip with some other kids, and even then another fellow had managed the boat.

"Edythe, show me, how do I get it going?" His voice shook.

She stepped into the boat, horrified to find him so helpless. "Watch," she said, and she showed him what to do. Soon the motor sputtered and took hold. She adjusted the gas, feeding it gently, talking to Paul, explaining.

"Paul, you've handled one of these things, haven't you?"

"Not by myself, actually. But there's nothing to it. I'll manage fine. Once I've started."

Edythe looked out at the river. "It's rough out there. You have to know how to ride the waves."

He took hold of the tiller. "I'll manage fine, Edythe."

But she couldn't leave him. She felt if she did he would never make it. She looked up at Emma, who stared back at her mutely, the water running off her sober face.

"Emma," she said, "I've got to go a ways with Paul. He doesn't have any experience with boats, and in this storm . . ."

Emma bent down close to them. "Madame, you must not!"

"Just to the other side of the city, Emma, out of reach of the searchlight, in case it comes on soon. He must get a good start on them. I can come to shore on the other side of the city."

"Madame," Emma said, "when you see a tall dead tree reaching out over the river, go in there. Sometimes boats go in there."

"Good, Emma. Now run home before you're seen. We'll be all right."

Paul was unlocking the padlock holding the boat to the wharf. He pulled the chain loose from the post and threw both it and the lock into the boat. There was the extra can of gasoline, the oars, and the air cushion. He reached a hand to Emma.

"Run, Emma. I love you, Emma. *Fi'a'manillah!*"

As he pushed the boat from the wharf, Edythe opened the throttle. She headed for the middle of the river. Emma melted back into the darkness. There was still no siren, and the tower light was still off. The city remained in darkness. Edythe turned the boat east. Paul crouched beside her and watched as she turned the stick so that they entered a rough wave on the diagonal, letting up on the gas as they met the crest, turning it on again as they fell into the water's trough. Lightning flashed across the water, followed by thunder. They felt as though they must have been seen by a thousand eyes in the brilliant light. Again darkness covered the river. The range of the inactive tower light must be behind them now. The water was swift. It would be fast running with the river, Edythe told Paul, if he could withstand the drive of the rain from the south and the waves. He must try to stay in deep water, but it would take effort to stay on course in places where the current ran strong.

The pitch of the waves grew more erratic and the small craft swerved dangerously. Edythe steadied the tiller, watching each wave. Paul was exultant with the excitement of being out of prison, on the river. All the worry, tension, and fear were falling away from him. I shall ride into the maw of Africa on *Father George*, he exulted. Mali, I come. Bamako, I come.

He looked back. The outlines of the city gradually folded into the darkness. No lights showed. No sound of a siren, no police boat searching the river.

"I'm in the clear, don't you think?" he shouted to Edythe above the sounds of the storm and the motor.

She looked at him and shook her head. His face was so alive. Yes, he was happy. She had never seen him looking that way before. Free. Alive. Vibrant. She was satisfied that she had come. It had been the right thing to do. And now it was time to let Paul take over. They exchanged places and she watched as he handled the tiller and the feeding of the gas as she had shown him. The river was getting narrower, and there was a stronger current that made the journey more hazardous. Edythe could feel it, and she showed Paul how to stay with it, to let it take the boat. He smiled at her.

"It's a clean fight out here. It's beautiful!" The water was running off his face.

Edythe pointed toward the shore. The dark outlines of palm trees were bending toward the east, lashed by the rain. The tall form of a naked tree stood silhouetted by the river's edge, one long branch extended outward.

"There it is, Paul. That's where Emma said we should come in."

The lightning flashed and they saw it clearly. There was no doubt about the landmark. Paul turned the tiller and at that moment a dark form came floating past them on the shoreside, probably a log or an overturned boat. Paul swerved the boat to avoid hitting it, swerved too sharply, and in a split second, as a wave lashed against them, the boat capsized. They were both in the water.

Edythe surfaced, looking wildly around for the boat, but it was nowhere to be seen. She saw Paul just a couple meters ahead of her. He seemed to be flailing around in a desperate motion. She struck out in a familiar stroke to reach him. She saw the air cushion bob past her. She grabbed for it, but did not reach it. It swept on down the river. Paul had disappeared. She swam toward where she had seen him, looking help-lessly around, calling, "Paul, Paul!" But the waves took away her voice, choking her.

His head emerged again very close to her, and she lunged for him and grabbed his arm, expecting the desperate embrace of a drowning man, but the arm was pulled out of her grasp. Whether the current pulled him or what, she did not know, but it was as if a force pulled him away, swept him down the river.

Oh, Paul, her thoughts cried, Paul, come back. She tried to swim ahead, but a wave washed over her and when she shook the water from her eyes again there was no one. Only the water as far ahead as she could see. She was alone on the river. Turning her face to-ward the shore and the old tree, she struck out to try to reach it. She could feel the current here pushing against her, pushing her on down, but she swam against it, using all her strength to get beyond its pull. A ter-rible weakness seemed to flow through her whole body and she longed to let go and let the river take her, too, as it took Paul, and then she thought of Heinrich sleeping in his cottage. She thought, I could not do this to him. He has suffered enough in his life. He will feel badly enough about Paul. I cannot let him mourn for me, too. She found some reserves of strength in the depths of her body and she pulled against the river, and soon she was out of the current and the water was calmer. She found that her toes were hitting sand and she pushed herself up on her feet and saw the great dead tree a little way up the riverbank. Dragging herself through the shallow water and staggering through the brush and high river weeds, she clasped her arms around the tree and fell weeping against its cool, wet trunk.

At the moment the boat capsized, Paul Marion knew that he was finished. That happiness in the boat, he told himself, was like the moments of peace and lucidity that people have just before death, for death was beside him now. He felt its presence. He knew he had not the strength to swim any distance at all. He only hoped Edythe could take care of herself. When he emerged the first time he tried to swim, but the current had been too strong and wave after wave had washed over him. He, also, had seen the air cushion bob past and tried helplessly to reach it. As he went under the next time in his mind's eye he saw his home again, a calm picture of flowerpots on the wooden porch, the Tennessee hills and the valley deep in rural peace, the wonderful red soil of his native land, and he thought, I wanted, oh I wanted to do so much yet, I wanted . . . Again the river threw him up and he felt the pressure of something against him, pulling on his arm, and his first panicky thought had been Crocodiles! and he had fought to pull away from it, and the current had pulled downward on him and the next time the river rolled over him, he thought, as his bursting lungs let the water come rushing in, Mali, here I come. Bamako, I'll float by on my way on my way.

The dark river churned and thrashed and fought with the storm at the spot where he last went under. There was no sign of the *Father George*.

45

HEINRICH HEARD SOMEONE REPEATING, "Doctor, Doctor!" He forced himself awake and sat up in bed, making an effort to be alert, to hear.

"What, what?" he gasped.

He saw Emma standing beside his bed. She was dripping wet. His ears registered the fact that it was still raining on his tin roof, and his eyes could see water running off the tall, familiar figure.

"Emma, what is it?"

"Doctor, Edythe went with Paul in boat."

Heinrich shook his head. "What are you saying, Emma?" Her words made no sense to him.

"Paul escape from jail, Doctor. We gave him boat. Paul not know well to drive boat so Edythe go with him."

Heinrich was on his feet. "Went with him? Where? Where?"

He looked so upset that Emma nearly lost her voice. She backed away from him.

"Madame go to other side of city, Doctor. I told her come in where big tree is. That's good place to come in."

Heinrich by now had caught the sense of what Emma was telling him, although he could still scarcely believe he was not dreaming. He had gone to sleep with the worry of Edythe and Emma and Paul.

"Emma." He was up now and pulling his clothes together. He had fallen asleep half dressed while waiting for Edythe.

"Emma, do you mean those two are out on the river

259

in this storm with Naby's men hunting them down with the police cruiser?" His hands were shaking as he fumbled with his belt.

"Siren not blow yet, Doctor."

But just as Emma spoke they heard above the sound of the storm the rising whine and scream of the prison siren. Higher, higher it rose and held its sustained note. Down, down it dropped, and then climbed again, demanding that the world know that wrong had been done the body politic, that all men must sit up and take notice, that justice must be done. The sounds cascaded again to repeat the accusation.

"Mein Gott, mein Gott!" Heinrich was saying, rubbing his head and staring at Emma. "What shall I do, Emma?"

"Madame need way to come home," Emma said. "After she come to land. Paul go on to Mali, to Bamako."

"How can I get there? I must go and find her before the police find her. But how?"

Emma said, "Sy Kanadu has brother who has taxi. Maybe I find him."

"Bien, Emma. We must take the chance on him."

"Bien sûr, Doctor."

"Do you know where they live, Emma?"

"Not far, Doctor."

"Then we'll go."

They went out into the rain, Emma leading the way, until after five minutes' walk they came to a small cottage in a back street near Avenue de Sékou Touré, and Emma pounded on the shutters and called until a sleepy voice answered.

People in Siguirre are at their best in responding to real need, and especially to the need of one as popular as the doctor. Soon a man stumbled out of the cottage. Emma spoke to him in Malinké, and then he gestured to the doctor and wordlessly they followed him a few buildings away to where his taxi was parked under the overhang of a shop. Emma explained to him where they must go. Heinrich told her to tell him also that it would be risky, for the police cars would be out and the man would be taking a chance, but he heard only grunts of assent from the driver who by now was starting up his motor. Heinrich got in front with him. The taxi was put into reverse and soon was backed slowly out of the alley, and when Heinrich looked for Emma she was gone.

They drove without lights to the east end of the quai by a circuitous route Heinrich did not recognize. They did not see any police cars. Heinrich knew he could not plan on much time. If only he could find Edythe at once. As they approached the end of the quai the streetlights suddenly came on again, and the light from the prison tower again perused its territory.

They took the dirt road going east, the one Heinrich and Alfoldi had often walked in the evenings. Here the driver from time to time flashed on his lights momentarily to be sure he was still on the road. When the road ended, he pulled off and parked between two huts. The siren was still wailing. Now it seemed like an agonized, soul-tearing cry for help. The blanket of its sound was some insulation against Heinrich's own fears, but the driver was nervous. He told the doctor to hurry, that they could not stay.

Heinrich walked toward the river, not knowing what he would do. He could see the tall silhouette of the dead tree and hoped that miraculously he would find Edythe there. But no one moved in the darkness and rain. He put his hands to his mouth and called, "Edythe, Edythe!" His cries were lashed back on his face by the rain.

"Edythe!" he called, knowing it was futile.

He could see, looking up the river, the slow circling of a light on the water. He was not sure if it was from the guard tower or a boat on the river itself. Turning his back and facing the east again, he cupped his hands to try to project the weak sounds he made against the storm. He walked through the shallow water at the edge of the river, feeling of the trunk of the big tree. Had Edythe been here? Had there been tragedy here? Would he ever see Edythe—or Paul—again?

He went back and found the path which the local people used to go farther down the river shore, and followed it, calling as he went. Ahead, he thought he saw a movement. He stood still, straining to see. Yes, something white was running, coming closer. God, was Edythe wearing her lab coat still? He called, and then he heard his name, "Heinrich, Heinrich." She came running out of the darkness, gasping and sobbing.

"Heinrich, I think Paul has drowned."

He held her close. "The boat, Edythe, where is it?"

"It capsized in the river. I tried to help Paul, but I couldn't. He pulled away from me. I swam to shore. There was no sign of him at all on the river when I started in. I thought maybe he was carried downstream. I've been looking." She was babbling, almost incoherent.

"Edythe, you've heard the sirens. We must go. There is a man waiting with a car."

"But Paul, Heinrich?"

"You've done your best. Come, it is vital for both of us."

She went compliantly. The sirens had ceased. The driver was impatiently waiting with the motor running and the taxi turned. Again in the same manner, driving through unfamiliar back streets and alleys they returned. The driver let them out some ways from where they lived and, hurrying through the dark streets, they made their way, hand in hand, to Heinrich's cottage.

"Now," said the doctor when they had closed the door behind them. "The police will be coming to search. Off with the wet clothes. I shall say we got wet coming from the hospital."

But Edythe only stood, the water running off her in a quickly spreading puddle, and Heinrich saw that she was crying, her face contorted, her mouth open as one in pain. He stripped off her clothes and put all their sodden garments in the shower. Then he rubbed her with a towel. She tried to talk, but her words were so mixed with her crying that he could hardly understand. She was telling about being in the boat and letting Paul take over, and the capsizing, and trying to get to him, and something about now she knew, she knew, and the words "Nicki Cordrey" caught in his mind and he understood that she must remember now. She had her memory back.

He put one of his shirts on her and they lay in the bed, and he tried to warm her by rubbing her with his hands, but she continued to cry. He wondered if he should get up and get a tranquilizer for her, but he wasn't sure he had any in the cottage.

"Edythe," he said, "don't think about it now. Think of me, Edythe."

She cried out, "But I'm not Edythe. I'm Nicki Cordrey. I remember, Heinrich. Everything is back now, and I don't want to be Nicki Cordrey. I want to be Edythe."

Both relief and anxiety flashed across his thoughts. "Do you remember everything, Edythe?"

She sat up and so did he. Looking toward him in the darkness she said, "I was on the plane with a friend, a young man, Ad Bouché-Leclerq. There were just the two of us. We were going to a regatta. We bickered about where we were going, though, and we got lost, the instruments didn't work, or at least the radio, and we got into a storm. Oh, now both of them are gone. Paul and Ad."

Again she burst out crying, and he tried to comfort her with his arms.

"Did you care for him?" he asked.

"Paul?" she said. "Of course, didn't you?"

"No, I mean the other. Ad."

"Oh, Heinrich, no, no, he was only a kid, like Paul, someone I knew. But I did persuade him to go, to take me. I was responsible."

"Dearest, no. It was an accident."

"I know that, Heinrich, and I know it was partly

263

Ad's own carelessness, but if I hadn't persuaded him to go, then he'd still be alive."

"He didn't have to go, Edythe. He had the choice, didn't he?"

"Yes, I know, but he did come, and I was the one who survived." She covered her face with her hands for a moment, and then looked up again and continued.

"I live in Dakar, Heinrich." Edythe put her hand over the doctor's hand lying in her lap, and held it firmly. "I know everything about myself now. But I almost wish I didn't remember. I was living such a useless, trivial life. I have a husband, Felix, but we haven't been living together. I don't know why we're still married except I've legal problems in Senegal, some technicality with my French citizenship. Maybe it's straightened out now. I don't love him, Heinrich, not the least, except maybe in a haunting, sad way when I remember him when he was younger."

"It's all right, Edythe. It will all straighten out."

"I love you, Heinrich."

"And I you, Edythe. Very much."

"Will I always be Edythe to you?" For the first time her voice sounded calm and normal.

He laughed a little, rubbing her back gently. "I guess so. At least, I'm not used to Nicole yet."

"Why hasn't anyone missed me back there? I'd never stay at a regatta all this time."

"There was a mix-up about the plane, Edythe, where it was going. But now they know about you."

"How do you know?"

"Édouard brought back news. We know who you are, where you live, your husband's name."

"What! You knew! Since when? Why didn't you tell me?"

"It's only been two or three days. I wanted to wait a little to see if you would remember by yourself. And see, you did."

She lay back again, thinking of all the implications of her life in Dakar and her relationships where she was.

"Is anyone coming to get me?" she asked, apprehensive at the thought. "I don't want to go back," she added, knowing as she spoke that she had to, that it was something still unfinished.

"I think they are sending your lawyer," Heinrich said, hating to bring out such a cold fact. "That is, when I tell them you are ready to go."

"That's like Felix," Edythe said. "Send the lawyer. But, of course, I'm not morally his responsibility anymore, since I left his house."

Heinrich spoke into the darkness. "Are you bound to him still, Edythe, in your own mind?"

"No, absolutely not." Her voice was firm. "We should have been divorced years ago. We haven't lived together for over a year; even before then we were strangers." She curled against him, seeking his warmth.

He caressed her face with his lips, his hand warming her body. "I almost lost you tonight, Edythe. I don't ever want to lose you again."

She replied, "We are bound together, Heinrich. By Paul, by all that has happened, by that river out there."

"My worry now," he said, finally, "is what the commissioner is going to do about you and Emma. He may consider you both highly suspect. I would send you out of Siguirre immediately if only there were a way."

"Where is Emma?" Edythe asked.

"She was here, of course, and told me where to look for you."

"Bless her," murmured Edythe. "Perhaps she is in our cottage."

She fell asleep then in exhaustion, but Heinrich lay awake. He felt certain the police would come to question and to search.

46

IN THE EARLY MORNING, when night was beginning to
lift itself from the upper Niger plateau, the storm began to lose its fury. The rain, however, continued to
fall, but dwindling hour by hour, preparing to drift
away for a few hours' respite. At this time the police
came to the hospital. They searched it room by room,
bed by bed, shining their flashlights into every closet,
corner, and basket from the storerooms and phar-
macy to the laundry and the kitchens.

They had come to the doctor's cottage after he had
fallen asleep watching for them. They had seen Edythe
asleep in his bed, and only asked who she was, and he
had replied, "It is the woman who walked out of the
forest at M'Boura."

They had looked at him strangely and said nothing
more than, "She will have to be questioned, too."

Herinrich had said, "It can wait until the daytime."

They did not insist and, finding no one hidden in his
cottage, they demanded to know where Emma was,
and he had truthfully answered that he did not know.

The police had attempted to search the cottage of
the nuns. Sister Hildegaard stood on the threshold sputtering resentment, forbidding them to enter. But Sister
Caroline said, "Yes, Sister, let them see for themselves.
Only they should not enter our chapel."

Since all this excitement and upheaval, the sisters
had had a difficult time settling down to a morning
routine. Sister Gertrude and Sister Hildegaard discussed the events back and forth, and back and forth.
They felt a justice in the escape of young Paul Marion,

and they didn't know who, if anyone, was involved, but because of the police search they were uneasy and worried. The police wanted to question Emma, but she could not be found. The sisters sent Fatou to look in Edythe's cottage, and the police followed, but they found no one. Fatou reported that neither Emma nor Edythe had slept there as far as she could tell. Emma did not show up at breakfast time. The sisters talked about this, and about Edythe's whereabouts, but the doctor came in and said that she was safe but still asleep, and did not comment further.

Sister Caroline said little. She took time for the chapel and sat for over an hour with her beads in her hands. The hospital work was light now that so many patients were gone.

Soon, however, there was a rush of new mothers. The first two Siguirre women delivered quickly, with Sister Gertrude assisting the doctor, but the third, brought in through the rain from some distance, hardly more than a child herself, and miscarrying, was in poor condition. Sister Gertrude and the doctor were shut up in the delivery room with her. The girl's cries echoed up and down the halls.

Edythe walked into the hospital wearing the wrap-around skirt and blouse of one of Emma's old *m'boubous*. As she went down the hall to the new wing she heard the cries and moans of someone in pain and knew the doctor must be busy with the patient. In the dining room there was an atmosphere of tension and agitation. Sister Hildegaard was talking to Fatou and Édouard Diallo. The kitchen help lingered in the doorway, listening. Sister Caroline entered from the outside entrance and seeing Edythe came to her and said, "You know that Paul escaped, Edythe?"

Edythe looked into the gray eyes and said quietly, "Yes, Sister, I know. Has Emma been in?"

The others turned to look at Edythe, and Fatou said that no one had seen Emma. Sister Caroline covered her face with her hands, and Edythe put an arm

267

around her. "I am sure Emma is all right, Sister. Don't worry."

Sister Caroline straightened up and smiled faintly at Edythe. "Yes, Edythe, I'm sure you are right. It is just all very disturbing."

The truth of the matter was, the sisters had not had enough sleep, and perhaps more than that, they were the only ones aware that this was Easter Sunday. No one else knew, no one cared. People were having babies, police were searching their hospital for an escaped prisoner, Emma was nowhere to be found. To distract the sisters, Edythe told them that something good had happened—she had her memory back. She could remember all about herself now, and she had a name of her own, although not as nice as the one Sister Caroline had given her. They congratulated Edythe, their faces brightened. Somehow, the night had brought one good thing.

Bakary, the cook, looking frightened, came in from the kitchen. He glanced around at the group. Sister Hildegaard noticed him and said, "What is it, Bakary?"

The cook motioned with a trembling hand toward the back. "Outside," he said hoarsely, "a man."

Sister Hildegaard followed him to the back door. The rest of them heard her exclaim, "Oh, heavens!"

Sister Caroline went out to her and returned immediately to give an order to Édouard Diallo.

"Édouard, have some one go and open the door from the morgue to the outside."

Édouard and Fatou disappeared toward the front of the hospital. Sister Hildegaard came back in and held onto the side of the kitchen door for support.

"What is it?" Edythe asked.

"My dear," said Sister Caroline, "they have brought the body of the prisoner, of Paul."

"Who has brought it?"

"Some *indigène*. They found it down the river. They should have taken it to the police. He is drowned, Edythe," Sister Caroline continued. "At least, he is dead."

"Armer Kerl, armer Kerl," repeated Sister Hildegaard, shaking her head and relapsing into German. "Poor young man."

"I must see him," Edythe said.

"Of course. The doctor must examine, though."

"Oh," groaned Sister Hildegaard, "if they would only finish in there."

"I shall go to the morgue and see about the body," Sister Caroline said. "Sister Hildegaard, please come too. Edythe, you may come if you wish. Édouard must notify the authorities at once."

Activity checked their emotions. They began to move. The hospital morgue was a small basement room under the old building. From the back of the foyer one descended to a basement level and into a concrete-lined room, as if the dead needed to be restrained by the strongest walls in the hospital. Several long tables stood there, and here they were now laying out a slender form wrapped in a torn and water-soaked sail. Edythe stood at the entrance from the hall, holding onto the door frame, feeling weak in the knees. Sister Hildegaard swept past her to assist Sister Caroline, and they straightened the limbs of the body and crossed the hands on the chest and closed the eyelids.

Edythe heard Sister Hildegaard ask, "Shouldn't we take off these trousers?"

Sister Caroline replied, "I think we should leave it as it is for the police. It is Paul, Edythe," she said, over her shoulder. "There's no doubt, and it appears to me that he drowned. Rigor mortis is just beginning."

Edythe watched without answering. Sister Hildegaard was putting some weights on the eyelids to keep them closed. Edythe thought that Paul might have been halfway to Bamako by now. The thought of the boat flashed through her mind, and a new worry. Probably Sister Caroline was thinking of it, too.

Édouard appeared on the basement stairs. "Tell sister," he told Edythe, "that the commissioner will come directly."

"Yes, Monsieur Diallo," Edythe replied, and she relayed the message.

Sister Caroline was drawing a white sheet over the body. She and Sister Hildegaard made the sign of the cross over it and said a prayer.

"Ask Édouard if the doctor is out yet," Sister Caroline told Edythe when she turned again. Édouard's No came down the stairs.

"We must all go back upstairs until the police arrive," Sister Caroline said. "Where is the man who brought the body?"

They looked outside, but the man had disappeared. "Oh, dear," said the sister. "The police won't like that. They will want to have his name and where he found it and all that. Why did he go off that way?"

"They always do," Sister Hildegaard said, trudging up the stairs, holding up her skirts. "He's too clever to stay around and have all that questioning by the police."

As they passed the delivery room a tremulous, shrill sound came through the walls. Edythe shuddered and wrapped her arms around herself.

"Edythe," said Sister Caroline as they reached the staff room, "have you a lab coat to put on before the commissioner gets here?"

"There is a clean one in Sister Gertrude's lab," Sister Hildegaard said.

"Yes, Sister."

Edythe went and found the coat and took off Emma's old clothes. She noticed her hands were trembling as she tried to button the coat. Outside, she could hear the sound of a large car pulling up under the portico. The three women stayed in the staff room, standing tense, staring at each other.

"Shouldn't we go up front?" asked Sister Hildegaard.

"No," said Sister Caroline. "Wait until he sends for us. Édouard will meet him."

In a few minutes, Fatou came down from the

270

foyer. "Sisters, we are all to go to the morgue." Her eyes were wide, her face stiff with tension.

"You do not need to come, Edythe," Sister Caroline said as they started to follow Fatou. "In a way, you are still a patient."

"The commissioner asked for her, too," Fatou said, turning. "He asked, 'Where is that white woman of the doctor's?'"

"I am coming," said Edythe, following Sister Hildegaard's back. Why should I be afraid? she asked herself. But she wished so much that Heinrich were with them. The door to the delivery room was still closed. There were no sounds coming from there now.

In the front hall a small group of *indigènes* stood at one side, staring in fear and apprehension at the police officers and all the people moving back and forth. It must be that girl's family, Edythe thought, passing them. Poor things, they look so afraid.

The group filed downstairs to the morgue again. Commissioner Equilbecq, heavy jowled and bulky, stood by the body of Paul. Two police officers were with him. They all wore jackets with official gold braid. The nuns went over to them and Edythe stayed by the doorway with Fatou and Édouard. Sy Kanadu was lucky to be off duty this day, she thought.

The officers asked the nuns to take off the clothes from the corpse. Edythe was glad they stood between her and the body. They found something which they handed to the commissioner, and he was examining it. He was counting money. They had Santillana's money. Would it reveal signs of the food it had been in? Her heart was racing. She felt the truth would be in her eyes if anyone were to look there. She saw the commissioner pass the money to one of the officers, who also counted it and put it away in his pocket. Sister Caroline was telling them about the man who had brought the body to the kitchen door, and sure enough, they were angry that the sisters had not detained the man.

271

"There was so much excitement; we did not notice him slip away," Sister Caroline was saying apologetically.

"Who can identify this body positively?" asked the commissioner in a loud voice.

"We both can," Sister Caroline said, a trifle irritably. "He was a patient at this hospital."

"One from the Church is enough. Is there no one else?"

One of the officers was taking out some paper forms and holding a pen for Sister Caroline to sign.

Edythe heard her own voice speak out. "I can identify the body."

"Come over here, please," the commissioner said.

Now that action was demanded of her, Edythe felt very calm. She went over to the group.

"Your name?" an officer asked.

"I am . . ." Edythe hesitated. Now she had her real name. Should she use it? "I am Nicole Armitage Cordrey," she said.

One of the officers said to the commissioner, "It is the woman from M'Boura."

"The doctor said you were amnesic, that you did not remember your name," the commissioner said to her sternly.

"Yes, monsieur, I have been, but yesterday I remembered everything. It all came back. I know my own name now."

The commissioner was inspecting her. So this was the woman he had heard so much about—from the doctor, from gossip in the hospital and the town, from his men who had searched the doctor's cottage in the night.

"You knew the prisoner?" he asked her.

"Yes, monsieur," Edythe said, looking at him directly. "He was a patient here the same as I. And then I visited him in the prison. I went with the doctor and I went with Emma, the girl who carried his food. He and I spoke English together."

"Please look at the body and tell us if you positively identify him."

Edythe turned and looked at Paul as an officer pulled the sheet back from his face. His face was white and rigid. There was a stubble of beard on his chin. He looked aged from the time they had faced each other in the boat on the river, when he had been so exultant and alive. Death had left pain on his face.

"Well?" asked the commissioner.

"Yes," said Edythe, turning her face away from Paul, thinking that with him everything was finished, no more trouble or worry or fear or joy or passion.

"It's Paul Marion," she told him.

Automatically she took the pen handed to her and bent over the paper. What name was she to write? Her hand wavered. Then, when she started the *N*, she found it easy to write Nicole Cordrey.

Suddenly a stench seemed to rise from the cold, wet concrete, a smell strong, fetid, putrescent. Edythe found herself swaying over the paper, a haze swimming over her mind, and she was caught by the commissioner himself, who kept his hands on her arms.

"Steady there," he said.

Edythe felt Sister Hildegaard's arm around her. The commissioner's voice boomed over all, "Let us find a place where we can talk now," and he turned and led the way out of the morgue.

"Are you all right, Edythe?" whispered Sister Hildegaard.

"Yes, I will be all right when we are outside, Sister. My stomach . . ."

"Yes, and I think you have not eaten either, poor dear."

Indeed, thought Edythe, I missed my dinner last night and breakfast this morning. She let herself be led up the stairs. The commissioner had established himself at the desk in Édouard's office. The officers and the rest of them stood around.

"Now then," said the commissioner, who seemed to

Edythe a little more human than she had thought at first. "Where is that girl called Emma, the one who carried the food basket?"

"We do not know," Sister Caroline said. "She has not come in today. She did not sleep last night in her usual place."

"Who saw her last?" he asked. An officer was writing things down in a notebook.

"I saw her last night," said Edythe in a weak voice. "I went to the prison with her when she took the food basket."

She felt Sister Caroline's sharp intake of breath as she spoke.

"And why would you go to the prison last night in all the rain?" asked the commissioner, looking at Edythe sharply.

"She is my friend. We live together," said Edythe.

"Did you see the prisoner last night?" he asked then, knowing very well already that the guard had not allowed her to enter.

Just then Doctor Heinrich's voice was heard in the foyer. Everyone's attention was diverted to him. He was talking to the group of *indigènes*. They were country people and their clothes and the bare legs of the men showed they had traveled far in the mud and the rain. Heinrich was saying something to them in Malinké. His face was gray-looking and sad. The family were nodding their heads at what he said, and then they turned and trudged out of the hospital.

"Will you answer the question, please?" the commissioner said to Edythe, turning toward her again with a frown.

"A moment please, Commissioner," put in Édouard Diallo. "The doctor would wish to be here."

Looking haggard, Heinrich came to the office door.

"What is going on here?" he demanded, looking at everyone and noticing Edythe's flushed face, the concerned looks of the nuns. The officers shifted their feet, the commissioner glowered. Sister Hildegaard spoke up.

274

"An *indigène* came to the hospital back door with the body of Paul Marion, Doctor. He was drowned."

"The body should have been taken to the police. They are free to remove it," Heinrich said gruffly, looking at the officers.

"That is not the point, Doctor," the commissioner said. "The prisoner is dead. I am now interested in finding who helped him escape."

"This is your concern, not ours, Commissioner. This is a hospital, not a courtroom."

"Slowly, Heinrich," said the commissioner. "The girl who carries the food basket to the prisoner, do you know where she is?"

"I do not," said Heinrich.

"Then I must address a few questions to this young woman." And he turned back to Edythe. "Tell me again your name."

"I am Nicole Armitage Cordrey," she answered. "I just remembered my real name last night. I have had amnesia."

"So," said the commissioner. "And you have identified the body as Paul Marion, the prisoner. Now, when did you last see the prisoner?"

Heinrich spoke again, "Commissioner, as director of this hospital, I must insist that this interrogation go no further. If there is to be such grilling of my patients and my employees then there must be proper legal procedures, with their lawyers present."

"Now, Heinrich," began the commissioner, moving in the tight desk chair uncomfortably. "Now, wait . . ."

"No, you wait, Commissioner," said Heinrich. "If you persist in your suspicions that these women—Edythe, here, that is what we called her, and Emma, the *indigène*—or any of my people here are involved in the escape of the prisoner, then I shall submit my resignation to the governor immediately. I cannot function under tension other than from the work itself. I will not tolerate it."

The sisters looked frightened. They had never heard

the doctor so stern. Commissioner Equilbecq got up, looking alarmed.

"Heinrich, there is no investigation. Marion is dead. It is the conclusion of a sad case. I'll see that Naby down there cleans house. I'm sure that is where the leak is, not these two young women of yours. I was just trying to sweep the floor clean as far as my office is concerned."

He looked at Edythe admiringly. He liked the doctor's taste.

"Come," he motioned to his officers, and they followed him to the foyer.

Outside, by the hospital steps, the big black limousine was parked. The rain dripped from its shiny surface and in the sky the clouds were beginning to thin and to lighten. All the out-of-doors glistened.

"The body is in our morgue?" Heinrich asked, following the commissioner to the foyer.

Someone answered Yes, and he asked, "Will you send for the body, Commissioner?"

"Oh," Equilbecq turned. "We will notify the American consul in Conakry and let them decide about its disposal. Ah, and I almost forgot. I have this cable I intended to give you."

And he took a crumpled cablegram from his pocket and handed it to the doctor. "It concerns your patient and the family lawyer."

Heinrich spread out the paper and read it. "Yes, Édouard Diallo brought us this information on Monday. We have been deluged with patients this week or I would have gotten in touch with you."

"D'accord, bien."

With dignity the commissioner, followed by his officers, went out. He climbed in the back seat of the limousine. The two officers crowded in beside the driver. The car sped away, its tires making smacking sounds against the wet tarmac.

The group in the hospital foyer felt the sudden release of tension as the limousine disappeared. Sister

Caroline went into the chapel and Sister Hildegaard followed her. Sister Gertrude was still cleaning up in the delivery room.

The doctor looked at Edythe, and she said, "Did you really mean it, Heinrich, that you would give your resignation?"

"Of course I meant it, Edythe, or I wouldn't have said it."

"But you were risking 'your whole work.' " Her eyes twinkled as she said it.

He smiled. "I decided a few days ago, Edythe, that there are some things worth the risk."

"Did the young girl die, Heinrich?"

"Yes, she did. I tried my best, but I couldn't save her or the child. Now, if I don't get some tea you'll have a fainting doctor on your hands."

"Come," she said, taking his arm. "I shall assist you myself."

47

THAT DAY the noontime meal was a special feast. The *indigène* staff had gone home to their families. The rest of them gathered in the staff dining room. Trays had been sent off to the patients, and now Sister Hildegaard supervised the carving of a large tinned ham baked in honey and pineapple. There were two bottles of French wine, kept for special occasions, brought out and served in juice glasses.

At the last moment, just as they were sitting down to the dinner, Alfoldi Santillana arrived, carrying a potted Easter lily and a box of chocolates, which he presented to the sisters.

"Pour le Pâques," he said. "The lily came all the way from Paris via Air France and our own local train service."

The nuns were so pleased that tears fell and handkerchiefs were brought out. "We hoped you'd come for dinner, *Monsieur le Professeur,*" Sister Gertrude said.

"I was with you last year, you may remember," the Italian replied.

He held the chairs for the sisters to sit. Doctor Heinrich and Edythe sat across from them.

"Now tell me what has happened about our unfortunate young friend," Alfoldi said, sitting down beside Heinrich. "I had an early-morning visit from the police, and now I am told that the case is closed."

"Yes, Alfoldi, the Niger claimed our young friend. His body lies in our morgue," said Heinrich heavily.

They talked of Paul. Everyone seemed to know and

278

accept, however, that there were certain aspects of the escape that could not be brought out in the open.

"I always believed in his innocence," said Alfoldi, taking out a white handkerchief and blowing his nose soundly. "I think I shall write a letter to his parents. I will need some help with the English, of course."

They ate slowly, in silence, as though the eating were a sacrament. No traffic passed the hospital. Someone, down the street, was singing. A freshness from the clean, cooled air drifted into the staff dining room. Gradually, as the food and wine were consumed, a sense of renewed life enveloped the group. The doctor crossed his knife and fork on his cleaned plate.

"Well," he said, "Paul met his death trying to escape. At least he did not die passively accepting the fate that befell him. This is what I shall remember about him. He died in his struggle to live."

They looked at the doctor, each of them thinking of his or her role in Paul's life in Siguirre. Edythe's thoughts turned inward and she saw herself and the turmoils that she had been through, the struggle with a mind that had held no memories, only an abyss she could not face, and it was clear to her that the abyss had been there as she had walked toward Ad's plane back in Dakar. It had been with her then, too. But now it was gone. It was not just remembering that filled that awful void. Somewhere, between that accident in the forest and the present, everything had changed—she had changed.

The others were still talking, and she heard Monsieur Santillana speaking of leaving.

". . . the day after tomorrow," he was saying. "In the morning I shall ship off my books and specimens. My notes, of course, I'll carry with me."

There was a general protest and murmur of regret at the announcement, even though it was not unexpected.

"We shall miss you, my friend," said Heinrich. "You

added a great deal to our small group here. You even added Edythe."

"Yes, Monsieur Santillana," said Edythe. "Will you put me in your book of tropical flora found in the jungle?"

"Mais, certainement!" Alfoldi answered, "although I would be more inclined, my dear, to include you in the fauna category; let us say, a fine specimen of *Tragelaphus scriptus* that one day wandered from the forest looking for its true mate."

Edythe laughed, her color rising. She looked inquiringly at Heinrich.

"I believe our friend refers to the antelope," he said. "Not a bad comparison."

"Well, I must be properly catalogued, of course," Edythe said, and then she added passionately, "I would feel so much better about everything if I only knew what has happened to Emma."

"Perhaps she is hiding," offered Sister Hildegaard. "They are very much afraid of the authorities."

Edythe thought to herself, but Emma is not "they." Emma would not be afraid.

Heinrich said, "I believe she has gone back to her village, or at least, that she is on her way."

"Like the others," murmured Sister Caroline.

"I think everything may have fit together. She may have been thinking of this for a long time, of this change."

"Some day," put in Alfoldi Santillana, as he reached for another sliver of ham, "a Fulani from Emma's tribe, a tall, strong man with tribal scars on his cheeks, wearing only a loin cloth of the brightest cotton, will come into town and come to Heinrich's, or else the hospital, and ask for Emma's box. He will lift it up on his head and stride off with it, taking all of her beautiful *m'boubous* to her."

"I shall have her box all ready for him," said Edythe, believing Alfoldi implicitly.

Heinrich had turned to Sister Caroline, noticing her

wipe her eyes, and he asked, "Sister, are you well today?"

"I am a little tired, Doctor," she replied, steadying her voice with an effort.

"Now you must take time off to go to Conakry for the ocean air. It is time for a change, and it would do you good."

"Yes, thank you, Doctor. I truly need to see Father Donnegan, too."

"Sister, you are free to go, and you can travel down with us, if you like."

Edythe looked at Heinrich quickly. "What! What are you saying?"

"I was thinking that perhaps I should take you back to Dakar instead of having that lawyer come to get you."

Everyone looked at him, amazed, and then at Edythe. Sister Hildegaard gave a satisfied nod at Sister Gertrude. Edythe's eyes were shining.

"Wonderful, Heinrich. Perfect!" She reached over and kissed his cheek.

"Here, here!" shouted Santillana. "Let's have a toast!" He got to his feet with his glass of wine. "To our goddess from M'Boura and the doctor of l'Hôpital Niger Plateau Supérieur!"

As they set down their glasses a clap of thunder rolled overhead and again the heavens burst open with rain. Sister Hildegaard jumped up and started to run. "I must close the windows," she said.